by Ivan Tritch

Novels

The Cain Connection
The Thought Network
The Prometheus Deception
Final Shift
The Reaper's Folly
The Woods
The Pilomotor Reaction

Collection

Dark Tapestries

Non-Fiction

WTF, Are You *Thinking?*
The Philosophies of an Ordinary Man

The Thought Network

a novel

Ivan Tritch

The Thought Network

Copyright © 1998, 2012 Ivan Tritch

Revised Version Copyright © 2012
by Ivan Tritch

All rights reserved. No part of this book may be reproduced in any form, except for the inclusion of brief quotations in a review, without permission in writing from the author or publisher

📖
A Heartsbane Production

THE THOUGHT NETWORK

Prologue

The woman sat in front of the television set, fretfully anticipating her husband's return from work. Last night his dinner had been late, and although tonight's meal simmered, ready, in the kitchen oven, she had the nagging feeling that she'd forgotten to do something; some little thing that might cause him to come down hard on her, as he had the previous evening. Her ribs still ached, and she noticed bruises on them when she looked in the mirror this morning. Nevertheless, she felt grateful—that they were only bruised instead of broken.

The children were upstairs playing quietly in their bedroom. They knew their father's broad range of stern rules brought harsh punishment if even the slightest of them was broken. The only sound in the downstairs den—aside from the TV—was the minute click of the grandfather clock in the hallway off the kitchen as it ticked off the seconds. The clock had been in the family for years on her husband's side, and for the past seven the woman had grown to hate it. There had been days that were too numerous to count, when she had listened, much as she was now, to the annoying tick of the wood and brass clock as she waited, wondering whether or not it would be one of the days when her husband had a bad day at work, or trouble with the car—or both.

Lately, it didn't have to be anything more than that.

She mentally evaluated the past thirty minutes, trying hard, but unsuccessfully, to put her finger on what it was she had forgotten. This agitated her further and made it harder to concentrate.

The children had watched the clock since a quarter past three, and had walked quietly up the stairs a little before three-thirty. The woman suspected the two of them had heard and saw a great deal yesterday. Each of their faces had held tight lines of tension all afternoon, and she had seen that tension intensify when they realized that it was 'time.' Although it was midsummer and the children should have been out playing and enjoying the freedom that summer brought each year, they were not allowed to at this time of the day. Their father might have some chores for them to do, and he liked them close at hand.

The dishes were washed, dried, and put neatly away in the cabinets over the sink, the handles on the morning's coffee cups turned to the front of the cabinet for easy access. Her husband hated it any other way. The floor was swept and mopped, the carpet throughout the house was vacuumed meticulously, as soon as she had put out the dog. She often wondered what her husband would think if he knew that she let the dog in sometimes during the day, when the kids were at school and loneliness wrapped itself around her like a thick scarf.

As far as she could see, everything was taken care of, in perfect order. Oh, and the laundry was also finished. She had taken the last load out of the dryer over an hour ago, had ironed the shirts and...

With a start, she remembered there *was* something she had

forgotten. Her husband had ripped one of his work shirts yesterday afternoon while doing the yardwork. He had been out back, trimming around the side hedges and slamming back can after can of beer, when he snagged the shirt on the branch of a nearby tree. He had told her to mend it today, and she had forgotten.

Panic seized her in a sudden and cold grip, and she went into the kitchen. Mind racing, her eyes searching for the clock over the stove, the single good thought going through her mind was that she was glad she couldn't see the grandfather clock down the hall. Sometimes she fancied she could hear it laughing at her at moments like this, telling her it had won once again and that time—ha, ha—was not on her side.

But surely there must be enough time left. She should have time to go upstairs, get the shirt, find her small sewing kit, choose the right thread and needle, and mend the garment before he returned from his day at work. A faraway glimmer of hope surfaced in her pacing mind, but she paid it no heed. That glimmer had once been like a roaring sun at midday, fierce, intense, but over the years it had dwindled so that it resembled a late-evening sun, sinking almost over the horizon, unable to hold on to another day. Today that diminishing sparkle of hope was like twilight.

She started down the hall for the stairs.

And that was when she heard the car pull up outside.

Fear seized her and froze her where she stood. Her mind screamed at her to do something—to *run*—but the rational part of her brain, the part that caused her to pay little attention to that faint glimmer of hope, told her calmly—and a little coldly—that running would do no good. Similar situations had occurred before, and she *had* run before. But only once, and once was enough. After that day, she had stayed indoors for two solid weeks, afraid of what the neighbors —or anyone, for that matter—might think if they saw her bruised and swollen face.

The motor from the car outside fell silent, and although her instincts continued to tell her to beat a path to greener pastures, she remained planted where she stood, afraid to do anything else, and all the while trying desperately to think of an excuse that would be acceptable to her soon-to-be-angry husband.

She could think of nothing.

She heard the rattle of keys in the front door, less than twenty feet from her.

Run out the back door, her mind screamed at her. *Run!* And on the heels of that: *What about the kids? Stay put!*

Before she could do anything, the front door was thrown open. It slammed into the wall and bounced back, vibrating on its hinges. Her husband stood framed in the doorway, his head hung forward slightly, his eyes vacant yet hauntingly piercing.

"Hi, hon," she tried, smiling, as though this was the way he made his entrance every evening.

He didn't respond as he put his hardhat and lunch pail on the small table next to the sofa.

Now, confusion and disillusionment crept into the woman's mind. Whether or not anything was wrong, she *always* got a reply of some sort from her husband, even if he was already angry with her. "The kids are upstairs," she offered. "They've been really good today." She tried a smile, but that didn't seem to work.

Maybe he wouldn't mention the shirt. At least, not if she kept his mind preoccupied with something else. Maybe he would forget all about his instructions for her to mend it. They said there was a first time for everything.

Numbly, he closed the door.

"Can I get you something to drink, dear?" she asked.

Instead of answering, he raised the lid of his lunch pail, a small Igloo cooler with a sandwich tray on top, beneath the lid.

She was finally able to move, after seeing an act that was normal for him. He would have his dirty silverware in the cooler for her to wash. He always took his own with him, along with leftovers from the previous night, because the little plastic forks in the breakroom in the construction site office-trailer never failed to break on the first or second bite.

So she walked toward him with relieved eagerness, already reaching out for the silverware that might keep her busy while she tried to think of an excuse for not doing his mending. Doing this one little normal thing might buy her enough time for that.

But she stopped short of him when she saw, with even greater confusion, that his right hand did not hold silverware. Instead, it held...

That can't be right, she thought, *what would he be doing with a...*

Suddenly her husband's hand slashed out, a pink blur, and the woman was blinded by a tremendous burst of pain in her left eye. She screamed and staggered backward.

He lashed out again, and her abdomen was filled with sudden, hot fire. Dimly, she could hear the patter of small feet in the upstairs hall, heading quickly to the stairwell.

"Stay in your room!" she yelled through the excruciating pain. *"Stay in—"* Her screams were cut off as her throat was filled with sudden pain, as well. She fell limply to her knees. Then there was even more pain; this time in her lower back.

And then more, in another place. And another.

As she fell on her stomach, heedless to stop the blows she was receiving from her husband, she looked at the television.

It was still on. She had been watching *General Hospital,* or at least looking at it as she contemplated the rest of her day, but what she saw on the screen now was a far cry from the serenity of tiled, hospital corridors, and the friendly medical staff who walked them. What she saw on the screen was another thing that was totally wrong on this afternoon of wrongness.

What she saw could not possibly be on the screen of her television. *Is that a newscaster? Why is he smiling at me?*

Her body, now blessedly numb, fell still. Darkness swayed in and out of her vision. The pain seemed to have left her, and now her sight was diminishing.

Were her thoughts leaving, too? Who would help her children?

She felt tingling prickles along her scalp like a thousand fingers, and an inner tugging at her mind. Was this part of dying?

The woman didn't live long enough to consider it. The last thing she heard was her children screaming. Their screams were like knives gouging out her heart. *My babies, oh God, not my babies.* With what little strength remained in her, she screamed out her husband's name. Even in her weakened state the scream was not a plea for help. Instead, it was a primitive yell of anger—and of *hate.*

She looked up. At the television set. That strange man was still there, laughing and pointing at her in a mock accusation.

And her last thought was an acceptance that what she was seeing was real. It was, indeed, real.

Then nothing.

*****

Part One

On the Edge of Reality

> So we beat on,
> boats against the current,
> borne back ceaselessly
> into the past...
>
> —F. Scott Fitzgerald

1

His name was Richard Raines, and he had been looking for a television set for the better part of two weeks. He did this in the evenings after work, checking in local flea markets, Bargain Barns, and small repair shops such as the one he was in now.

He had even made a special trip last weekend to Ravenden, to the huge flea markets held in that area. He took a bottle of bourbon with him on that excursion, and that had been a mistake; he'd ended up at the edge of Spring River, away from all the weekend tourists, and spent the afternoon staring across the cool churning water, thinking about old dreams and dulling the clarity of those thoughts with shot after shot of *Jim Beam*. So, he had yet to locate the right place or the right television set.

What about that one over there?" he asked, pointing to a low shelf at the back of the room. The room was actually part of a small repair shop that looked as though it might have been a garage at one point in time.

"Well, let's go over and take a look," said the shop owner.

"Okay," Richard agreed. His light brown hair had thinned somewhat over the past three years, and although he was approaching thirty-five years of age, his face maintained a cool, youthful complexion for which most of his friends and business associates envied him.

"Don't many people come by this way anymore," said the shop's owner, who had introduced himself to Richard as George Morrison. He was about the roundest man Richard had ever seen. His hair was a grayish-white that seemed to be the trademark of all small shop owners, and the trace of beard stubble on his rounded cheeks and formidable chin was the same color. He walked with a noticeable limp to the back of the shop, and Richard followed him, wondering if the man had polio, or if he might have lost part, or all, of a leg in one war or another.

He decided not to ask.

"Nope, not many at all," Mr. Morrison continued, as though Richard had prodded him to go on. "Business just kind of came to a screeching halt about three months ago when that new video and appliance store opened up a couple a blocks down the street. Not that business *here* was doing so great. But it still gets me. A guy works all his life doing the only thing he's good at making a living at—just getting by, mostly—and then some confangled company with all the money they could ever want decides they want to make some *more* money, and *who cares* if it puts old George Morrison under further than he already is?" He stopped and turned around to face Richard. "People are greedy. Always remember that." He ran a liver-spotted hand over the stubble on his chin, as though he were examining the whiskers there for the first time. "Make any sense to you?"

"No," Richard said, unaware of what the old man was talking about. He had tuned out Mr. Morrison's prattling almost completely since they had started toward the back of the shop, catching only fragments of the conversation here and there. He was too awestruck with the TV to do anything more than nod and shake his head in the right places.

Now, looking at the set in front of him, he felt a little swoonish, and oddly excited. He was looking for a TV set for what seemed like, on the surface, a very simple reason: his was gone. Yet it wasn't that simple, and he knew he couldn't pretend it was. As he looked at the set, he remembered part of his childhood in Jacksonville, Florida. His parents had, at one time, owned a television set similar to this. He had not seen one like it since, and was surprised that he had come across a TV that resembled his parents' old one so completely.

It was an older set with four squat legs made of a dark stained wood that was the same color as the console encasing the screen. The screen itself was a dull green color, rounded on the sides, and framed by about two inches of metal on all four sides, likening it to an old picture frame. The controls—volume, tone, and channel selector—were located directly below the metal at the bottom of the screen. A light film of dust covered the top of the TV. In his mind, Richard could see this set sitting in the vacant spot next to his bookshelf, where the other set had been before...

Before Tina left.

That's it, bring her up again. Can't you ever stop?

He pushed the thought away with a mental hand and looked at the old man. "How much?"

George Morrison looked at him as though Richard was a man preparing to jump from the fortieth floor of a high building: cautiously, with puzzlement, and with more than a little trepidation. "You sure this is the one you want?" he asked as he pointed to the TV.

Richard thought about it briefly, but in his mind's eye it seemed to take longer, for his thoughts, as though on ball bearings, swiveled around to the day he had asked Tina a similar question: *Are you sure this is what you really want?*

"Yes, I'm positive," he said, echoing the response she had given him. He mentally shook his head. He needed to focus. He knew that, but it was tough sometimes.

Originally, he had not set out to replace the set that he'd let his ex-wife take with her. He didn't watch much television in the first place, because books offered so much more. Aside from that—and the second determining factor in him giving Tina the set—was that he hadn't like the looks of it. It had been given to them by her mother as a wedding gift, but its color, a light tan wood finish, clashed with his bookshelves, which had been on either side of it. In the end, it could have been this one thing that prompted him to purchase a replacement set, but the truth was this; he was lonely. He was past the point of worrying what people would think, partly due to the fact that he had been spending a lot of his time inside a bottle. He was lonely, and in the end he had set about looking for another television in hopes that it would get his mind off Tina. Everything that had happened had been popping into his mind at odd but frequent moments, often when he least expected it.

On one of his few sober evenings, he had decided that maybe a TV would help. But it wouldn't resemble the ugly, off-colored thing that had sat between his bookshelves for the past three years.

"Yeah, this it is," he said.

"It's a black and white, you know," the old man said. He looked at Richard questionably, his eyebrows raised.

"That doesn't matter," Richard told him, never taking his eyes off the set. "This is the one. Definitely. I've been looking for one just like this for a pretty good while."

Mr. Morrison looked agitated for some reason, and Richard suspected he knew why. His first instinct upon coming into the shop was to be on his guard when it came to dickering on a price if he found something he liked. He had almost bought a set four blocks over, at a pawn shop—one not as nice as this one, but which would accent his shelves nicely—but he'd felt that the pawnbroker was trying to hoodoo him on the price. Now, oddly, he wasn't so concerned with the business end of the deal. This was the set. He could picture himself in front of it watching reruns of his favorite sitcoms (although there weren't many that qualified) and old westerns. All of that would be flavored with a bit of sweet nostalgia because of the similarity between this set and the one he'd grown up with back home. Thinking of his family in that retrospective manner might also help rid his mind of Tina. *No* price could be too high for that.

"Seventy-five dollars," George Morrison told him.

Richard frowned, but not too hard. He would have laughed and walked out of the store—and had done so many times during the past couple of weeks—but, oddly, the price seemed secondary. "Care if I plug it in and try it out?"

George jerked as though startled, as if the question had caught him off guard. "The price is seventy-five dollars, as is," he said, a little coldly. "Surely you saw the sign outside. This television is in good working order. I guarantee it."

"Okay," Richard said passively, his eyes still roaming over the set. He looked up in time to see George Morrison roll his eyes, before limping his way toward the front of the shop. Richard followed him.

"Most of the time I can't move a black and white bigger than ten inches. That one's been on display for quite some time. Thought I was going to have to throw the damn thing out." And then, in a softer voice, perhaps to himself: "I wish I had."

"Sounds like a reasonable price," Richard said when he got to the register. He knew he sounded like the most gullible guy in the world at the moment, but the old man hadn't charged as much as he had been expecting or what, in his mind, he would have been willing to pay.

Richard handed the old man four twenties and told him to keep the change.

That done, the two of them managed to load the set onto the back of Richard's pickup truck, both men breaking out in a light sweat before the task was completed. The temperature outside was in the lower eighties and, although that was fairly cool for late summer in Jonesboro, Arkansas, moving the TV had been a real job.

Richard closed the tailgate and then leaned back against it, breathing hard. "Heavy son-of-a-bitch, isn't it?"

"It is, at that," Mr. Morrison said as he wiped sweat from the back of his thick neck with a hanky he fetched from a hip pocket. "And black and white, too." He looked solemnly at Richard.

"I told you—"

"Listen," George Morrison said sharply. The look on his face and the tone of his voice was as serious as any Richard had ever seen or heard. "I could have sold you a nice color set for about the same price as this...*this* one. Might have been smaller, but you would have been happier with it. And that's the truth."

Having spoken his piece, he tucked the hanky back into his pocket and limped slowly toward his shop.

Richard was flabbergasted. He had bought something from this old man, and this was the gratitude he got? He watched in stunned silence as the man made his way to his shop.

Mr. Morrison turned around a faced him once more before disappearing inside the open front door. "You won't be happy with *that* set, Richard Raines. Not happy at all."

"Wha—?"

But the old man was gone.

Must be something wrong with it, Richard told himself. *Maybe I should have tried it out.* But he hadn't needed to, had he? He had seen the sign out front, just above the door, before he'd gone into the shop. He looked at it again now. It said:

USED TV'S and APPLIANCES

And underneath that, in smaller letters:

with warranty

And he had the warranty in his pocket, along with the bill of sale.

No, he was confident the set would work. The old fart was more than likely pissed off because he couldn't sell him a more expensive set. One salesman is like the next, Richard concluded. They want to milk all the money out of you that is humanly possible, and if what you buy is not exactly what you had in mind it was just tough shit.

He had found the television set that he'd so painstakingly sought over a two-week duration, and now he couldn't wait to get it home and plug it in and

and did he call me by my name?

Sure did. Probably saw my driver's license when I paid him.

Yeah, right. Open your wallet, dummy, and you'll see that your license isn't even visible unless you remove your photos and credit cards.

He shook these thoughts from his head, and automatically began to think about Tina. It seemed as though he spent most of his time doing that these days. That, and talking to a bottle; or, to be more apt, talking to himself *through* a bottle.

At least the house would be a *little* less empty now. Not that it was missing a lot of things—just the things she had wanted that he had allowed her to take...and herself, of course; she wasn't there, either. Maybe the TV would be the distraction he needed to finally get his mind off her and the things that had transpired between the two of them.

Well, between her and *them.*

But, like always, it hurt to even think those thoughts, and so he began whistling, something he did when trying to get something—anything—off his mind. He'd been whistling a lot lately.

He looked up at the clear sky, and at the sun, which was lowering in the west toward a twilight that was only a few hours away, and decided that not even Tina could ruin this day for him. If he didn't allow her to, at least.

He checked the tailgate once more to make certain that it was secure, and then he realized why the old man had known his name. He had a copy of the warranty that Richard had in his hip pocket. Richard had filled out the form at the counter after paying the man. He had been so preoccupied with the TV set that it had escaped his mind. He shrugged his shoulders, climbed into the cab of his truck, and headed home with his new find—the television of his dreams.

But hadn't he been living a dream? He *thought* he had been. Before it came tumbling down on him, anyway. He was a grown man, but he still knew—from bitter experience—that dreams can turn into nightmares.

2

Richard pulled into the driveway of his home, an apartment at 2900 Crestwood, around five-thirty on the evening of September sixth. The sun was lower on the western horizon, and the oak trees in the front yard that shaded the driveway at this time of day were rustling in a light breeze. A few leaves fluttered around the yard as if happy that they had so much room to themselves before the surrounding trees would begin to litter the lawn with the rest of their passengers in a month or so.

The apartment was actually a condo that was three payments away from being Richard's free and clear, but he had never liked the word 'condo' (it was too similar to condom), and so he thought of his place as just an apartment, although it was much more luxurious than most of the apartments located throughout the city. It was a single unit, and could have been thought of as a house, if there weren't forty more identical 'condos' in the neighborhood.

He had purchased it shortly after he and Tina were wed three years ago, when he had been making good money as a supervisor at a struggling factory on the industrial side of town. He had put down a third of the price, and he had surprised Tina with her expensive wedding gift ten days after they returned from a honeymoon trip to the Bahamas. Ironically, he had surprised her again just three weeks ago when, ten days after she left him, he told her that she couldn't have the apartment in the divorce settlement.

She had been upset to say the least, but after conferring with Richard's attorney—and then her own—she found that her name was not on any documents pertaining to the condo, and that he had submitted his offer to purchase it just before they were married. This had been done intentionally by Richard, although he couldn't have said why he'd been determined to do so. It was something for which he was now proud.

Tina was informed that her only alternative was to take him to court, and she hadn't been about to do that. No, sir. She wanted *something* out of the divorce, and she only took whatever Richard allowed her to take from the apartment (mostly furniture) and he guessed she was satisfied.

Richard knew this, also.

But still…

"Hey, Richie, can I give you a hand with that thing?"

Richard had been unlocking his front door, and now he turned to face the familiar voice of his friend and neighbor, Paul Frazier. "You sure can. In fact, I was fixing to come over and ask you for some help. You saved me a trip."

"Oh, *really?*" Paul said laughing. He walked over and clapped Richard on the shoulder. Then he coughed, an obvious fake one. "You know, I may be coming down with something. I may have to go in and rest."

They both laughed, and Richard said, "This thing is heavier than it looks."

Paul eyed the set. "Looks like it. You know, I haven't seen you much lately, outside of work. Is everything okay?"

"Oh, yeah," Richard said. "Everything's great."

"Good deal," Paul said, He nodded and looked at the television.

Paul Frazier was Richard's neighbor, co-worker, and best friend. He had, in fact, been his best friend since junior high school, when Paul and his family had first moved into town. He was about Richard's height (5'10") and of similar build, but blonde headed. His small mustache looked nearly white compared to his dark brown eyes, which seemed piercing at first glance. However, if you looked closely enough, you saw that there was a pretty easy-going guy behind them. He had been Richard's neighbor for almost two years now. Their friendship, always strong, had played a major role in Richard talking Paul and his wife into buying the apartment next to his. Things had been great since, and both parties liked the arrangements okay. The most positive factor for both men was that they didn't have to go more than twenty yards to share a beer or two during a ball game, or get together for work-related business, or just for conversation.

Yet for the past two or three weeks they had rarely seen each other in the evenings, or on weekends.

"So, what do you think?" Richard said, as he watched Paul make his way around the back of the pickup, where he was getting a look at the television set from all angles.

Paul looked up and scratched his head idly, "Kind of old, isn't it?"

"Yeah, well…but just *look* at it."

"I *am,* I *am,*" Paul said, looking from the TV set to Richard, and then back again. "I can see that it's old. If it was much older, Moses could have watched it as he crossed the Red Sea."

Richard stared at him for a few seconds, the only sound coming from two baby robins chirping from high atop one of the oaks, and then they both (Richard and Paul, not the robins) burst out laughing at that old joke.

"Just help me get in inside, will you?"

*****

My God, Richie, I think you've finally begun to lose it, pal, Paul thought to himself as they lifted the television from the truck. *If you could only get that bitch out of your mind for good, there might still be some hope.*

Paul had never liked Tina, and he guessed he never would. He also guessed that Richard sensed this from time to time, although he never said so. Her arrogant ways and the manner in which she manipulated Richard and threw his feelings around aggravated him to no end. Yet he'd always made it a point to keep this to himself, as hard as it was to do sometimes. Richard was obviously happy, and that's what mattered. At least, he had been happy.

Anything for Richie's sake, man. And don't forget our *sake —mine and Richard's. Better give it a little more time. He'll come around.*

"Shit, you're right, this thing *is* one heavy mother," Paul said as they made their way awkwardly through the front door.

"We're almost there," Richard said.

There were only a few pieces of furniture in the front room, so they made it over to the spot by the bookshelves without bumping into anything.

Having set down his end of the set, Paul grunted, sat heavily on the sofa, and surveyed the room. It had been two weeks or so since he'd been in here, and things had changed during that time. The gray carpet covering the floor was still in excellent shape, but there were spots that were brighter than others, outlining places where other pieces of furniture had been. Over by the north wall was the largest clean spot, where a beautiful twelve-piece sectional sofa had been in front of the fireplace. Now that area looked empty and foreboding. The two oil paintings that had always hung on either side of the fireplace were still there, as was the bar at the east end of the room. There were a couple more bare spots in the room where two expensive solid-oak end tables had been.

And then, of course, there was the place next to the bookshelves where they had set the old television.

The bookshelves were made of dark maple and covered one-half of the south wall—the rest of which was bare, save for one window—and went up to within a foot of the ceiling. Most of the shelves were full. Richard was an avid reader and he saved anything he read, and this was not the only bookshelf in the place; the one in his bedroom was nearly as big, and just as full. He collected everything from mystery and suspense novels, to science fiction and horror, and was more than proud of his small collection of rare and out-of-print first editions.

Richard stood, stretching, and asked Paul if he wanted a beer. "We should celebrate getting this thing in here without dropping it on our feet."

"Sure. You know how hard work makes me thirsty."

"I hear you. But hard work or not, I want a cold beer when I sit down in front of the television," Richard said. He lit a cigarette and headed toward the kitchen. When he returned, Paul was looking at the television. "Well, what do you think?" Richard asked.

"It looks okay, I guess," Paul said after a brief pause. "I just didn't think you were the type of guy to buy an antique.

Especially when it's a television set that you plan on using regularly. Antique books, yes, but this…"

"Maybe you're right, but I don't know," Richard said. "It reminds me of my parents' old house, and growing up there, and I guess I just need a little of that right now." He took a swallow of his beer and looked at Paul. "Sentimental bullshit. Sounds pretty corny, huh?"

"Not at all, m'man. Not at all," Paul said. He could swallow that easily enough. After what happened with Tina, he knew that Richard had needed something else to occupy his mind and rid it of memories of her. He would have liked for Richard to turn to him after Tina left, but Paul knew him well enough to know that he would—eventually. That was just Richard. When something stressed him, he usually looked for comfort in some object—such as a photograph—before he turned to a friend. He had to first work it out himself. Paul had thought on more than one occasion that Richard would have made a damn fine writer.

He drained his beer and stood. "I'm gonna head on over to the homestead before Margie wonders what happened to me. I was taking out the garbage when you pulled up. I've been helping her with the housework all afternoon, and she's going to think I bailed on her."

Richard laughed. "Okay. I'll see you in the morning."

*****

After Paul left, Richard put the empty beer cans in the trash under the kitchen sink. Then—after looking for roughly five minutes—he found a bottle of glass cleaner and an old rag and began to wipe down the television set. Before he was finished, he had made an extra trip to the bathroom closet for more rags and a bottle of wood polish.

He stood and looked at the completed chore, stretching backward to relieve the tightness in his lower back that came from bending over the set. *Not bad,* he thought.

The TV *did* look like an antique, but weren't a lot of antiques relics of beauty, whose purpose was to preserve art—and history? It really didn't look that bad. Certainly quite a bit better than it had before he'd taken the polish to it. It was in remarkably good condition for its age, with only light dings and scratches on its wood exterior. It accented his shelves nicely and was almost the same color as the paneled wall behind it.

He placed the cleaners in a cupboard, swiped two cans of beer from the refrigerator, and returned to the front room.

He looked at the television, and for a few seconds a feeling of dread wormed its way into his stomach. A cold chill; and with the chill came a bleak thought, passing through his mind before he could grasp it clearly. *Why did I buy this television?* Briefly, his face held a quizzical look, as though he had come across some fine piece of information and had forgotten exactly what it was.

The fleeting feeling passed and he shrugged once before popping the tab on one of the cans of beer. He hunkered down on his knees in front of the set.

No remote, but what the hell. I'm not that *lazy.*

He reached for the volume control and turned the TV on.

3

Tina Raines awakened shortly after midnight, alone. The bedclothes lay scattered and crumpled near the foot of the bed, where they had ended up during her latest sexual romp with a man she'd met that evening, downtown at The Scene. Of course, she had gotten what she had gone to the small night club for in the first place.

A man. Any man.

Although she had thought that the guy who had told her his name was Jim—he wouldn't tell her his last name—might be different, he hadn't been. He had silently and conveniently slipped out of bed while she slept, and there was no telling where he had gone—her guess was home to a wife she knew nothing about. She would never see him again, and was not surprised to find that she really didn't give a shit, one way or the other.

She rubbed her head slowly with one manicured hand, pushing away a lock of her golden hair, feeling the slight throb of a premature hangover that she knew would soon turn into a thumping headache if she didn't go back to sleep. As she sat up, still in the nude, her head began to ache with greater force, and she reached for the bottle of aspirin on the end table next to the bed.

That is when she discovered the crumpled twenty-dollar bill next to the bottle of white pills.

The bastard.

But what should she be so angry about? Most of her male …acquaintances…didn't give her any money at all, and besides, it wasn't as though she couldn't use the money this guy Jim—if that was truly his name—had left for her. It upset her when a guy left money after a night with her, because she wasn't a hooker, or a whore, or any other of the many names commonly used to refer to girls of easy virtue. And the main reason it upset her was because, deep down, she *did* feel like a whore whenever someone left her money after a sexual relationship—no matter how brief that relationship was. Nevertheless, she couldn't find it in her heart to blame herself for feeling this way. It wasn't her fault.

It's Richard's fault.

It was never her fault, and although she would not openly admit it, her whole life seemed to have followed a path where there was a sign along the side of the road every fifty feet or so that said in big, black letter: *IT'S NOT YOUR FAULT!* To her it seemed like a perfectly normal road to take. Afterall, she had been born and bred somewhere along that path.

As a young girl growing up in Jonesboro, with something of a perfectionist for a mother, she learned early in life that when something went wrong—or if she did something bad—it was not her fault. Tina did no wrong. When she came home one day in the fifth grade and told her mother that three boys had lifted up her dress and felt her panties, her mother had soothed and crooned over her little girl as though she had been raped. She had told Tina that it *wasn't her fault.* It was those the fault of those brats, and she would call the school and take care of the matter—which she did. Tina's mother was a member-in-good-standing of the Parent-Teachers-Association, and the three boys in question had gotten suspensions.

What her mother hadn't know, of course, was that Tina had *let* those boys raise her dress and feel her panties. When she had told her mother about it, she had mentioned it with the sort of childlike excitement she would show if she'd gotten an *A* on her spelling test. Her mother had undoubtedly mistaken her emotions.

And there was the time, years later while she was in high school, that she had come home drunk from a date one evening wearing only her denim skirt and her bra, which was covered with dark brown stains, as though she had eaten dinner without her blouse—and sloppily at that. She couldn't remember what had happened to the blouse, and they had never found it, but her mother had made one thing perfectly clear that night over a cold shower and coffee: *It wasn't her fault.* Tina had been able to live with it.

There was always someone else to blame.

She had eventually met Richard, and he had opened up a whole new world for her—a world in which a lot of mistakes *were* her fault. The transition from the way her mother had raised her, to the things that he showed her about herself, should have been a painstaking one, but Richard had pointed things out to her so simply and innocently that she couldn't take them for granted. She had then, for perhaps the first time, found a true fault about her in someone else; her mother. It was *her* fault that she had been raised thinking she could do no wrong.

But those ingrown tendencies wouldn't stay pushed aside for long. Things rolled along smoothly with her and Richard for a while, and then she had really messed things up. She had...

Tina crawled out of the bed and lit a cigarette from the pack on the nightstand in the small bedroom, and then she slipped into a long, navy-blue bathrobe that had been a Christmas present from Richard two years ago. Her head still ached, but it was a numbing ache, as the aspirin began its work.

She went to the window and looked out at the night from her fourth-floor apartment. A cool, refreshing breeze, only slightly chilly, wafted into the bedroom and over her robed body, bringing an alertness to her that made her headache seem less of an annoyance.

As she smoked, she thought about the day ahead of her. Mrs. Murphy downstairs would be up and around before seven. She would most likely still be in her nightgown and slippers, and complaining noisily about how that numbskull Brad Patterson in 1C had thrown up and left a mess in the first-floor bathroom coming in late from one of his nightly drunks. At seven-thirty, Tina would have to be downtown at Maurice's Café, where she would wait on tables until she got off at five. And from there—if she wasn't too tired—she would likely end up at The Scene, or maybe Snow's Bar and Grill, for an afterwork drink. Since the divorce, that was pretty much an ordinary day for her, and not one that she looked forward to with any real pleasure.

Unless, of course, she was picked up at the bar.

Her mother, who had died of a heart attack eighteen months ago, had left her entire savings—over two-hundred-thousand dollars—to various charities around the city, and in Tina's eyes she would never forgive her for that. Part of it was because she knew her mother had done so because they had not agreed that Richard was the right husband for her.

The lifestyle she now had, at least since she and Richard had first separated, then divorced, was the type she'd loathed even thinking about most of her life. Richard had given her—or to put it into truer perspective, had let her have—only some of the furniture, her clothes and personal things, and five-hundred dollars cash, and she had used most of that money to rent the small three-room apartment in which she now lived. And to top that off, she had to share a bathroom with the rest of the fourth floor. She had just started her job at Maurice's, and was less than twenty dollars from being flat broke, when she had realized that no matter how distressful and embarrassing her current situation, the job was at present her only means of survival.

Her mother's money was gone, and now so was Richard's and she had never before had to depend upon herself to furnish a means of living. The sudden change of lifestyle should have been devastating, but in her foremind she had never blamed herself for any of it. First it had been her mother's fault, and now it was Richard's. If he had not made her believe—*want* to believe—everything that he told her, especially about the way her mother raised her, then things might have been different and she might not be living in this shithole, where mice infested the kitchen at night and cockroaches were was plentiful as dust.

Yes, if it wasn't for that poor excuse of a man who was now her ex-husband, she would have still been in the good graces of her mother and would have likely inherited some—if not all—of her estate.

But this.

This was not the way she was meant to live. Richard had single-handedly ruined her life. She hadn't helped the situation by occasionally stepping out of the marriage—and sometimes more than occasionally—but he had caused *that,* also. At least in her mind he had.

But things weren't going to stay the same. No. Richard might have taken the mine and given her the shaft, but the whole thing had gone too smoothly on his end. There had to be something he had overlooked that she could use to squeeze something more out of him. At least some money, because she wasn't going to live like this for long, and it wasn't her fault in the first place. She remembered how he had managed to keep the condo, and suspected he was sneakier than she'd thought.

She stubbed the cigarette and then crawled back into bed. Pulling the covers up to her neck, she went pleasantly back to sleep, filled with a new motivation to better her current lifestyle—a feeling that was new and very much attractive to her.

4

At first there was only static across the screen, and Richard began to think that maybe he *should* have tried the damn thing out at the shop. And following that thought: *the old man was right, I* won't *be happy with this set.*

Then he remembered that he hadn't hooked it up to cable. The channel selector was on 10, and of course he couldn't get anything but channel 8 without cable. He thought randomly that forgetting mundane things such as this was becoming an increasingly frequent habit for him. Two days ago, he had got to work only to discover that he'd left his briefcase—full of important papers he needed for a presentation that day—at home. On another occasion, he had forgotten to lock the doors of his truck, something he never failed to do, only to find the next morning that all of his compact discs had been stolen out of the console. He had been halfway to work before he discovered that his radio and CD player were missing, as well.

Of course, the television wasn't cable compatible, so Richard went into the kitchen to his odds-and-ends drawer to look for the adapter he knew was there somewhere. It took less than a minute for him to paw through the nuts, screws, miscellaneous tools, and other items to find what he was looking for.

The adapter fit the end of the cable, while two wires with little u-shaped posts protruded from the opposite end. These posts fit the antenna hook-up on the back of the set. He and Tina had purchased the adapter over a year ago, when their set went on the blink so that they could hook the cable up to the portable set Paul and Margie Frazier had loaned them while theirs was repaired.

He grabbed a flat screwdriver from the drawer and returned to the living room.

Static still resonated from the television, and he turned the volume all the way down before moving the set (with some effort) to one side to allow himself access behind it.

Feels like a refrigerator instead of a television.

He hooked the adaptor to the cable and had one wire from the other one hooked to the set when the room was suddenly filled with crackling, popping static. Richard was so startled by the sudden noise that he bumped his head on the bookshelf and barked his shin on the corner of the TV. Swearing out loud, he leaned over the set and turned the volume all the way down. The room fell silent once more.

He squeezed his way from behind the set and stood in front of it, staring. The screen was still white with snowy static. He rubbed his head, where a small bump was already forming.

Although he wasn't finished connecting the cable, he had come around to the front of the set because, while he was leaning over it to turn down the volume, he had seen—or thought he had seen—a clear picture of his arm *on the screen*. It had been there for a split second before the static returned, filling the screen with its white snowy lines and pulses; not just a reflection off the screen, but a real image, as though it were being broadcast through the television.

The screen remained white and mute as he stared at it.

Just your imagination. Probably caused by the bump on your head.

I saw it.

Sure, you did.

But an uneasy feeling had come over him. Fear? Yes, he believed it was. Not fear because he saw *(or thought you saw,* his mind screamed at him) his arm on the screen, because he knew that sort of thing didn't happen. But a small, growing fear because, for the first time, his mind openly entertained the idea that the pressures over the past two months—driven primarily from the divorce—were draining him to the point where he imagined seeing things.

How do you explain the volume escalating like that?

I bumped the TV with my shin, and it probably jarred the volume control.

Right. But you bumped your shin because the increase in volume startled you.

But had it? He couldn't remember. Nonsensical worrying such as this was not going to help his mental state, anyway. He laughed in the darkening room. The sun outside was sinking and shadows loomed long and dark inside the apartment; the only illumination came from the white fuzz on the TV screen.

He drained his beer, picked up the screwdriver, and finished connecting the cable. That completed, the static vanished and the screen was filled with the laughing face of Fred Sanford, of

Sanford and Son, who was mouthing something to his son, Lamont. Richard pushed the TV back into its spot and returned the screwdriver to the kitchen drawer.

After grabbing another beer on his way past the fridge, he turned the volume up to a respectable level, turned on the lamp beside the sofa, and lit a cigarette, inhaling deeply. The small sofa was the only other piece of furniture he'd purchased—he had to sit *somewhere.*

He watched the rest of *Sanford and Son,* a thirty-minute edition of the evening news, and was watching the last half-hour of the *Movie of the Week* when something strange happened.

Although the TV was black and white, Richard had decided that it produced a clearer picture than any set he had ever owned. And when the picture suddenly went off and was replaced by noisy static, it awakened him from the semi-doze into which he had fallen just minutes before (he had by that time finished eight beers).

"What the...?" *Cable must be out,* was his first thought. Hell, it had happened before—seemingly once a month, like a reminder from the cable company to pay the bill—and usually at a crucial point in some movie or show. The first impulsive thing to do when the cable goes out is to check all the stations and see if they, too, are out. That is what he did now, cursing under his breath. He ran through the channels, receiving nothing but static on all stations, and left the channel selector on six.

He turned the volume down and sat on the floor in front of the set. *I should call the damn cable company.* But had he paid his bill this month? He couldn't remember, but thought he had. He was meticulous about paying his bills on time. Well. Normally. He waited a few minutes, hoping that the picture would return, and then decided that he would just go to bed, after a look at his watch.

He was ordinarily a late-night person, but for the past three weeks he had been catching up on sleep—something he usually got only four or five hours of nightly. Now he was to the point where he was beginning to rely on the extra three or four hours a night he'd been getting.

Since Tina left, he hadn't felt the urge to stay up late with a good book and a cold beer, as was his past custom. In fact, he hadn't felt much of an urge to do anything but work and sleep.

And think about what Tina did.

He began whistling quietly, and he was reaching to turn the TV set off when suddenly the picture and volume came on simultaneously, making him jump back in surprise.

Must be a news channel, was his first thought.

The man on the screen was wearing a black suit with a red tie fastened around the collar of a white dress shirt. His hair was a dark brown, almost black, his eyes as green as emeralds. He was sitting behind a desk and smiling at the camera. In the background, Richard could hear laughter and applause from an unseen audience, and he supposed that his idea of this being a news channel was shot to hell.

Thinking that he might go ahead and watch the last fifteen minutes of the movie he'd been watching when the cable went out, he reached for the channel selector.

"Don't touch that dial!" the man on the screen said, smiling. He tipped a wink at the camera.

"Wha...?" And then Richard was smiling, too. For just a second there he could have sworn that the man was talking to him. Boy, he *needed* to go to bed.

"That's right," the man on the TV said. "Don't touch that dial, but keep that smile, Richard Raines, because you're watching channel 94, the network that shows you more." More applause from the unseen audience. "And now..."

But that is all Richard heard, because he did something that he had never in his life done before. He fainted dead away.

5

As soon as Richard Raines pulled away in his truck with the television, George Morrison closed up his TV and appliance shop a little earlier than usual. After putting up the 'closed' sign in the front door and drawing the shades on the windows facing the street, he went into the small apartment in the back half of the building and made himself a drink.

He did not close early because business had been extremely good that day—it hadn't been a good day at all. Mrs. Wilkins, who lived over on Irving Street, had come by early this morning to pick up a toaster that had been dropped off for repair. She had bitched profusely over the ten dollars he charged her, put paid it anyway. She had been doing business with George for fifteen years and raised such a fuss every time he fixed something for her.

When she came by this morning, she had looked more than casually at the old TV set next to the Zenith, and George had been dreadfully worried that she would be the one to buy it. After a short while she seemed to lose interest in it and went on about her way, out the door and down the street.

George had been both relieved and thankful.

He relied heavily on his long-time customers. His business would be shut down without the handful of them that he managed to keep by giving them a price on his work that was much lower than his competitors charged. Perhaps the prices he charged were too low, for more often than not he wouldn't realize much, if any, profit from his cheap labor for this small group of customers. He supposed the main reason he did this was just to stay busy around the place. The shop was paid for, so his overhead was low, but he still had to eat, didn't he?

As he sat at his small kitchen table, slowly nursing his drink, George thought back to the time, less than an hour ago, when the young lanky man had come into his small shop. Call it intuition, instinct—maybe there wasn't a term for it—but as soon as George had seen him, he had known by the chill that clutched his spine and the anxiety that began in his stomach and nearly overtook him, that this man with the light-colored hair was looking for a television.

But not just any television.

He had known right off that the old black and white at the back of the shop was the one Richard Raines would buy from him, and that he, George, would be scanning the papers a little more closely the next several days.

It seemed like things began happening the same way every time.

He remembered the first time the television had found its way into his shop. At the time, he had simply figured he'd gotten a good deal on an old set for which he might be able to turn a buck or two. The person who sold him the TV was a young man in his twenties who'd brought the set to George's shop some eight years ago, claiming that his wife had been bitching at him for the last eight months to buy her a color television and get rid of 'that damned black and white set.'

George hadn't been surprised. He'd heard similar stories before in his many years in the business, and he sometimes wondered why people always seemed to have a story to tell about what they were trying to sell. Sentimental, he guessed.

It wasn't until he'd paid the young man, who signed the receipt as Victor Haynes, with a crisp new twenty-dollar bill that George realized the young man wasn't just feeding him a line of bologna about the TV. It was evident that he didn't want to sell the set (George thought for just a second that the young man was going to cry as he pocketed the twenty), but he seemed to have come to some sort of crossroad with the whole thing. Perhaps his wife had told him that either that damned black and white set went out the door, or she did.

Or maybe there were other reasons.

George didn't really think about that particular transaction until three days later, when he was reading the *Jonesboro Journal* and happened upon Victor Haynes' photo in the obituaries near the back of the newspaper. According to the brief column beneath his picture, Victor had died of a massive coronary two days earlier while lifting a new television set from the back of his truck. It wouldn't strike George until later how odd it was for a seemingly healthy twenty-three-year-old to have a 'massive coronary.' Without thinking about what he was doing, he had cut the obit out of the newspaper and stuck it in one of his desk drawers. He had then thrown the rest of the newspaper in the garbage out back, for some reason uneasy.

Although he wouldn't have told anyone at the time, George had somehow felt linked to Victor Haynes' passing. Afterall, he had shelled out a measly twenty bucks for the old black and white, knowing inside that from what Victor Haynes had told him, he was only selling the set (and so cheaply) to please his wife and, ultimately, to save his marriage.

And though George also knew that he was in no legal way linked to the death of the young man, he somehow *did* feel guilty. He had thrown away the rest of that newspaper as though he had killed the young man himself and was disposing of the murder weapon.

Less than a week later, he sold the old TV.

He had marked a price of fifty-dollars on it without a second thought, and the older man who bought it from him later in the week hadn't seemed to mind the outlandish price. Afterall, the set worked, didn't it? Of course it did. George had tried it out himself one night after closing. He had turned it on and…and…

He shook his head and swallowed the last of his drink. He didn't want to think about that. Not at the moment. The whole thing was a puzzle he had been working on for the better part of eight years now, and although he felt like he had come close to solving it more than once, the whole strange business with the old TV set remained a puzzle to George Morrison. Not a complete puzzle, though, for he had put in a piece here and there, and eight years later he was sure that he only needed two or three more 'pieces' to complete the odd mystery.

He was intensely obsessed with the old television and the way that he seemed to stay perpetually linked with it.

He had first begun work on his 'puzzle' four days after selling the set to the older man, whose obit in the *Journal* that day said his name was Merv Calhoun. The cause of Merv's death was not *massive coronary*, as had been Victor Haynes'. The cause of Merv's death was something else altogether—something that put a different perspective on things. The *Journal* had stated that the cause of death was *unknown,* and that may have been *the* one thing that started George's mind to thinking—the *unknown.*

Merv Calhoun's widow had held an auction two weeks later in order to liquidate her late husband's belongings. Going through the legal process with her attorney was a hassle, and she had told a local reporter that she just couldn't stay in the house that she and Merv had shared, and that she had decided to go up to Springfield, Missouri, and move in with her older sister, who was also widowed. She would need the money now that poor Merv couldn't support her anymore.

George had read about the auction in the paper (along with Mrs. Calhoun's heartbreaking words). It was on a Saturday, and he went out early to the Calhoun farm just outside the city limits, hoping to find a few items worth bidding on that he might be able to get at a good price. He was also curious about how the two deaths seemed linked somehow to him and the television. That sounded outrageous, but he was a man who could not fathom coincidences.

On that Saturday afternoon, he was the only person to make a bid on the television. He bid twenty dollars on it, sure that it would be raised by some man or woman who thought that he or she could use an old black and white in their guest bedroom. But no one had.

After two onlookers helped him load the TV onto his old Chevy truck, George took it back to his shop, along with a toaster, an automatic coffee maker, and some garden tools.

He sold the TV again three weeks later, and it was going on a year before some kid who looked no older than sixteen brought it into George's shop to unload it for whatever he could get out of it.

Over the years, George had followed the television's owners almost obsessively, slowly realizing that something was happening, and trying desperately to find a patter in order to get on top of the situation, which became progressively horrifying to him. He had done quite a bit of research, and a more than average share of speculation, and all he had come away with so far were several disturbing facts. The least of them was this: when Richard Raines had entered his shop this afternoon, George had known that he was looking for a television.

But not just *any* television—*That* television. *These lame brains,* George had thought to himself. *I wish guys like him were looking for refrigerators or something. I could probably take them for a ride.* But, of course, he could never bring himself to do that. He had hiked the price up to seventy-five dollars in the hopes that the man would shy away and look at a different television set. That hadn't worked.

George Morrison knew what he would be doing over the next several days, if not longer. He poured himself another dose of gin, added a shot of tonic, and stirred it meticulously with his index finger. He knew that the first thing he would do about this new development in his 'puzzle' would be to wait.

And watch.

6

At first, he didn't know what had happened, or how long he had been sleeping on the floor in front of the television. He had vague memories of the cable returning, and then…and then…

Channel 94? Did he say Channel 94?

And then the guy on the screen had spoken to him—had said his *name* for Christ's sake. The fuzziness from the fainting spell was leaving his head in slow increments, but he could remember that much quite plainly.

He looked at the screen.

White snow, no sound.

He looked at his watch.

11:45.

Just a dream, then.

But was *it a dream, Richard?*

Of course, it was.

Just a dream, or are you just too afraid to admit that it really happened?

Shit like that doesn't *happen, so it* didn't *happen.*

Yet, something inside him—a gut feeling, perhaps instinct—told him that it had *indeed* happened. It was just too vivid for it to have been a dream.

He turned the TV off and trudged wearily to his bedroom, which to him was now the loneliest place in the apartment. But he wasn't able to shake what had happened from his mind. His head throbbed where he had bumped it against the bookshelf. The amount of beer he'd drunk didn't help in that area, either.

It wasn't until the sky clouded over, until the first drops of rain hit his bedroom window a little past two o'clock, that he was able to fall asleep.

Only then did he dream. But not of the TV, as he thought he might. He dreamed instead of something more frightening to him at this point in time than even that.

He dreamed of Tina.

*****

In his dream—and he had lost count of how many times he'd dreamed this same dream, or a version of it—Tina was telling him once again that she was leaving him.

Although he had replayed that moment in his mind time and time again—the tone of her voice cold and stony, the look in her blue eyes somehow a bleary red—this time was different. In reality, she had left him only because she knew he had found out what she'd been doing behind his back. In this dream, however, the chain of events was completely different.

Because...what?

Because she was *laughing* at him. Yes, laughing—her head thrown back in a wild fit of screams, laughter, and giggles that chilled his heart. And when at last the laughter subsided, she brought her head down slowly, and to Richard's horror her upper canines had grown incredibly long. But not just long ...they looked painfully sharp. They bit into her lower lip, puncturing it repeatedly as she talked.

"I did it, Richard. I fucked *all* of them. Rob, Billy, Kerry, Pat...hell, I even let two guys I didn't even *know* put it in me at the same time. *At the same time, Richard! At the same time!*"

"*No—*"

"Yeah, that's what your buddy Paul said, that little wimp. If he wasn't so much like you, I would have fucked *him,* too. But I didn't need him. I got all I wanted *when* I wanted it, and you were too fucking blind to see what was going on until it was too late." She went into another screaming fit of laughter, a sound that was nothing like the smooth, gentle laugh that Tina possessed.

"Fucked them *all,* Richard."

"I did it, Richard…"

"At the same time, Richard!"

"At the same time…fucked them *all,* Richard…at the same time…I *did* it, Richard…!"

"Did it…"

"Time…"

And then she was coming at him, fangs bared, arms outstretched, grinning, a distorted facsimile of the woman she had been.

That is when Richard woke, stifling a scream behind his pursed lips, cold sweat zigzagging down his forehead and face in small rivulets.

The rain outside had stopped, but a brisk wind still whispered around the eaves, producing a low, eerie sound that he had gotten used to over the last three years. He looked at the clock on the nightstand: 5:17a.m.

He got up and sat on the edge of the bed, running a trembling hand through his tussled hair. God, what a dream.

What a nightmare.

He didn't know why he had dreamed about the fangs and the laughing, but the rest…well, he knew damn well why he might have dreamed of those events.

He went into the kitchen and put on a pot of coffee, the images of his dream lingering, fading slowly. He figured he wouldn't be able to sleep again in the next long hour before dawn, but before his *Mr. Coffee* had finished its job he was sprawled out on the living room sofa, one arm dangling down to the floor, the other tucked behind his head, sound asleep.

And this time there were no dreams.

8

Richard was awakened by the sound of the telephone ringing; faintly at first, and then much louder as he came up from the depths of sleep.

The phone was on the floor next to the fireplace, and he crawled to it groggily, blinking his eyes against the morning sunlight that slanted into the room from the east-facing windows.

He managed to get the receiver to his ear, rubbing sleep from his eyes with his free hand. "Yeah."

"Hey, where have you *been,* man? Do you know what time it is?" It was Paul.

"Oh shit," Richard said, realizing suddenly what the call meant. He looked at his watch. Half past nine. He was late for work. "I fell asleep on the sofa...didn't hear the alarm clock in the bedroom."

"You'd better hurry and get here. Patrick is on the warpath." Paul's voice was disquieting.

"What has he said?" Richard asked. He now had the phone cradled against his shoulder and was hastily undressing.

"Not much yet, but..."

"Then what in hell is he on the warpath about? I'm only thirty minutes late."

"I know that," Paul said. "and *he* knows that, but if you're not here for the presentation for the Anderson and Son's account, well..."

"Oh Christ. Oh boy."

"Yeah."

"I forgot all about that being today. Shit."

"You've got all the layouts for it together, don't you?" Paul asked.

"Yeah. I've had them ready since last Tuesday. It's just that I sure picked one hell of a day to oversleep."

"I'll say."

"Damn."

"Well listen," Paul said. "Is there anything up here that needs to be done that I can do while you're on your way?"

Richard paused for a minute, considering. "Nothing off the top of my head, but thanks anyway. I'm pretty sure I've got everything here with me." And then, as an afterthought: "At least I think so."

"Okay. The presentation is at ten-fifteen, so…" he trailed off.

"I'll be there in less than thirty minutes, Paul. Tell Pat not to shit his drawers or anything. We've got this account nailed down as tight as a coffin."

"Okay." The relief in Paul's voice was quite evident.

"And Paul?"

"Yeah?"

"Thanks for calling and waking me up. You're a life saver. I really appreciate it."

"No problem. Try not to worry about it."

"I won't. This thing will be wrapped up in a few hours and then we can talk about it over drinks, at lunch."

"Sounds like a plan."

Richard laid the phone onto the cradle and hurried to the bathroom for a quick shower.

As he finished showering and began dressing, he thought about the morning's upcoming presentation. Anderson and Sons was a real estate company on the west side of town near the Jonesboro city limits. The company that Richard—as well as Paul—worked for, the Jonesboro Advertising Corporation, carried accounts for several local real estate agencies, but none were anywhere near as large as Anderson and Sons, whose account would total more than five million dollars. Patrick Garnell had reminded Richard of this countless times during the two weeks Richard had spent preparing the presentation. Although Paul had helped him with some of the layouts, most of it was on Richard's shoulders, and if he and Paul made an above average presentation and acquired the real estate company's business, there would be a least a decent raise in it for him, and perhaps even a promotion.

Or maybe we won't even get the account.
Don't be so pessimistic, Richard.
I've lost counts before. Not many, but...
Big deal.
Yeah, big deal.

Richard was surprised to find—since the divorce—how easy it had become to say 'big deal' about many things, no matter how vast or significant.

He finished dressing, went into the living room, and turned on the television to check the weather forecast on Channel 11: Partly cloudy this morning, clearing this afternoon with temperatures in the low eighties. Good. It would be a nice day. At least as far as the weather was concerned.

As he bent forward to turn the TV off, the screen was abruptly filled with the face of someone that Richard didn't at first recognize; a newscaster, perhaps.

But then a chill swept through him as recognition dawned on his face. It wasn't a newscaster smiling serenely at him from the TV screen. It was the guy

Channel 94

who had been on the set last night; the man who had spoken to him, although that had been—and still was—impossible.

Richard backed up a step, mouth and eyes gaping at the screen. His throat felt dry and sticky, and his head swirled.

And then, incredibly, the man said: "A newscaster, huh? Jesus, Richard, give will a break, will you?" The man began

48

picking lint from his black suit as he talked. "And please don't faint on my again. Last night was enough, although I had been expecting as much. It's just that it gets so...frustrating sometimes."

"Wha—who are you?" Richard finally managed. He had felt just seconds ago as if he *might* faint again.

"That's not really important right now, Richard. We'll talk later, perhaps as soon as this evening. My people will be here then. What's important now is that you get to your presentation. It's going to be a success, you know. The man smiled at him as though Richard was his grandson; a kind smile.

Richard reacted to the absurdity of the whole situation with the first coherent thought that entered his reeling mind.

Losing it, that's what it is. I'm losing my mind.

"No, you're not losing your mind," the man said, startling him once again.

"But—"

"Now hurry along, before you're later than you already are." The man made a shewing motion with his hand, and then the screen went blank. In the TV's wake, the sudden silence filled the room like a tomb.

He stared stupidly at the TV for about fifteen seconds, and then he picked up the advertising layouts, locked the apartment door behind him, and was soon sitting in the cab of his truck, breathing heavily and sweating.

All he could think of on the way to the office was the same thing he had thought earlier in his living room, when the man on the screen had somehow heard his thoughts.

I'm losing my mind. I'm losing my fucking mind.

9

At five minutes of five o'clock, the pay phone in the back room of Maurice's Café rang shrilly, startling Tina Raines, who was changing into a fresh set of clothes before her shift ended at five. The phone, which was mounted along the back wall next to a small row of shabby lockers, was labeled with a rough piece of cardboard and a black marker as *Employee Telephone*. The sign was hung there years ago by the café's owner, Maurice Carmine, who disliked the idea of his employees using his business phone. Tina knew that he didn't like his waitresses to change out of their uniforms even five minutes before their shifts ended, but she also knew that a large part of the customers that patronized the small café enjoyed her waiting on them, and she figured Maurice himself knew that good waitresses were hard to come by. So, screw him if he had a problem with her quitting a little early.

Now the phone rang a second time, echoing loudly in the deserted room.

The other waitresses on shift, Melanie Stevens and Gayle Lombard, were staying on until seven, picking up a little overtime that Tina knew she could use herself, and so she was alone in the dimly lit room.

Wriggling the rest of the way into her jeans, she made her way over to the phone and answered it after the third ring. "Hello?"

The voice on the other end was male, coarse yet smooth. "Yes, I'm trying to get in touch with Tina Raines. Is she by chance still there?"

Before she answered, Tina tried mentally to place the man's voice, and then she tried to remember to whom she had given this number. She could do neither, but the man sounded nice enough. "This is her speaking," she said, a small, flattered grin spreading across her face.

"Tina! This is Biff."

"Biff?"

"Yes, Biff. Don't you remember? We have a date tonight."

Tina detected slight disappointment in his voice. "I was just calling to see if you were going to be ready by seven.

Biff.

Suddenly she remembered, and felt stupid and foolish. "Of course I remember, Biff. I'm sorry. It's just been a long day."

Biff sighed audibly on the other end. He sounded relieved. "So. See you at seven? Snow's Bar and Grille?"

"Yes," Tina said. "Seven o'clock will be fine."

"Great. See you then." He hung up.

Tina put the phone on the hook and, without thinking, stuck her middle finger in the coin return slot to make sure one of the other girls hadn't left a free call in there somewhere.

Going to her locker and standing in front of the small mirror at the top of the door, she thought about the evening ahead of her. How could she have forgotten Biff Larento? She had met him at The Scene four days ago, after admiring him for nearly two hours from two tables away, while she drank about four too many drinks. His short, coal-black hair, high cheekbones and square jawline, topped off with two sparkling emerald-green eyes, immediately appealed to her. He was handsome.

Yet to her he was, upon first sight, more than that. His lean, muscular body was downright god-like, pressing against the black jeans and red muscle shirt that he'd been wearing as though at any minute his broad chest and robust legs would simply shed the clothes like some sort of excess skin.

She had finally, after noticing that he was there by himself—although he fielded quite a few appraising looks from some of the other females at the club—asked him to dance. After three dances, he asked her to join him at his table, and before she knew it, they were at his place on the south side of town, in bed together. When the lovemaking was over, she returned to her own apartment, feeling—aside from drunk—fresh and alive.

And feeling something else, as well. Something that she hadn't felt in a long time, not even with the two guys she had slept with since she had met Biff (and part of her felt really awful about *that*). Tina felt as though she could fall for Biff Larento without a look back; could fall for him as easily as a young child falls for the cute puppy or kitten that his mother or father brings home for him.

She could fall more easily than that...if it wasn't for Richard, and the way he had screwed her over in the divorce settlement.

She realized now that one thing was the real reason she had forgotten about her date with Biff—had momentarily forgotten his name. She had spent the entire morning and most of the day thinking of how she could get revenge on Richard for what he had done to her life.

Her mother wasn't alive to help her out of the jam she was in, and she couldn't—*wouldn't*—go to Richard about it in any straightforward way. It simply would not work. She had no one she could turn to, no one she could rely on, except for herself.

A part of her wondered passingly if this was the reason she felt the way she did about Biff Larento—that it wasn't a symptom of love at all, or the closeness provided by sex—only a need to be heard by a friendly, understanding ear, and to have someone tell her that what she was doing wasn't wrong; wasn't her fault. Almost fearfully, she wondered if she felt that way because she needed help turning her life around—that she couldn't do it alone.

She pushed these uncharitable thoughts aside with a brisk rake of mental fingers.

She didn't need Biff's or anyone else's help—at least at the moment—to set her life straight and make Richard pay for what he had done to her. On her lunchbreak that day at noon, she finally came to a decision about what to do and called Richard's attorney, a man by the name of Thomas Harrington, to set up an appointment for the following morning. He had been disagreeable at first with the idea of an appointment with him after she told him its purpose, but quickly complied to the meeting when Tina told him that she would go over his head—possibly to a judge, or another lawyer—to the get the information she was after.

So, the appointment was made and she hadn't needed any outside help to do *that.*

The idea she had was undoubtedly a shot in the dark, but more than that, it was a start. And she couldn't help herself or do anything about her situation without starting *somewhere.*

She finished brushing her hair, added a little make-up to the soft skin of her face, picked up her handbag, and clocked out at the employee time clock.

If she hurried, she would have time for a few drinks on the way home, before preparing further for her date with Biff Larento.

10

"Paul, I need to talk to you about something," Richard said.

They were at The Faria, having after-lunch drinks from a bottle of *Dom Perignon* with which Patrick had surprised them after the presentation. The *successful* presentation. It had gone very smoothly, and the executives for Anderson and Sons had been impressed and confident in Richard's ideas for promoting their businesses, and had told him as much. Patrick had given them both the rest of the day off.

Now, sitting here with their drinks in hand and their bodies full of rich food, the morning's festivities seemed days old, although the bright afternoon sun was still hours away from setting.

"Sure, Richie, anything," Paul said, sipping his champagne.

"Well, maybe it can wait for later," Richard said, cutting his eyes away from Paul's. "I'd hate to put a damper on our little celebration."

Paul looked concerned. "Nothing serious, is it?" He put down his wine glass.

If you only knew, Richard thought. *If I only knew how to tell you about it.* "No," he said. "Nothing so serious it can't wait until later."

Paul picked up his glass and emptied it, reaching for the bottle. "Are you sure?"

"Yes," Richard said. He picked up his own glass. "Pretty good, isn't it?"

"Yeah. Best I've ever tasted. But it still hasn't calmed me down much. I was *so* nervous this morning."

"It's a large account."

Paul let out a deep sigh. "I'm just glad it's over."

"Me, too."

For his part, Richard had been more than nervous when he arrived at work. He had been distraught with thoughts about what had happened at his apartment that morning. First oversleeping, and then the business with the television. But shortly after starting his presentation he had settled into a comfortable groove: stable, sure of himself, with unfailing speech that was his trademark while giving such a presentation.

Thoughts about the TV had seemed to fragment into tiny, unimportant pieces.

But now, something—the champagne, perhaps—seemed to be gluing those pieces back into complete thoughts.

If you tell Paul, he'll think you're crazy.

And that would just confirm my own doubts. Maybe I am.

But are *you going crazy, Richard? Are* you losing your mind?

He decided he would have to do some more thinking on that one, and so, after first considering telling Paul, he shied away from the idea, hoping that he could first work the answer out by himself. Or at least try. And this wasn't the right time, anyway, if he were to be honest with himself.

"...to you?"

"Hmm? I'm sorry, I didn't catch all of that. Woolgathering."

"I said, do you suppose you'll get the raise you have coming to you?"

Richard brightened a little. "I had better get at *least* a raise, because if I don't, I'll tell Patrick that he can start doing this crap himself." He emptied his glass and Paul poured it full for him again. Richard seemed to think about it. "In fact, we had *both* better get raises."

"Think so?"

"Of course. You were a big help, man. You put a lot of work into it, and I've already made sure Patrick knows it. And from the way he was acting when we left the office, I'd say the chances are looking pretty good."

"He *was* happy, wasn't he?"

"Happy isn't the word for it. He was ecstatic," Richard said, thinking about all the claps on the back and the zany smiles Patrick had given him after the presentation was over and the executives from Anderson and Sons had left.

"So," Paul said, raising his glass above the table. "Suppose we propose a toast."

"Sure," Richard said, raising his own. "You call it, hombre."

"To us," Paul said, with a smile at the corner of his lips. "Screw Patrick for now."

Richard smiled as they brought their glasses together. "To us." *And to my sanity,* he thought to himself.

They emptied their glasses and slammed them down on the small table at roughly the same time. Then they both burst out laughing, attracting odd stares from three older ladies who were two tables over.

Richard poured the remaining contents of the bottle into the empty glasses, a blank, thoughtful look suddenly clouding his reddening face. His thoughts had gone unexpectedly to the dream he'd had the night before: Tina, and the fangs poking through her lips, mutilating them.

"So, how are you handling the divorce?" Paul asked.

Jeez, my mind must be an open window today."

"Pretty well," Richard said. "Why?"

"I don't know. Just wondering." Paul looked as though he wanted to say more but wasn't sure how to go about it. "Listen, Richie, you know that I'm here if you ever need to talk to me about anything. Anything at all."

"I know that," Richard said. "I didn't mean to sound hateful. I just...I've got it. Thanks for being concerned."

"No problem, man."

"I've had a lot on my mind lately. I should be relieved that the presentation is over, and I guess I am." He finished his glass and looked out over the pleasant view of Highland Drive and then, almost as an afterthought, added. "Now if I could only get *this* shit off my mind."

"What?"

"Nothing," Richard said after a moment. "You about ready to blow this joint?"

"Sure," Paul said. "And what do you say we stop by Hal's Liquor Store on the way to the house? Feel like a little more celebrating?

Richard smiled. "That sounds like a *damn* good idea. But we can skip Hal's if you want. I've got two pints of Jim Beam and a fifth of Crown Royal at home beneath the bar just waiting for the right situation and the right men for the job."

"Well now," Paul said, slipping an arm around Richard's shoulders as they made their way out of the restaurant. "I believe this is as good a situation as any, and we *definitely* qualify as the right men for the job. Don't you think?"

"I sure as shit do," Richard said, feeling light-headed from the expensive bubbly. "Maybe we'll see what's on the tube afterwhile, too," he said, thinking suddenly about the television again.

And maybe my new friend will show up again. Wouldn't that be funny?

"We'll talk later, perhaps as soon as this evening."

And just what will Paul think if he does?

"My people will be here then."

Richard shook his head numbly. Of course, that was it! He had thought about telling Paul about the TV and had back out of the idea at the last minute, but now he could just *show* it to him.

And if nothing happens?

If nothing happens, I'll know for a fact that I'm going bananas. Won't that be a riot?

"Sure, we might even watch a little television," Paul said. "It's been a long time since I watched a black and white, anyway."

They both laughed, and then they were on their way to Richard's apartment, the sun cascading brightly from an almost clear sky.

11

By the time they arrived at his place, Richard was beginning to feel the full effect of the bottle of *Dom Perignon,* and he had to fumble with his keys for about thirty seconds before he could fit the right one into the slot in the front door, finally succeeding, and half-stumbling through the open door into the living room. He went straight to the bar and mixed two drinks while Paul dropped down heavily on the sofa, sighing.

Richard brought the drinks over and sat down in the floor opposite the sofa. There they sat idly for better than two hours, drinking one mixed drink after another, smoking cigarettes, and talking—mostly about the stressful yet wonderful day at work, but about other things, as well.

It was about four o'clock when Richard remembered the TV.

"Want to see what's on?"

"Sure. What the hell," Paul said. "I've got a helluva buzz. How about you?"

"Buzz isn't the word for it," Richard told him. "I'd almost say that I was on my way to being shit-faced drunk." He made his way to the TV, staggering and almost falling more than once. They had gone through half of the fifth of Crown Royal and had started on one of the pints of Beam.

"What's on this time of day, anyway?" Paul said.

"The Munsters just started a few minutes ago. Of course it's in black and white, anyway."

"Sounds okay to me," Paul said. He laid his had on the armrest of the sofa and closed his eyes, moaning softly.

Richard turned the set on and turned the channel selector to 10. They were just a few minutes into the show when the phone rang, startling both of them. Richard picked it up on the fifth ring. It had taken him that long to move fifteen feet across the living room floor. "It's for you, man," he said, handing the phone to Paul after almost dropping it twice.

"The old lady?"

"You got it."

"Oh shit." He took the receiver and talked into it while Richard turned his attention back to The Munsters.

From what Richard couldn't help overhearing, it sounded as though Margie was on Paul's case pretty hard, probably for not calling or going next door to tell her where he was. Or perhaps she was having problems understanding his slurry voice. It had never been like that until Tina left. Before that, the two of them—Paul and Margie—would visit together on occasion, and the two women had gotten along fairly well, even though they had very dissimilar personalities. He supposed some things change, though, and he didn't see much of Margie anymore. He generally assumed she had chosen to be on Tina's side of the divorce, but he didn't know for sure. "That's women for ya," Paul often told him, and Richard thought he was beginning to see some sense in that ancient male statement.

Paul slammed the phone down and got up sluggishly. "Richie, I hate to drink and run, but I've got to get over to the house. It slipped my mind that Margie's parents were coming over tonight."

"Okay. No problem."

Paul seemed to consider this. "You're right, you know. The state I'm in, I can put up with just about anything. Even in-laws."

They both laughed and then Paul left, stumbling across the front yard toward his own apartment. Richard closed the door and shut out the last of the remaining daylight. The sudden silence was unsettling.

But quiet? The TV was on and...no, not quite quiet. Richard turned around slowly, already anticipating what he was hearing. A faint, staticky sound was emanating from the end of the room next to the bookshelf. His scalp tingled as though being massaged by a million fingers.

The television.

Oh, God, not again.

Richard stared hard at the floor, trying not to look at the TV, but he couldn't help but hear the voice that came from it.

"Oh yes, Richard. Again. Didn't I tell you that we'd get together for a little chat tonight?"

It was the man from channel 94 *(the network that shows you more),* and although Richard felt he shouldn't have been surprised, he was. What surprised him even more was that the man had kept good on his other promise; he could hear an unseen audience applauding, laughing, and shouting.

The man on the screen leaned forward across the table, counter, or desk he was behind (it favored a desk more than anything). "What's the matter, Richard? A little rough on the bourbon this evening?" The hidden audience fell silent.

Richard managed to reach the sofa, and he plopped down on it with another groan. "Yeah, a little rough on the bourbon. You could say that."

"Well, what do you know?" the man on the screen said. "He *does* talk. I *knew* he did!" The crowd in the background went wild them, and Richard was reminded of the unseen audience that was nevertheless there on the game shows he had stopped watching years ago.

The man on the screen was wearing the same black suit he had been wearing the two prior times Richard had seen him, only instead of a red tie, the man wore a bright yellow one around the collar of his white dress shirt. It seemed to Richard to glare like the sun in the early hours of morning—bright but soft on the eye.

"Wh—who are you?" he finally managed.

"Who am *I? Who am I,* Richard?" The man chuckled heartily and his audience—if that was indeed what it was—laughed along with him. "Why, I'm *yours,* Richard. You own me. You bought me, and now you own me. It's a hell of a deal, isn't it? Who did you think I was, anyway, Bob Barker?" The man's audience really got going on that one, and Richard felt his face begin to flush. Not with anger, but with embarrassment.

What the hell are you embarrassed about? Must be because you're talking to your damn television set.

"You're not talking to your set, Richard," the man cajoled. "You're talking to *me.*"

"But who are you besides…besides…mine."

"That's a good question. And I will answer it for you if you'll do two simple things for me. Now listen."

Feeling more curious than he did frightened, and also feeling sobriety making a dim return, Richard listened to his TV.

12

When Paul told Margie about that morning's presentation, her demeanor changed quickly from a light anger to a gleeful mood, and it seemed to no longer bother her so much that he had been next door celebrating.

She kissed him lightly on the forehead, told him to just sit back and relax, brought him a cup of hot coffee, and went to the kitchen to finish preparing dinner. Margie Frazier was six-feet-one, three inches taller than Paul, and although they attracted some odd stares from people in public, neither one of them saw anything in their differing sizes that prohibited their relationship in any way. Margie's dark, elegant hair and deep brown eyes gave her a gentle look that betrayed her size. The only thing Paul had ever found even remotely wrong with their relationship was that, occasionally, she seemed overly protective and worrisome over him. And tonight she had been that way again—at least at first. As was usually the case, Paul explained to her in detail the reasons for his actions and she quickly became her usual self; gentle, cheerful.

Paul wondered how he had ever been so lucky to marry a woman who was so understanding.

While she was out in the kitchen putting the finishing touches on the steak dinners she was preparing, he sat in the front room, sipping strong black coffee, and thought about the day's events, especially the way his friend had acted, off and on, during most of the morning and afternoon.

Something was bothering Richard, and although Paul at first thought it was the divorce, he now considered, in his drunken state, that it might just be something else, as well.

Although Patrick Garnell would not have noticed any subtle change in Richard from day to day, at work or anywhere else, Paul could. He and Richard had been friends for too long for him *not* to notice even the slightest change. You couldn't fool your closest friends very often. And from the time Paul had realized Richard was going to be late for work, and called him, he had known something was wrong.

For one thing, Richard was *never* late for work, and as far as Paul knew, he wasn't in the habit of falling asleep on the sofa, away from the alarm clock. A dependable, reliable man, he had always been punctual when it came to his work habits.

This was what first caused Paul to think that the only thing bothering his friend was the divorce. Richard hadn't talked to him much about it, and now Paul was beginning to fear that his friend was closing up like a shell and would never let him know how he was coping, how he was taking the sudden change in a life that had been so neat, orderly, and well-kept.

Paul would give him some more time to come around, but he was going to have to say something to Richard soon.

The doorbell chimed throughout the condo, startling Paul out of his thoughts about Richard, and into thoughts about something not quite as problematic: his in-laws were here.

He groaned, and as Margie hustled in from the kitchen to answer to door (frowning at him as she passed the sofa) Paul prepared himself for one of the occasions he dreaded most in life—dinner with his sweet wife's parents.

13

That night after dinner—which hadn't turned out so badly after all—and after making love with his wife, Paul Frazier lay awake until almost one o'clock in the morning thinking about his friend. He would give it a couple of days, and if Richard didn't confide in him about what was on his mind—what had caused him to alienate himself from him—then Paul was going to bring the subject up himself. It couldn't hurt.

Under no circumstances would he allow such a close friendship to come apart. Not because of a divorce from a woman who never truly loved Richard.

Not for anything.

14

"Don't turn me off," the man on the screen said.

"What?"

"You heard me. I don't stutter and your ears don't flap. I said, don't turn me off. That's the first thing. Simple enough?"

"You mean, don't turn you off *ever?*"

The man rolled his eyes. *"No,* I don't mean ever. Just don't turn me off until we're through with tonight's little...show. Fair enough?"

"Fair enough." *Tonight's little show? Is that what he said?*

"Don't worry, Richard," the man said. "It's nothing bad, really. You might even have fun, who knows?" The man seemed to gaze past the screen, over Richard's shoulder. "Isn't that right, gang?" This time the applause was deafening.

Richard cleared his throat. His head had cleared remarkably since the man had first come onto the screen, but he still felt light-headed, almost as if he was hung over instead of on his way to becoming rat-faced drunk. And the tingling sensation along his scalp wouldn't seem to go away. "What's the second thing?" he asked.

"The second thing is even more simple than the first. All you have to do is answer a question for me. Think you can do that?"

"I can try, I guess," Richard said, wondering why the man's patronizing voice seemed to be grating on his nerves.

"Good." The man smiled and swallowed visibly, as if he were a woman fixing to tell her neighbor some hot gossip. "Are you ready for the question?"

"As I'll ever be."

"Okay, here it is: What's two plus two?"

Richard was stunned. He had been expecting something more along the line of 'what's the population of Flagstaff Arizona?' Something like that would fit in nicely with his mind's increasing insistence that the man was a game show host. He started laughing.

"Well, what's the answer?"

And if I get it right, Richard thought crazily, *do I get what's behind curtain number one, or curtain number two?*

The man's audience fell silent, and Richard managed to stop laughing.

"Four," he said. "The answer is four."

"That's correct!" the man yelled happily. The crowd in the background went wild once again.

For some reason agitated by this, a new thought popped into Richard's head. He reached for the volume control.

"No, *wait!*" the man hollered, stilling the noisy audience. The smile was gone from his face and it was replaced by…what? Fear? Yes, Richard thought maybe it was.

He had to smile at that. The man wasn't in *total* control of the situation, then. He pulled his hand back a little. "What's wrong?" he asked the man on the screen.

"Don't turn me off. You said that you wouldn't." The man's voice was clearly a plea.

"Well look here, Mr. whoever-you-are. If all you can do is insult my intelligence by asking me a silly question, and then laugh at me, I don't want to hear anything you have to say."

"Okay, okay. I'm just joking around. I didn't mean anything by it. After all, I told you it would be a simple question. I mean, I *could* have asked you, for instance, the population of Flagstaff, Arizona. Right?" He tipped a wink at Richard.

"Right."

"Then you would never know who I am, would you?"

Richard sighed heavily. "No."

"Now, I'm sorry if I've upset you. I just like to clown around sometimes, that's all. You ought to do it more often yourself. You'd be surprised what a good sense of humor can do for a person."

Richard suddenly, helplessly, felt bad. The man was right. But hell, this all seemed so crazy. It *was* crazy. Nevertheless, the bad feeling was there. Or maybe it was the alcohol fogging his brain. "I'm sorry, whatever your name is."

"Jerry, please," the man said.

At least we're on a first name basis now, Richard thought, and almost laughed.

"I'm sorry, *Jerry*. I guess I'm just a little drunk right now. And it's not every day that I have my television talking to me, and me to it." He walked to the bar and made another drink from the bottle of Jim Beam.

"That's quite alright, and I understand. Actually, there's a reason behind me asking you that particular question."

Richard sat back down on the sofa and lit a cigarette.

"I asked that question because of its answer.

"Four."

"Right. That is the number I had in mind. Now, let me ask you something else. If you don't mind, that is," Jerry added.

"Shoot."

"Does the number four hold any significance to you?"

"As a matter of fact, it does," Richard said. "It just so happens that four is my favorite number."

"And why is that?" Jerry asked conversationally.

"Hell, I don't know. I guess everyone has their own favorite number, and mine just happens to be four. Not any real reason for it. Call it superstition if you want."

"Is that right?"

Richard thought for a moment. "Well, I was born on the fourth of October, if that matters any."

"It doesn't," Jerry said. "What about when you were four years old? That's what I'm trying to get at."

"What about it?"

"Do you remember anything...important...happening to you at that time of your life?"

"Are you kidding? I'm almost thirty-five and you're asking if I remember anything important that happened to me when I was just *four?* You've *got* to be kidding." Richard laughed and took a sip from his drink. "What could have been so important that I should remember it, when I was so young at the time?"

"Oh, lots of things," Jerry said. "Anything that happens in *anyone's* life is important. It may not seem like it to them at the time, but it is. People learn more from experience than they do from anything else. Do you agree with that?"

"I guess that's a pretty safe thing to say," Richard said. It felt as though his buzz was rekindling, a fuzzy-numb feeling that wasn't totally unpleasant.

"Right. But the thing is, most people take all but the largest lessons in life for granted. I'll give you an example," the man said, as though Richard had specifically requested one.

Most parents tell their children to look both ways before crossing the street—good common sense—but little kids still get run over nearly every day. It just happens. Whether they were told to look both ways, or whether they just know to, it still happens. And do you know why, Richard?"

"I give up. Why?"

Jerry said, "Because they were only *told* not to cross the street until after they've looked both ways. They haven't been creamed by a Mack truck doing fifty miles an hour, or thirty, so they really couldn't tell you *why* they look both ways before crossing a street. Sure, they *think* they know what would happen—they might get ran over—and to a certain extent they are correct, but until it happens, they can't really tell you why they look both ways. Not really. It would *scare* them to know the real reason why.

"Now on the other hand, take a child who has crossed without looking and has come within an inch of being hit by a passing vehicle—whether he'd been chasing a ball or simply not paying attention. Now *that* child understands a little better the reason why you should look both ways before crossing the street. He or she doesn't *totally* understand, but better than anyone who hasn't had the same experience.

"And then there are the children who *do* chase the ball into the street, and the ones who don't pay attention to what they're doing, who *do* get ran over by the Mack truck. Now *they* could tell you the *real* reason why you don't cross the street before looking both ways first. But of course, for them, it's usually too late."

Jerry stopped here, lit a cigarette (a brand called *Demptus* that Richard had never seen nor heard of before), and stared at him while he smoked.

Richard felt as though Jerry was waiting for him to say something, and he was right. "Well?" Jerry asked.

"What has this got to do with me being four years old? I never an *experience* while crossing the street."

"I know that," Jerry said, letting a smile spread across his face again. "What I'm trying to say is that *life* is that way, too. The child who comes within an inch of being hit by that Mack truck might forget about it even happening on down the road— no pun intended—but inside, *inside,* he doesn't forget, and he's instinctively more cautious when he crosses the street. He might seem to have forgotten the close call with that truck, but in reality, *inside,* no one ever forgets anything that happens to them, *or* what they learned from it. Do you understand what I'm saying?"

"I...guess I do," Richard said, although he wasn't positive about it. "I just don't see what this has to do with—"

"Does the name Peter Irons ring a bell?"

Richard suddenly dropped his glass onto the carpet and whiskey and coke, ice cubes included, spilled in all directions on the thick carpet.

"Ah-h," Jerry said contently. He leaned back in his chair and looked at Richard. His unseen audience had been relatively quiet for the last few minutes, and now they were so silent they might not have been there at all.

A light sweat appeared on Richard's forehead. "I-I...How did you know about...? I'd forgotten all *about* him."

"Yet really you haven't. Not inside. You're like the child that came within an inch of being hit while crossing the street, and who thought *he'd* forgotten about *that.* And let's just say that I can see what's hidden inside of you, even if you consciously can't. And I'll help *you* see what's there, too, if you will let me."

"But I don't *want* to remember him," Richard said, almost childishly, as those old memories began to nudge at the front of his mind. He began whistling loudly and his eyes began searching the living room ceiling. He was clearly trying his best to pay no attention to what this man, Jerry, had said. But he couldn't. No amount of whistling could keep away the thought. It had nibbled a hole through the block in his mind and was now up front, ready to be dealt with. "Oh, God."

"Listen, Richard," Jerry said in a calm voice. "I'm only going to help you. That's what I'm here for. What happened with Peter Irons is in the past. You're a grown man now. *Think* about what happened, and live with it. And then, maybe..." Jerry shrugged his shoulders. "And then maybe something can be done about it."

Richard sighed heavily. "I can't *help* but think about it now. It's *there*."

"Then go ahead, Richard. *Think* about it. That's the only way."

Richard leaned back on the sofa, and since he could do nothing *but* think about it—the memory was now like a wave cascading over his entire body, mind, and soul—he did the most natural thing in the world.

He remembered…

15

Summertime, 1966. Jacksonville, Florida

Four-year-old Richie Raines walked along Neptune Beach, holding his mother's hand, as water from the Atlantic Ocean rippled between his bare feet. Great white seagulls cried shrilly above the sandy beach, as if telling the last of the day's swimmers that the sun would be going down soon and that they had overstayed their visit and it was time for them to go home—it was their beach.

"But can't I go with you, Mom?"

"No, Richie. I've already told you that you can't. Your father and I won't be back until late tonight, and that's much too late for a little boy like you to be up. Besides, Audrey will be there with you. You like her, don't you?"

"Yeah, I guess," Richie said. "But sometimes her boyfriend comes over, and then she won't play with me or read me any stories before I go to bed. She just wants to smooch with her 'ol boyfriend." He kicked a shell that was sticking up from the sand and then stared down at his feet as they walked.

His mother ruffled his sandy brown hair and laughed. She was a dark-haired woman with an appreciative smile, beautiful blue eyes, and a rather thin neck that made her resemble Olive Oyl on the *Popeye* cartoons. "I know how you feel, honey," she said. "But Audrey sometimes has things of her own to do while she's watching you. Things that she would do on her own time, anyway. Like homework and...her boyfriend. I'm just glad that she doesn't mind sitting for your father and me. It's very nice of her. And she likes you."

"I like her, too, but..." He trailed off and looked out at the waves rolling in from the wide expanse of water.

"But what, honey?" she asked, stopping and turning Richie around to face her. "What is it?"

Tears began to run in two small streams down Richie's tanned face. He wiped them off with the palms of his little hands, but they kept coming. Finally, he said, "I don't like Audrey's boyfriend. Peter."

His mother was shocked at this sudden outburst of tears. Richie had never before cried without at least a hint that the tears were forthcoming. She was even more astounded that he seemed to be crying because of Audrey's boyfriend. Peter Irons seemed like a nice enough young man to her: the Honor Roll every semester in high school, even in this his senior year, an athletic scholarship to attend the University of Florida next fall, good healthy looks, and an air about him that said he knew he was going somewhere and was going to make his mark in life.

What could be so wrong about Peter that it made Richie dislike him—make him cry like this?

"Honey," she said. "Why don't you like Peter?"

It was only three words, but it caused a fresh batch of tears to spill down his upturned face. "He scares me."

His mother uttered a short laugh that sounded to Richie like one of relief, and then she picked him up and hugged him close. "Oh, Richie, I'm sure that Peter is only playing with you. You shouldn't be upset about it. He's a very nice boy, and Audrey says that he helps her out quite a bit when he's over while your father and I are gone. You don't have anything to be afraid of about Peter. Okay?"

"Okay," Richie said, wiping his eyes, although he had been rather reluctant to say anything.

She set him back onto the sand and they walked across it to the parking lot.

But he didn't think it was okay. No, sir. In his four short years he had learned to trust and believe everything that his mother told him, and when she asked him 'okay,' it usually was.

But this...

For the first time in his early life, Richard Elliot Raines did not believe what his mother told him. Not by a long shot. It was *not* 'okay'. And if he knew how to go about telling his mother that, he would do it. He would tell her that it was definitely not 'okay' and he would make her believe him, too.

Was it okay when Audrey didn't feel like smooching with Peter and he took it out on Richie while they—he and Peter—played wrestling, like they sometimes did? Play-wrestle that was supposed to be *playful*. It had started out that way, yes, but one night a few months back, when Audrey hadn't felt like doing the smooching thing and Peter and Richie had begun to play-wrestle up in Richie's room, Richie had noticed a change in Peter that, had Richie been older, he would have identified as a hot annoyance, as though something were bothering him. But he *hadn't* known that something was on Peter's mind, or that perhaps he was mad at Audrey for something. All he knew was that their playful little game of wrestling soon became very lopsided, with Richie taking all of the punches and not getting a good chance to return any.

And the punches that he was receiving one after the other had suddenly become *real* punches, not play punches that made light contact, and kind of tickled. No, these punches *hurt,* and Richie soon began crying because of the flares of pain that seemed to come from all directions. Richie was beginning to believe that Audrey—who was downstairs in the living room—was either on the phone, or asleep on the sofa, and couldn't hear his cries.

Peter must have known better, because he quit punching on Richie and, just before he left the room, tossed Richie in the air, away from him, and Richie's head hit the headboard hard enough to knock him out cold. But just before he succumbed to a thick black cloud of confusion, Audrey had slammed into the bedroom, asking what was wrong. And Peter was telling her it was okay, that Richie had just banged his head while they were play-wrestling, had started crying, that he, Peter, had calmed him down, and Richie was now falling asleep, everything was 'okay.'

But it wasn't.

It wasn't okay. And neither was the bump that was on Richie's forehead when he woke from his 'nap.' That bump *hurt*. But of course he wasn't able to tell his parents about it, because Peter beat him to that, also. His mother questioned him about what had happened when she saw the ugly lump on the head of her little four-year-old, and Peter had answered for him, telling his mother and father that Richie had fallen against the headboard during their regular game of play-wrestle, and that he was 'okay.'

His mother said he looked 'okay' and, surprisingly, so did Audrey. His father looked at the purple bruise and playfully asked Richie when he was going to turn into a pro wrestler. Then he ruffled Richie's hair and told him—to make the decision almost, but not quite, unanimous—that it was 'okay.'

Richie started to tell them they were wrong, that it was *not* okay, but as chance would have it he looked at Peter first, and the look Peter gave him made him change his mind. That look told Richie that it *was* okay, and that it was *always* going to be okay, and he had better not get any ideas. Otherwise...

So, frightened as much as a four-year-old can be, Richie had remained silent. It was not 'okay', but he said nothing anyway. Somehow the idea of telling on Peter began to look much less attractive than it had when his parents had first come through the front door that night.

Peter's rough-housing had gotten progressively worse. There were increasingly frequent 'accidents' while play-wrestling; hurtful ones to Richie, but they, too, went unnoticed by his parents. Once, even, he had heard his father telling Peter that he was proud that he and Richie got along so well, and that their play-wrestling was going to help make Richie a stronger man when he got older and life became a little tougher.

Richie's father thought everything was 'okay,' and perhaps it *was* by him, but had he ever sat down and seriously *talked* to Richie about his bruised arm, or the newest bump on his head, he would have discovered that he was being fooled into thinking everything was 'okay', when actually his son was being abused behind his back.

It was almost three weeks ago that the play-wrestling had abruptly come to a halt. But if Richie had known at the time what Peter had in mind for him after the wrestling stopped, he would have gladly chosen to be knocked around his bedroom a little more. He would have jumped up and down with anticipation at the idea.

But what Peter had in mind was not at all something to jump up and down about. He began making Richie get under his small single bed, and he would not let him out for long periods of time, sitting on top of the bed, and pressing down on Richie's hand with a sneakered foot, just hard enough to pinch it good, whenever he tried to crawl out one side or the other.

This little game went on for about three occasions that Peter was there with Audrey, and then Richie was introduced to his closet. The *dark* closet. He was too short to reach the string to the sixty-watt bulb that swayed above him somewhere in the darkness like a tempting oracle, and he was too scared to scream for Audrey. Peter had told him in a very serious way that if he screamed or cried, he would put Richie in the clothes hamper that occupied a corner of the bedroom, and that he would sit on top of it and not let Richie out—*ever.*

Richie believed him. He hated being trapped under the bed, but at least he could see around him, could see his room (and every now and then a sneakered foot darting down on one side of him or the other). The closet was worse, and when Richie was trapped in there, he thought he just might die. He couldn't see anything, and the only comfort he had was knowing some of his toys were trapped inside the closet with him; his cars, a few of his trucks, a set of building blocks. He held onto some of these toys when Peter trapped him in the closet, and it seemed to take away some of the fear. The only time they didn't was when he had reached around for one and, instead of picking up a toy truck or some blocks, his hand happened upon his plastic Godzilla monster. That time the black, sticky panic, the *knowledge* of what was happening to him, was overwhelming and would not go away until Peter let him out of the closet, laughing and telling him that he had better not tell his parents...or Audrey.

But the *clothes hamper?*

He was small and vulnerable, and he tried his best to be strong, but he wanted no part of *that.* He held Peter's threat as the truth, and so far had been lucky. Yet small as he was, he believed that his luck would soon run out. He could see, as much as a child in his position could, the sparkle in Peter's eyes whenever he threatened him with the clothes hamper. He knew that it was going to happen. Peter's eyes said so.

And you can bet your bottom dollar that Richie believed him. It was, to coin a phrase, '*not* okay.'

Richie and his mother arrived home from Neptune Beach a little past seven, and thirty minutes later the doorbell rang, a pleasant, bell-tolling sound that Richie had come to fear on nights—such as this one—when his parents were going out. He stood in the hallway at the far side of the living room, a dull, nauseating feeling in his stomach, and watched his mother cross the room to the door, putting in her earrings as she went.

His chest tightened. He was hoping against hope that tonight was one of the rare nights that Peter stayed home, and was more than relieved when Audrey stepped through the front door, alone, and smiled sweetly at him.

"Hi, Richie."

He said hello to her shyly. He was always shy whenever Audrey first came through the door, although he knew and liked her, and he usually loosened up shortly after his parents were gone. And then his mother was kissing him, leaving bright red lipstick stains on both his cheeks, and his father was hugging him tightly, telling him to be good. And then his parents were gone.

"What are you watching?" Audrey asked him. He had sat down in the floor in front of the television.

"Nothing, yet," Richie said. "But the *Mickey Mouse Club* is coming on in a few minutes." He loved watching Mickey and all his funny friends, and he never missed a show if he could help it. "Wanna watch it with me?"

"Sure. For a little while, anyway," Audrey said.

Richie turned and looked at her. A lock of her dark brown hair had fallen over one of her blue-green eyes; a look that a guy her age would think sexy. But that wasn't why Richie was looking at her. No, it wasn't her looks at all. It was the tone of her voice that had caught his attention. *For a little while, anyway.*

A chill went up his spine like icy fingers.

"How come you don't want to watch *all* of it?" He had to ask because he had to know. He was too young to understand precisely how he felt, but he knew that there had to be a reason why she couldn't watch the entire show with him.

By some instinct that he didn't comprehend or understand he knew why before she even said it.

"Well, Richie, I thought I would make some popcorn and lemonade before Peter gets here."

Richie's face turned white. Not pale like it usually did whenever he heard Peter's name, but *white.*

Audrey noticed this and seemed puzzled. "Richie, what's wrong?"

But instead of answering her, he ran to the stairs and bound up them as fast as his little legs would carry him.

He reached his room, closed the door, and laid down on his bed, crying softly to himself. The relief he had felt when Peter hadn't shown up with Audrey was completely forgotten. But had he actually *felt* that relief? No. Not totally. He knew it had been too good to be true.

When his parents were out and Audrey babysat him, he wasn't sure about *anything.* It wasn't always that way. He used to feel so big and grown up when his parents were out and he was with Audrey. He was hyper, he was happy, and he felt an uncontrollable, overwhelming sense of freedom that was beyond his reasoning.

Now he felt lost, afraid. Alone.

"Richie?" Audrey called. It sounded as though she was coming up the stairs. "Richie? Are you alright? Richie?"

The doorbell suddenly began its bell-tolling.

Richie's head had been buried in his pillow, and now he raised it slowly. "I'm okay," he yelled. He thought she heard him, even through the closed door, and he could hear her footsteps as she retreated back down the stairs to answer the door.

But he wasn't okay. Not since she'd told him that Peter was coming over, and especially not since he was here now, for it was likely him at the door.

Hugging his pillow close, he sat up in his bed and listened.

Their voices were faint, but they were obviously close to the stairs, and he could make out enough to cause fear's cold hand to embrace him once again.

"—and he ran upstairs…his bedroom door."

"Why?" That loud voice was undoubtedly Peter's. Richie hugged his pillow tighter.

"I don't know why," Audrey said, this time loud enough for Richie to hear everything. "I was just about to talk to him when you rang the bell. He said he was okay, though."

"Probably just needs a man to talk to him." Peter again. Richie thought that he would soon be paying a visit upstairs to his room.

Audrey's voice rose, but Richie couldn't make anything out. The two of them must have moved to another room, probably the kitchen, but he could tell they were arguing now. Whether or not it was about him wasn't very clear. In fact, from the few pieces of conversation that he *could* hear, Richie surmised that Peter had taken the opportunity at hand to try and do the smooching thing with Audrey.

"Is that all you *ever* think about?" Audrey screamed, and Richie heard the anger in her voice quite clearly.

There came the unmistakable sound of a slap, followed by Audrey crying.

And then footfalls on the stairs, heavy and swift.

Richie cringed on his bed and hugged his pillow even tighter. It seemed that feathers would burst from it at any time, he held it so tightly.

The doorknob began to rattle.

"Richie," came Peter's muffled voice from the other side of the door. "Richie, it's me, Peter. Open up. You can talk to me about what's wrong." And then, in a softer voice: "Nothing is going to happen to you. Richie?"

From his bed, Richie somehow managed to find his voice, although it was choked with fear. *"No!"* he yelled as loud as his dry throat would allow. *"No!"*

"Richie, listen to me." Peter lowered his voice even more, and Richie knew that he was making sure Audrey couldn't overhear what he said. "If you don't open this door right now, then I'm going to put you in the hamper and never let you out until your parents come home."

Richie imagined he could see the sparkle in Peter's eyes as the voice came through the closed door. "You can't 'cause I won't let you in," he yelled back to Peter.

"You can't stay in there forever," Peter said, still talking low. "If you don't open this door right now, then it's going to be a whole lot worse for you, Richie. Don't make me mad, okay?"

The sincere clarity and inherent madness of that statement made Richie climb slowly off the bed and walk to the locked door. He knew that Peter was telling him the truth, and if he wasn't, well, he had to believe Peter anyway. "Okay, I'll open the door," he said.

"Wise choice, my man," came Peter's reply.

With shaking hands, Richie unlocked his bedroom door, his fear escalating to a feverish pitch. But before he could turn the handle to open it, Peter shoved it wide open from the other side and grabbed Richie up, placing one large hand over his mouth. With his left foot, Peter pushed the door shut again, and with his free hand locked it.

Richie struggled wildly but his frantic kicks and muffled screams were in vain.

"You should have opened the door when I told you to, you little shit," Peter said. There was a maniacal grin on his reddened face. He twisted Richie's right ear, causing more tears to well up in red eyes. Then he carried him over to the clothes hamper and, with one hand, turned it over and dumped the few clothes that were in it to the floor. "I guess there's only one way for you to learn to listen to me when I tell you to," Peter said. He turned the hamper upright and it hit the floor with a thud.

Richie's eyes widened when he saw what Peter planned to do with him, and he struggled even harder, all to no avail.

He had time to think that if his parents found out about this, they would never believe it. At least not if Richie told them. But who *would* tell them?

He looked down at the floor at two pairs of his socks and a pair of his jeans which had been in the hamper only seconds ago, and wished longingly to be down there with them on the floor, free from the clothes hamper. Free from Peter Irons. And he also had time to wonder *why* Peter did these things to him. He didn't think he was such a bad kid, and his parents didn't seem to think so, either. He honestly didn't believe he had ever given them a reason to.

So, why?

He didn't know.

He struggled briefly against Peter one last time, and then fell limp from exhaustion and cried quietly as Peter put him feet first into the clothes hamper and closed the lid.

Richie didn't even try to push up on the lid; if he had it wouldn't have done him a bit of good. Peter was sitting on it.

Richie closed his eyes tightly and tried not to let this dark, cramped place cause more panic than it already was. He could hear Peter saying something, lots of things, but he couldn't understand much of it because his head was pinned between his knees.

He cried openly for what seemed to him like forever, panic running rampant in his head, totally encompassing his entire being, and then began to feel as though he was dying. He almost welcomed it. He tried to think of his mother, holding his hand just this afternoon as they walked along Neptune Beach in all that open space, and that thought only doubled his panic. He cried some more.

Then something even more terrible happened.

He felt himself being turned. Not just him, but the clothes

hamper, as Peter turned it upside down and then sat on its bottom side.

The fear and panic he felt when he realized what was happening was incredible. His heart raced like he had never felt before. He couldn't move. He was in a black void that had him in a death grip. His breathing was difficult, his breath nothing but hot, shallow draws. And, because he was upside down, and because most of his blood was rushing to his cramped head, Richie was saved from quite possibly going mad at the age of four.

The rush of blood to his head caused him to pass out.

And although he was spared (at least consciously) the last ten minutes or so of that blood-chilling ordeal, it was better than two years, and more than a few nightmares, before his young, growing mind forgot about his incident with Peter Irons.

16

It was forty minutes past twilight, and Richard got up from the sofa, rubbing his eyes with his free hand, and turning on a lamp close to the fireplace. His other hand held the last of a fresh drink, and he swallowed it, stumbling to the bar as he did so to make another. His hands were shaking, his entire body trembling.

"You know, that stuff can kill you," a voice said from behind him.

He turned around and saw that it was Jerry, on the television set. He had almost forgotten that he was not the only person in the apartment. The vivid memories that had come to his mind for the past thirty minutes or so had commanded most of his attention, seeming to propel him into the past and the past into sparkling reality.

The images were so damn *clear.*

And there was another feeling underlying the clarity of those bleak, terrible memories, one he was surprised to feel; anger. A confusing anger that came from within a deep inner part of himself he had never explored; a part of his soul he had never come face to face with. He wasn't sure if that was good, or bad.

"It really can kill you," Jerry said. "I'm not joking."

"Yeah, I know it can kill me, but it's a helluva good way to deal with stress, and that's the *only* reason I drink."

"Is it?" Jerry asked.

"Yeah." But that was all Richard offered for an answer. He would have to think about that small question later, perhaps when he was sober and his head was clear. Right now, he was too caught up in memories from the past, and in his growing anger, which seemed to have spawned directly from them.

"Let me ask *you* something, Jerry, if you don't mind."

"Not at all. Anything."

"Whatever happened to Peter Irons after the day he put me in the clothes hamper? I don't remember ever seeing him again after that."

"No, you wouldn't be expected to remember that," Jerry said. "Not with your conscious mind, at any rate. Aside from your ordeals with Peter—the bed, the closet, the clothes hamper— you also inadvertently played a major roll in he and your baby-sitter, Audrey, splitting up. So, in a sense, you also saved yourself from further abuse by that demented young man."

"How's that?" Richard asked.

"It seems that Peter and Audrey had quite an argument before he came up the stairs and stuffed you in that hamper."

"I remember them arguing about something," Richard said. "But I thought it was over Peter's sexual advances toward her."

"It wasn't over that," Jerry said. "although some of their previous arguments were. But the truth of the matter is that they were arguing over Peter going up to your room. You see, it had become something of an obsession with him. He was beginning to spend more time up in your room on his visits than he was with Audrey, and that was the root of their problems. At least to her it was. In fact, she was beginning to suspect that Peter wasn't as friendly to you as he let on to be—not only to her, but to your parents. There was also the fact that he had smacked Audrey around a few times in the months leading up to it."

"So, what happened?"

Jerry said, "She broke up with Peter the day after the bastard crammed you into that clothes hamper. When your mother asked Audrey about Peter, she went as far as telling her that she broke up with him for your sake, and it was all she would say. Your parents, of course, couldn't for the life of them figure out what she meant by that. But...sometimes parents are just out and out blind to their children's needs and worries. It's just a fact of life. Wouldn't you agree?"

"Yeah, I guess I would," Richard said, although he had no children of his own as a basis for his answer. "But I was only four, for Chrissakes." The rising anger in his voice was very pronounced. "Who's going to believe a four-year-old when it comes to something like that?"

"Exactly," Jerry said. "That's why a large percentage of child abuse goes unnoticed, even today, although these days a closer eye is kept on such things. I would even go so far as saying—and this is only my opinion, mind you—that parents neglecting what their children have to say, even at as young an age as four, is *also* child abuse. Adults seem to be too preoccupied with their own lives to listen more than casually to their children, whether it be about school, or about their babysitters. Or their babysitter's boyfriend, as was your case. Thus, the basic difference in the way children and adults form opinions. The difference in the way they *think.* Your mother had a drastically different opinion about Peter Irons than you did. Her opinion of him was pretty high, as a matter of fact. But she didn't know enough about his relationship with you. She didn't *know* what he was doing to you while she was away with your father. And the reason she didn't know was because she didn't take you seriously when you told her Peter scared you. In fact, she laughed about it as if you were being silly."

Richard interrupted him here. He had heard enough. "Don't you go and blame what happened on my mother. I'm not angry at her the least little bit. The only person to blame here is Peter Irons, so you just leave her out of it." He had retrieved the half-finished pint of Jim Beam from the bar while Jerry was talking, and now he tipped it up and swallowed hugely from the neck of it.

"Hold on just a minute," Jerry said. "I'm not trying to pin blame on your mother for anything."

"Well, it sure sounds like it."

"I know it does, but—"

"Then how come you say you aren't?"

Jerry looked exasperated. He looked at his unseen audience, which had been completely silent for the better part of an hour. "What do you think, gang? Am I trying to blame any of this on Richard's mother? Am I trying to put her down in any way?"

The crowd in front of Jerry, whoever they were, and whatever they were there for, all shouted one loud *no!* in unison, in voices that sounded dull and grating.

Richard's confusion at this insane revelation by what seemed like hundreds of people whom he couldn't even see, left him disoriented. And on top of that, he was just about sauced. The pint of whiskey was nearly gone, and in the ensuing silence from the crowd in the television, he wondered briefly if he had only imagined their response to Jerry's question.

No, I'm just losing my mind. This is too much.
"Richard...Richard?"
"Yeah."
"I've already told you that you are *not* losing your mind, okay?"

"Gotcha," Richard said drunkenly. He plopped down on the sofa and chuckled. Not just at Jerry, but at the whole situation.

Here he was, alone in his apartment, drunker than a shithouse rat, upholding one end of an argument with a guy who was on his *television,* for crying out loud. The excess amount of bourbon he had consumed was helping to dim the craziness of it all, but it helped only marginally. The colors from objects in the room and the black and white of Jerry's face on the television seemed to be meshing together, doubling, tripling, and then coming back into some sort of focus. Jerry's last words were floating somewhere in that drunken haze, and Richard found them laughable as hell.

Because it was the truth.

That thought struck him like a cold winter wind. How could he possible be experiencing all of this if he was losing his mind? He couldn't come up with an answer. Perhaps there wasn't one. He pinched himself hard on the cheek and then grimaced at the slight burst of pain. No, he wasn't dreaming, either.

This was his life this night, and it *was* happening.

"Richard, you're something else, you know it?"

"He looked at the TV screen. "How's that?"

Jerry said, "You are getting so drunk that your train of thought is about as short as a poodle's pecker."

Richard laughed. "That's a good one, but m'not drunk," he said, sitting on the edge of the sofa, swaying back and forth, and trying hard to focus on the conversation.

"That's arguable," Jerry muttered, more to himself than to Richard. "Now then. Do I have your undivided attention?"

"Sure," Richard said, chuckling lightly. This was a riot, a scream.

"Before you forgot what we were discussing and started thinking about your sanity, I was attempting to explain to you what I meant about your mother."

At the mention of his mother, Richard recalled, with a slight touch of returning anger, what Jerry had told him "Go on," he said evenly.

"What I wanted to tell you," Jerry began, "is this—I'm not singling your mother out when I talk about parents not paying enough attention to what their children feel, think, and say. Although I used your case as an example, what happened with you and Peter Irons was not your mother's fault. I just wanted to show you how your abuse at the hands of that deranged boy could have been prevented. Maybe everything that happened wasn't preventable, but it never should have gone as far as it did."

"I think I'm beginning to see your point," Richard said in response to this more tactful approach, although part of him didn't want to see anything.

Part of him wanted to kill Peter Irons, or at least something close to it. This feeling caught him by surprise, because he realized—even in his drunken state—that it was the first time in his life that a desire so deadly and dark had entered his mind. Even what Tina had done could not be considered bad when compared to this—this memory of a childhood incident that had somehow stayed locked up in his subconscious for thirty years. To Richard, it was frightening that a memory buried for so long could hold so much power.

And there was some sense to what Jerry said. Richard's mother *wasn't* to blame. What happened there was just a basic lack of real communication between a child and his parent, as much Richard's fault as it was hers—if either of them could be blamed at all.

No, there was only one person who could have, without a doubt, prevented it; only one person to hold responsible. That person was Peter Irons.

Another thought followed that; something Jerry had told him earlier: *You're a grown man now. Think about what happened and learn to live with it. And then, maybe... something can be done about it.*

What had he meant by that?

Jerry's voice startled him from his thoughts. I'm glad that you're beginning to come to terms with this, Richard."

Richard's face took on a serious, studious look. Jerry was grinning, as if the ball was formed and Richard was about to make it roll.

He looked at Jerry, the light from the television casting an eerie light on Richard's face, shadowing his forehead, beneath his eyes, and below his bottom lip. In that one moment, he had never looked more sober.

"Where is Peter Irons now?" he asked.

On the screen, Jerry leaned back in his chair and folded his hands across his lap. He looked pleased. "I'm glad you asked that," he said, "because it's quite interesting, really."

"You mean you know where he is? You actually *know?*" He had not expected an answer to that question, but he had asked it anyway, as that is where the conversation had led him, yet also fearful inside that he might actually get one, and not sure how he would handle it if he did.

"Of course I know," said Jerry, as if this were a foregone conclusion. "And so would you, if you watched the news more often instead of those silly half-hour comedies that you indulge in."

"Just another way to deal with stress," Richard said, and smiled.

Jerry didn't appear to have heard him. "Do you remember anything at all about a guy over in West Memphis, Arkansas, who came home from work one evening and, according to the police in that city, for no apparent reason at all stabbed his wife to death with a ballpoint pen, and then beat his two children to death with an axe handle?"

"Sure," Richard said. "It was in all the papers at the time. Happened about two years ago, didn't it?"

"Yes."

"I remember."

"I'm surprised," Jerry said.

"You may be right about me not watching the news as much as I should, but I *do* read the papers. And it's hard to forget something that bizarre, especially when it happened in a city less than eighty miles from here." Richard paused a moment and then said, "Wait a minute. The article about the murders gave a grisly description of the bodies and how they were killed, but not any names. At least not that of the murderer. I didn't follow the story after that first article."

Jerry said, "At the time, they had yet to apprehend the killer. Police don't always broadcast their suspects nationwide. It takes away the element of surprise—especially if they know who did it, whether from witnesses or evidence found at the scene of the crime."

"And the killer was…"

"You got it," Jerry said. "Peter Irons."

"I'll be damned," Richard said. It gave him goosebumps to think that Peter Irons, after last seeing him in Jacksonville, Florida, in 1966, had been living this close to him. "So, what happened to him?" he asked. "Where is he now?"

Jerry lit a *Demptus* from the pack that was laying on his desk and inhaled deeply. He let the smoke out in a long white cloud. "Well, Mr. Irons is presently serving life without parole down in Little Rock, at the state penitentiary. He has been there eighteen months, give or take."

Richard thought about it for a minute. Peter Irons had tortured him ceaselessly for a period of more than four months when he was only four-years-old, and there had been no justice to come out of that. In Richard's mind—his conscious mind, at least—he and Peter Irons had gone their separate ways, the incident forgotten in the mind of a four-year-old, a mind in which there was so much fresh input coming in that not everything could be sorted and filed away for future reference. The mind didn't seem capable of mastering that trick until later. And this memory had ultimately been found in the part of the mind where it seemed that everything that *didn't* get filed and sorted was at least saved in some remote, dark corner.

And now this.

Peter Irons' sadistic behavior had escalated with time, and he had ultimately murdered his own family. He had murdered first his wife, and then his children, in cold blood; had taken their lives as though he were God and had the power to do so. And had justice been served?

Well, the man was down in Little Rock, behind bars, where he would be getting three hot meals and a place to lay his diseased head for the rest of his life; a free roof over his head, and a social life to boot. Even if it was with criminal-types like himself, they were still *people*, and he could associate with them, become friends with them. He didn't have to deal with the hassles and headaches that everyone outside of that prison had to deal with on a daily basis. He didn't have to worry about getting audited by the IRS, paying taxes, paying bills, or meeting a budget. He was down there in Little Rock with less stress and worries than most of the people in the entire country.

But to the outside world—and especially to the lawmakers—justice had been served, and that seemed to be enough for them.

But was that justice? Was it real, *true* justice with no virtue as to what the law—and most people—recognized as justice? That was the question that came to Richard now, and it caused a black flash of anger and hate to form in his mind. A dark hate that had perhaps been buried somewhere deep inside him since the age of four, when justice had been something little understood and elusive.

He looked at the screen at Jerry for countless seconds, the anger rising in him the way a diver swims toward the surface to air, to life. "Prison isn't good enough punishment for him," he said finally.

Jerry stubbed his cigarette in an ashtray at one corner of his desk, letting out a breath of white smoke as he did so. He smiled at Richard and nodded his head in perfect understanding. "I couldn't have put it a better way myself."

"He should have been killed," Richard said.

"I know."

"Sent to the gas chamber, electrocuted...something." The anger in his voice was apparent, but it felt good to tell Jerry this; to vent some of the anger and hate that he felt. He lit a cigarette and snapped his lighter shut. "Even death by gas or electrocution wouldn't have been good enough for that bastard."

"My sentiments, exactly," Jerry said.

"Why the hell would he do those things to me? No, forget that for now. How the hell could he kill his wife, his *children?*" He was talking as much to himself now as he was to Jerry. "Tina did a lot of bad things to me, probably things that wouldn't seem right in the eyes of most people, and certainly not right in mine, but I would never consider *murder* as a solution to the problem. That..."

"Richard—"

"would be..."

"*Richard!*"

He stopped and looked at Jerry, who was regarding him with a keen sort of interest; a look like that from a cat when it first sees the piece of yarn dangling in front of it.

"What?" It came out as a question, but still contained an

undertone of aggravated anger.

"You are right," Jerry said. "Murder...cold blooded murder ...doesn't solve anything. But think about this. What about the murder of a murderer? What would you call that?" Jerry sat back in his chair again, seeming to study him.

Richard didn't have to think long on that one. The fury at Peter Irons was still just below the surface, bubbling dangerously close to the top. And something else had risen up, perhaps born with that dark anger; the maddening need for revenge. He suddenly saw with perfect clarity what the whole evening's conversation with Jerry meant. It all led to this. One single question from the man triggered it, and that one question could be responded to with one answer, one *word*, and that word was at the front of Richard's mind, straining at his vocal cords, ready to be released.

The veins on his neck stood out in cords, but he was able to answer the question quite easily. "I'd call that *justice!*"

Jerry's audience, which had been quiet for some time now, suddenly burst into a deafening applause, which startled Richard. Right now, he could not even begin to contemplate who that audience consisted of, or what their purpose might be. Perhaps he would find that out later. Right now, the issue at hand was not them, but a man. A child abuser, a child *killer,* named Peter Irons.

"Justice," Richard said again. He liked the way that word sounded, how it made him feel. The word seemed to hold some sort of power. It had backbone. And he realized that it was the one word, above any others in the language, that *should* have backbone. *Justice.*

"You are exactly right," Jerry said. "That would be justice in the highest sense of the word."

Richard composed himself a little, standing up (getting one hell of a rush in the process), and running a shaking hand through his tussled hair.

"So, what can *I* do about it?" he asked. "He's behind bars down there, protected by the state, and most likely pretty content in the fact that he didn't ride the lightning for what he did. I'd kill the son-of-a-bitch myself if I could get my hands on him, but I can't."

"Maybe not," Jerry said. "But some of my people *can.*"

"How?"

"That's not important, nor relevant to you, Richard. Sometimes what you don't know really is better for you. All I need from you is to know one thing"

"What's that?"

"Do you want justice…*true* justice served to Peter Irons?" He looked at him somberly, and Richard could see that there was no joke written on his face. That look, those cold, sharp eyes, told him that Jerry meant business.

"You know I do," Richard said.

"Okay. Good."

"What do I have to do?"

"Nothing," Jerry said. "Absolutely nothing. But you can read about it in the papers if you'd like."

Before Richard could respond, Jerry disappeared from the screen in a crackling of white static, and then Archie Bunker was on the screen, yelling for his son-in-law, 'meathead', to get out of his chair.

Dumbfounded, feeling suddenly very drowsy, and *very* drunk, Richard settled back on the sofa and tried to get involved in the comedy. But he couldn't. Jerry's last words echoed in every part of his mind, seeming to bounce off every side until they inevitably found a cozy place at the front. Mixed with the evening's load of liquor, those words made coherent thought impossible.

*****

17

On the seventh of September, a day after he had sold the television, George Morrison sat behind his desk in the small office of his shop, going meticulously through the information he'd received from two phone calls made earlier in the day. The sun from a clear, cloudless sky was two hours diminished, and now darkness ruled Chestnut Avenue, suppressed only by two dimly lit street lamps on either side of the downtown street. Except for an occasional passing vehicle, the night was quiet and empty outside George's small shop.

His day at the shop had been reasonably profitable, though it had nevertheless been slow, as it was nearly every business day. He sold an old Frigidaire refrigerator around nine-thirty that morning, and an electric range an hour or so after that. All hopes of a busy day disappeared from his mind around one o'clock, when no one else had entered the store, and he realized that it was going to be another slow one. He saw no business at all the rest of the afternoon, and while he had his nightly after-work drink at five, he reflected that, if that refrigerator hadn't been in his shop for so long, and if he hadn't marked it down repeatedly, the day wouldn't have been as good as it was.

Of course it had been good in other ways, also.

He'd sold the TV set again just yesterday, and since business had been slow today, he'd had time to work on his 'puzzle.' First by going over the items he had, and then by making a couple of phone calls to a friend of his named Larry Vincent, who worked down at the Federal Building. Larry, who had drunk countless beers—and played as many hands of cribbage—with George over the years, and who had done this type of favor for him before, had been able to give George some information that he accessed—rather easily—from the computer network in his office.

George learned from Larry that Richard Raines lived at 2900 Crestwood here in Jonesboro, a rather nice section of town about fifteen blocks over. George had been curious about where Richard worked, and Larry had given him that information, also. Mr. Raines worked at JAC—the Jonesboro Advertising Corporation—a company that received a majority of its business from real estate developers.

George had thanked Larry for the information, and it had been an hour or so later before he called Larry again, wanting to know Richard's marital status. Divorced. George had expected as much, so he wasn't surprised.

He had copied all of this down carefully on a yellow legal pad, and now he sat in his office comparing this information to that of the past owners of the television set. Over the past eight years, Larry Vincent had been able to give him the same type of information he'd provided today, and although George suspected he was more than a little curious about the calls, Larry seldom questioned him about *why* he needed to know this or that about someone George had no ties to outside of business.

As always, George was grateful that he had such an understanding friend in Larry.

He shuffled through the different pieces of paper and notes that were on his desk and made the comparisons he knew formed a pattern.

With the exception of Merv Calhoun, the second owner of the television, every person who had bought the TV from George had either been divorced, or on the brink of it, as was the case with Victor Haynes, the young man who had first brought the television into the shop.

The second thing that most of the TV's owners had in common was that they all had—with the exception of Merv

Calhoun once again—well-paying jobs, and lived in nice neighborhoods. Although George doubted this had anything to do with the overall pattern of his 'puzzle,' he had made a note of it, anyway.

The third thing, and something they *all* had in common, was the fact that each owner of the TV set had been killed within ten days after purchasing the set from him. *That* was the one that bothered him most. He knew it was no coincidence; knew that even after Merv Calhoun died suddenly from an *unknown* cause. That cause of death had soon become a pretty popular association with the TV. George had made a list of the past owners, their job titles, and their causes of death. Now he filled in the information he had on Richard Raines, in all but the last column:

NAME	OCCUPATION	CAUSE OF DEATH
Victor Haynes	Factory Supervisor	Heart Attack
Merv Calhoun	Farmer	UNKNOWN
Donald Forrester	Business Executive	UNKNOWN
Phil Clayton	Restaurant Owner	UNKNOWN
Gary Grisham	Business Executive	Stabbing*
Wade Crosset	Attorney	Mutilation*
Martha Stonewall	Police Officer	UNKNOWN
Louis Griffin	Hdwr. Store Owner	UNKNOWN
Richard Raines	Advert. Executive	

He glanced over this list, remembering when he had made each entry. The *unknown* cause of death had occurred five out of eight times, so far, but he knew in his heart that the cause of death all eight times had been *unknown.* He had newspaper articles on all of them in a neatly compiled notebook on his desk, and he knew from them alone that in the cases of Gary Grisham and Wade Crosset, the police had known how these two men died, but they didn't know who had killed them. To George, that was still *unknown*. It was still a mystery, still a puzzle. Thus, the asterisks on his list.

Putting this list aside, George put another one in front of him and glanced over is slowly, carefully, although he had looked at this list hundreds of times before. This one was a little different:

NAME	DATE BOUGHT TV	DATE DECEASED
Victor Haynes	7/21/89 (sold TV)	7/22/89
Merv Calhoun	7/27/89	7/30/89
Donald Forrester	8/21/89	8/25/89
Phil Clayton	7/24/90	7/30/90
Gary Grisham	8/27/92	9/06/92
Wade Crosset	8/16/93	8/26/93
Martha Stonewall	9/14/95	9/22/95
Louis Griffin	8/18/96	8/26/96
Richard Raines	9/06/97	

George put this list on top of the other one after filling in Richard's name and the date that he bought the television. This list bothered him more than the other. He managed to sell the TV only in the late summer or early autumn, and each owner died only a short time after that.

What did that mean?

He had asked himself *that* question more than once.

He had a couple more lists to go over, but he realized that it was getting late—for him, anyway—and he hadn't needed to go any further than that second list to realize that it was going to take a lot more ambition and effort on his part if he was going to prevent another mysterious death from happening.

And he wanted to do that. This had gone on a long time, and the guilt he'd felt over the years was pressing on his shoulders with more and more force, leading him to believe that something was wrong with him to have let this go on for so long. It sounded crazy, but felt true. Guilt was a heavy burden.

Closing his notebooks and extinguishing the desk lamp, he made his slow way to the small apartment at the back of his shop, thinking that this time, whether he liked it or not, he was going to have to have some outside help to prevent Richard Raines' certain death.

He couldn't fathom the guilt of even one more death on his shoulders…or his mind.

*****

Part Two

On the Brink of Insanity

Justice should not only be done,
but should manifestly and undoubtedly
be seen to be done.

—Gordon Hewart
Judicial opinion (1924)

1

Tina Raines left the offices of Thomas Harrington, walked briskly to her car, keyed the ignition, put the auto in gear, and then sped out of the small parking lot. The car's tires squealed loudly in the relative quietness of the afternoon.

She was pissed. *Royally* pissed.

Her visit to Richard's attorney hadn't done her a whole lot of good as far as she was concerned, and although she knew it hadn't been Tom Harrington's fault, she blamed him anyway. She had always hated featherweights like him; the type of attorney who knew his way around the courtroom—or up a girl's dress if she'd let him—yet was as timid as a mouse when confronted head-to-head about something that wasn't on his current agenda.

Things like the appointment with Tina.

She didn't know exactly what he had expected the meeting to be about, but he most certainly must not have thought it was about any regular course of business. He'd seemed to have only one thing on his mind when she'd entered his office at nine-thirty this morning—and that was sex. Although sex wasn't such an outlandish idea to Tina in even the worse circumstances, it wasn't the purpose for the appointment. Especially not with a wimp like Thomas Harrington.

But then, nearly every man was a wimp compared to Biff Larento, who was even now still in bed at her place after the wild night the two of them had spent together.

Biff had met Tina at Snow's Bar and Grill last night, as planned, where the two of them had a couple of drinks before hitting a popular nightclub downtown for dancing and more drinks. The music was loud, the band excellent, and the atmosphere of the smoke-filled club had put her in a very sensual mood. The two of them left after an hour or so of dancing, deciding to go to Tina's place because it was closer. She had been all over Biff on the way to her place, and once they were upstairs there followed a series of wild sex in various places, starting in the floor in front of the door when they first entered the apartment, and culminating in her bed—with an encounter in the short hallway on the way *to* the bedroom. Tina hadn't experienced such a night—or as many orgasms—in years.

Compared to Biff, Tom Harrington was like a toy poodle next to a pit bull. Whereas Biff was sturdy, lean, muscular, and handsome, the attorney was short, skinny, very timid, and would probably weight one-forty soaking wet. Aside from *those* unappealing characteristics, he was also going bald, and Tina was a woman who was not turned on by thinning hair, or a shiny head—at least not one on top of some idiot's brain.

She had made the appointment with the attorney for only one thing—information. And, although she hadn't catered to his sexual wants, Tina had made sure that he didn't lose interest in what she was there for by making sure he got a look at plenty of healthy thigh from her side-slitted skirt, and several sexy smiles from her unblemished face.

Patting his perspiring forehead with a handkerchief every five minutes or so, and being none too discrete about looking her body over every *two* minutes or so, Tom had pulled the file on the divorce, which she had asked him to do.

Together they had reviewed the details of the divorce, primarily the property and financial matters, after Tom had first locked the door to his office and drawn the shades. He knew as well as she did that what he was doing was illegal—at least as far as his client's privacy was concerned. Tina came around the desk and stood next to him as she bent over to look at the papers, making sure he got a good look down her low blouse.

The condo was in Richard's name, and he had kept it, knowing full well that a battle in court would be embarrassing for her after what she'd done. Tina hadn't argued there.

The charge cards—Mastercard, American Express, Sears, Discover, and thirteen others—were all in Richard's name, and so she hadn't been able to help herself financially there, and she was no longer covered by the medical insurance that Richard held at JAC. On top of that, the bank accounts—checking, savings, and an IRA—were also in his name, and the only way for her to get her hands on any of those monies was to sue, something that she didn't—and wouldn't—contemplate.

She knew all of these facts already, and was feeling like the appointment with Thomas Harrington was just a waste of time when he had caught her by complete surprise.

"There *is* one other thing," he'd said, "although I don't have any proof of it via a copy here. I only know what Richard has told me of it." He had wiped his forehead with his damp handkerchief and eyed her coolly. "I don't suppose you'd be interested, would you?"

Realizing that he might have the piece of information she was looking for, and knowing the only way that she was going to get it, Tina had hiked her skirt up two or three inches on her tantalizing thighs and smiled sweetly at him. "Of *course* I would be interested," she said. "Now, just what *is* this other thing that I know you're so anxious to tell me about?"

Wiping his forehead again, perhaps thinking that he was going to get laid in about five short minutes, he told her that

Richard had purchased a life insurance policy four years ago and had paid it off just last year. It was something that didn't really pertain to the divorce, but had been overlooked nevertheless. Thomas didn't know how much the policy was worth, or who the beneficiary was. He had not been Richard's attorney at the time he'd purchased it, so he hadn't handled that particular transaction.

Holding back a deep outrage, Tina wanted to ask a dozen or more questions, but asked only one—the one she felt was the most important; "Are you sure about this?"

"No," he'd said. "Like I've told you, I only know what Richard has told me. He mentioned it once right after I began handling his business, and then once more last year, when he told me he had paid it off. Surely he must have told you..."

"I don't know anything about it."

Thomas had looked surprised (although to Tina the surprised look seemed feigned), and then he had wiped his forehead for the umpteenth time. "Well, maybe we could discuss all of this over dinner tonight. My place?"

Tina had been nonplussed. "I'll tell you what, Mr. Harrington..."

"Tom...please."

"I'll tell you what, Tom," she'd said, standing up and straightening his tie for him. "When I find out for sure that Richard has this life insurance policy you talk about, I'll give you a call and we'll have dinner anywhere you want. Okay?"

The attorney, who was perspiring freely now, said that it was okay. Tina could almost smell his anxiety.

Now, as she sped down Main Street, she tried to vent some of the anger she felt. Although she wanted to be angry with the attorney, she really couldn't be. After a little more thought as she drove to her apartment, she realized that, although she'd at first thought the meeting with Tom Harrington had been hopeless, she had come away with something, after all— the potential of Richard's life insurance policy. If it even existed, of course.

But Tina knew it did. She felt it. It made sense.

And she wouldn't put it past Richard. He had put the condo in his name, the charge accounts, and practically every other financial instrument the two of them had held. And why should she have been upset about that? His reason for all of this was that if something should ever happen to his job and they fell into credit and financial problems, her name and credit would still be good. He loved her and didn't want to ever see her get into any misunderstandings with their creditors. Or so he had said, anyway, and she had believed him. After all, she had loved him, too (or so she had thought and sincerely believed, at the time).

What upset her the most, what *angered* her the most, was that he had failed to tell her about the insurance policy. According to Tom Harrington, Richard had purchased it four years ago. Of course, they hadn't been married then, but *also* according to the attorney, Richard had paid this policy off just last year. They *had* been married then, and if there indeed *was* a policy, he had failed to mention it to her for *years*. Neglecting to mention something like that to your spouse was not a charitable thing to do. It was deceptive and sneaky.

She should have listened to her mother when it came to Richard Raines. Tina had heard that love was blind, and had come to think that it was also deaf. Her mother had been right, and the only consolation was that she was no longer here to tell Tina 'I told you so.'

What was she to do now?

The first answer to come to her mind was to forget the whole thing. Forget Richard Raines, forget the mistake of the marriage, and forget what he had done to make her current lifestyle so degrading. Forget, and just get on with her life.

But she couldn't.

She could forget none of that, and now she couldn't forget about the life insurance policy that he may or may not have purchased, although she could think of no reason why he would lie to his attorney about something so important. Worse, she wasn't confident enough in what Tom Harrington said to believe that the policy actually existed.

As she pulled into the small parking lot outside her apartment building, she realized she could not let this sleeping dog lie until she knew for sure.

There was a payphone downstairs, near the entrance, and she picked it up, wrinkling her nose at the disgusting smells coming from either the first-floor toilet, or whoever had recently used the phone. Dialing from memory, she called the apartment that she and Richard had shared.

She let it ring seven times before she hung up.

Damn!

She knew from experience that if Richard was home, he would have picked up the telephone before the fourth ring, but she had let it ring three times more on the off chance that he was asleep, or in the bathroom, or not there at all.

She checked her watch—another gift from Richard, this one from two years ago on her birthday—and saw that it was just after eleven-thirty. Although she knew that occasionally he would take off work in the middle of the day on a whim, she knew instinctively that today was not such a day. If Richard took off early, he would be at home, mostly likely reading a book and drinking something with alcohol in it. He therefore had to be at work. *Had* to be.

She began dialing the number at JAC—again from memory—and was halfway through the sequence when she had an even better idea. She hung up and returned to her car.

She didn't need to confront Richard about this. It would only cause trouble. She thought there might be a way to handle this herself.

2

As Tina neared Richard's apartment, she saw with a good deal of relief that his truck was not in the driveway. Not only that, but the Frazier's driveway was also empty. She couldn't have asked for better timing.

She parked in Richard's driveway, and fished around on her keyring for the key to the front door that was still on there somewhere. He had never asked her for it, and she'd never offered to give it back to him. Although that was the case, she knew that if she used it, the law would see her as a criminal, and part of her couldn't help feeling like one at this particular moment.

Less than a minute later she was inside.

The first thing she noticed was how empty and barren the place looked. Evidently, Richard hadn't made an attempt to replace the things she'd been able to take with her.

Then she noticed the television set over by the bookshelf. So he had made an effort after all. What was stranger to her than the antique look of the set (she would have never allowed him to purchase such a despicable TV), was the fact that it was on. White, snowy static covered the screen. It wasn't like Richard at all to go somewhere and leave the TV on, even if he only planned to be gone less than thirty minutes.

What if he's here? her mind screamed at her. *What if he let someone borrow his truck to move furniture or something, and he's only in the bathroom... dead in his bedroom from a heart attack or something?*

She pushed these thoughts from her mind. She didn't think anyone was home. "Richard?" she called tentatively.

No answer.

She suddenly felt unseen eyes staring at her. Her scalp began to feel as though thousands of fingers were tickling her skin.

Calm down, girl, you're just nervous. After all, you're breaking the law here.

She walked over to the set and turned the volume control down until the set clicked off. The feeling of being watched seemed to fade as fast as the snowy static.

Now that the uneasy feeling was no longer with her, she took a deep breath and hurried to the master bedroom, where she knew he kept his important papers and documents. To her dismay, the gray metal box in which he kept those papers was not in its usual place on the top shelf of the wide walk-in closet. Not that *she* had ever been allowed to look inside it. However, this ruined everything. He had moved the box.

She rummaged around the complete length of the shelf, being careful to put everything back in its proper place, but still did not happen upon the fireproof box. Feeling extremely disappointed, she cast her eyes downward…

…and saw the box.

It was in a far corner of the closet, on the floor, next to a pile of shoes she knew were Richard's discards; shoes he had worn out, shoes he no longer liked, and shoes he only wore for special occasions, such as playing softball or tag-football with his buddies from work. He termed them 'junk-shoes,' and they were piled askew, some of them covering nearly half of the gray metal box.

Getting a firm picture in her mind of the way the shoes were stacked, in order to put them back the same way, she slowly and carefully pulled the box from beneath the small pile. She took the box out of the closet and set it on the unmade bed, noticing only casually that he was getting out of habit on more than one thing. He'd always made sure the bed was made before going to work, and most of the time he'd made it himself.

Something thumped softly, quickly, in the front room.

She froze, listening intently, her eyes scanning the hall in front of the open bedroom door, fully expecting to hear footfalls start toward the back of the condo. Her heart pounded fiercely. A thick, hot sweat broke out under her hairline.

She listened for the sound again but heard nothing.

After a silent minute or so she pried at the top of the box with her fingers, and was relieved to find that it was not locked. If it had been, she would have been out of luck. Richard kept the key on the keychain that he always kept in his pocket. But it was unlocked, and that was something. He *always* kept this box locked. He was slipping about a *lot* of things. She was also glad that she didn't have to take the box with her, and try to open it later. That would complicate things more than she wanted to think about.

She told herself that she had been lucky thus far, but she still felt a maddening need to hurry. If Richard returned right now—or even Paul or Margie—she would find herself in an unexplainable situation.

Hi, there. Just thought I'd stop by and see how the old homestead was holding up. Or, better yet, *just thought I'd stop by and drop off your housekey. Still works, you know.*

Right.

She thumbed through the papers as fast as she could allow without overlooking anything. Old credit card receipts, cancelled checks, paid bills, income tax papers, and other items.

Near the back of the box, she found a long, beige, hardboard envelope. She pulled it out of the box, her heart pounding again, but for a different reason. Whatever was in this envelope, she had not seen it before (actually, she rarely saw *any* of this stuff, and when she had it was only when Richard showed something to her). And if he really did have a life insurance policy, this had to be it. With silent trepidation, she opened the envelope.

It *was* a life insurance policy.

She couldn't believe it. Tom Harrington had been right after all. Wimp or not, he had been right. She bypassed all the small print and found what she wanted to know the most:

Insurance Value: *$200,000.00*

And a little farther down from that:

Policy Beneficiary: *Tina Raines*
Secondary Beneficiary: *none*

Tina was shocked. Not only to find that there actually was a life insurance policy, but that she was the sole beneficiary of the policy insurance. She had merely been hoping that she could threaten him with a lawsuit to cash in the policy—if one existed—and split the proceeds with her; she didn't expect to be the beneficiary. Why hadn't he changed *that?*

She put the policy back into the beige envelope and placed the envelope back into the box in the space she had marked when she'd taken it out. That done, she closed the box and carried it back to the closet. In her excitement over the policy, she had forgotten the exact order the shoes had been in around and on the box, but after restacking them, she thought she'd done a pretty good job.

She made her way through the condo to the front door, ducking low in front of the kitchen window, where the curtains were open to the beautiful day outside.

Before she opened the door to leave, she noticed once again the odd television set. What had gotten into Richard, anyway? He seemed to be getting careless about a lot of things these days. Especially things like the life insurance policy he hadn't told her about. She smiled at that.

But that TV. There was something about it. It seemed to stare hungrily at her, the dullish-green screen a huge, yawning mouth, waiting to be fed.

Shaking those thoughts from her mind, she exited the condo, relieved to find as she got into her car and drove away that the Fraziers still hadn't made it home.

She drove toward her own apartment wearing a sunny smile that was as bright as the day, and a dangerous idea beginning to form in her mind.

3

Little Rock State Penitentiary, in Little Rock, Arkansas, sat on the northern banks of the Arkansas River. It was the oldest prison in the state, and because of that fact—and because of its obsolete design and furnishings—a brand new facility was presently under construction less than half a mile east of the site where this one now stood.

LRSP was small for a maximum-security prison, and although the new prison would boast nearly twelve-hundred cells, LRSP consisted of just four-hundred, counting solitary and the old stockade, which could not be used these days because of crumbling walls and giant vermin that roamed freely in the depths of those holding cells. In fact, it hadn't been used since the time a con named Weisel Malone (who had been put there for clubbing one of the night watchmen with a corner of his cell bunk that he'd somehow worked free) had been pulled out dead his third day in from infectious rat bits. Rat bites were what went on the report, but had you asked the guard who found him, an unfortunate man named Joey McIntosh (who had quietly resigned the next day and was now working at a carwash in Conway), he would have told you that ole Weisel had been nearly totally consumed by those collie-sized vermin.

So, the stockade was no longer used. It was sealed off quietly and inconspicuously from the rest of the prison with a new mortar wall, just as the prisoners were sealed off from the outside world by the thirty-feet high cement wall that surrounded the prison grounds. There were guard-posts along the top of that wall, three to a side, and each was equipped with machine guns on tripods, and riot guns and flood lights. Between each post was a spiraled tangle of barbed wire, which at night housed about fifteen-thousand volts of electricity. Any con attempting to scale the wall would be shaking in his boots, and cooked well down, if he came in contact with the wire, and over the years a good many had.

The cells inside the prison were small but adequate, nine-feet wide by twelve deep, one toilet, and one or two bunks, depending on the number of prisoners assigned to each cell. The cells were dank and cold in the wintertime, hot and stuffy in the summer, but they held their occupants well, which was the only thing that really mattered to the state.

In the early hours of morning on September 8, 1997, in cell number 4, located in cellblock 8, Peter Irons was awakened from a troubled sleep by a soft thump that he, in his groggy state, was sure had come from inside his cell—and if not from his cell, then from the dream he'd been having.

He was back in West Memphis in the dream, at the two-bedroom house he shared with his family. Although this dream seemed vivid, it couldn't have been real because in it he had been waiting for Mary to get home from work, and Mary didn't work. *He* did. *He* made the money in this family, *he* wore the boots, and by God she had better not forget it, either. But in his dream, this wasn't so. And the kids...the kids were nagging him about supper, and when it was going to be ready, but that wasn't his job, either, and Mary had better not forget *that*. And then she was coming through the front door, setting her hard hat and lunch pail on the small table next to the sofa. He asked her where the hell she had been and what she thought she was doing, but she only smiled and opened her lunch pail...and pulled out a ball-point pen.

The ball-point pen.

That is when he had awakened to the soft thump. It could have been made by her closing the lunch pail in his dream—could very easily have been that—but Peter was pretty sure that sound had come from behind him, somewhere in his cell.

He was facing the west wall of his cell, the position he had slept in since he'd been here, and although he was suddenly filled with a cold, dread contemplation, he turned over more quickly than he might have had he known what had made that gentle thump.

It was her. It was Mary. And on either side of her were the kids. *His* kids, who he had murdered in a frenzy of rage some twenty-four months ago.

Only now they were here.

But that wasn't right, *couldn't* be right, because his kids were dead, and so was Mary. They were dead two years ago, and they were dead now. What was left of both of Mary's eyes trickled down her cheeks in a slow, gelatin stream of thick puss, just as they had done when Peter poked the ball-point pen through each of them, one at a time. Of course, she had been dead by the time he'd made it to her other eye (the first stab had been in one eye), but he'd poked them out anyway, what the hell. From the neck down she was bleeding from over fifty places where he had stabbed her with the pen, the dark red blood running out in steamy rivulets as she stood near the door of the cell. There was no compassion in her eyeless sockets as she stood there, and Peter felt none himself. A part of his confused mind still told him that he was only dreaming.

The kids were what shook him up the most.

His son, Pete, stood to the right of his mother, and in the dim light cast through the cell door from the corridor of the cell block, Peter could see the raised, purple knots on the right side of the boy's head, and the swollen eye that was totally closed from the blows of the axe handle. Blood trickled from the youngster's nose and mouth, and the drops made dime-sized drops as they fell, like a dripping faucet, to the cement floor of the small cell.

His daughter, Sheila, stood to the left of Mary, holding her mother's hand companionably. She didn't look as bad as Little Pete did; two blows with the axe handle had finished her quite quickly. He had struck her first directly of top of her head, and had then caved in the left side of her chest with the handle, causing two ribs to pierce her left lung and her heart. She had died instantly from that, although she had been well on her way from the blow to the head. Now, blood was welling out from her left side in a steady flow, and some ran a jagged course down the front of her face from the gouge in the top of her head, where a few pieces of her scalp stuck up like crooked tombstones.

The kids.

Something inside of him, a part of him that still had some humanity left in it, always regretted what he had done to them. He had tried to tell himself over and over that Mary was the only one he'd really wanted to kill, that the kids, Pete six, and Sheila four, had just been in the wrong place at the wrong time, but that didn't change what had happened. Wasn't even close to the truth, anyway, no matter how much he tried to convince himself otherwise.

The naked truth was simple enough, regardless of the denials he often tried to make in his twisted mind. He had wanted to kill *all* of them—*because of the man,* he told himself. He *made me do it*—and in the end, he had.

And it looked to him as though he was going to have to kill them again, because he saw now that this was *not* a dream. He realized this even before little Pete laid a cold, blood-stained hand on his blanketed shoulder and smiled at him with a puffy, purplish-black mouth that was missing a total of six teeth.

"Hi, Daddy," this hellish thing that was his dead son said.

And then Sheila was there too, alongside Pete. "Hi, Daddy." Her one-lunged voice sounded full of gravel.

Peter tried to scream but found that his voice seemed to have forgotten how to make any sound at all. His throat felt as though he'd just eaten a mouthful of sand.

And then, incredibly, Mary was between the kids, smiling at Peter lovingly...and holding up a pen.

The ball-point pen.

"I forgot to mend your shirt," she said, "but I remembered this." She held it up directly in front of him...and smiled.

Peter had time to notice the dark stains on the pen, a black and white Bic. He had thrown the pen away in an alley after the murders, and the police had never found it. He thought he knew *why* they hadn't found it, oh yeah. *Now* he knew. And suddenly he found his voice. It rose in his throat and spewed from his mouth, high-pitched and very loud in the sleeping prison...

...and was cutoff in mid-scream as Mary drove the ball-point through his larynx, the back of his neck, and into the mattress beneath him.

He looked one last time through the fire coming from his torn throat at the grotesque, grinning family that he had murdered, and realized that prison wasn't so bad compared to some things.

And then all three were on him.

4

Article from the ARKANSAS TIMES, Sept. 10, 1997, p.2

CONVICT SLAIN IN BIZARRE MURDER AT LITTLE ROCK STATE PENITENTIARY

Little Rock, Ark.—In an incident that has authorities baffled, a prisoner serving a life sentence at Little Rock State Penitentiary was apparently murdered sometime late Wednesday evening. Peter Wayne Irons was found dead inside his locked cell by prison Security Guard, Nathan Riles, after Riles and other prisoners heard screams coming from cellblock 8 in the maximum security prison. It has been reported that Mr. Irons was stabbed to death with an as yet unknown object that "was not a blade or knife of any kind." This according to Little Rock Chief of Police, Carl Filmore, who was on the scene following a call from Prison Warden Elmer Isely. Both the police and prison authorities were unable to ascertain how the perpetrator got into the cell with Irons, but Chief Filmore state that a full investigation into the matter would begin immediately. Warden Elmer Isely could not be reached for comment. Peter Irons had been serving a life sentence for...

Article from pg 6 of THE JONESBORO DAILY JOURNAL, September 10, 1997

MURDER AT LITTLE ROCK STATE PENITENTIARY

(AP) Little Rock, Ark.—A West Memphis man, serving a life sentence for murdering his wife and two children twenty-four months ago, was found dead in his cell at Little Rock State Penitentiary late Wednesday evening, the victim of an apparent murder. Peter Wayne Irons was found brutally mutilated by an unknown assailant shortly after midnight by a prison security guard, who reported hearing a "loud scream that was suddenly cut off." Prison authorities said they "have no clues as of yet," and Little Rock Chief of Police, Carl Filmore, who was on scene shortly after the murder, is heading a full investigation that was to have gotten underway early Thursday morning. Unconfirmed sources say that some of the prisoners at the penitentiary claim that the "assailant" could have been rats, but details are sketchy, pending further investigation and the State Coroner's report, scheduled for release sometime this afternoon.

5

Richard lay the newspaper down on his desk at the offices of the Jonesboro Advertising Corporation and ran a sweaty palm through his tussled hair. He hadn't slept at all the night before, nor had he shaved this morning, something that was almost a ritual to him. A rough, black stubble covered most of his tired face, and he rubbed his fingers back and forth over it absently as he thought about what he had just read in this morning's papers.

Peter Irons had been killed by an 'unknown assailant,' and the police had 'no clues as of yet.' At least according to whatever dipshit had covered the story in the papers. But to Richard's racing mind, the assailant was not unknown—not completely—and there were plenty of clues.

A thought, unbidden and sudden, popped into his mind. A brief memory of a conversation not too long past; *Think about it...and then, maybe...something can be done about it.* Another thought followed that one. A question; *Do you want justice...true justice served to Peter Irons?* Jerry's words.

But he couldn't believe what he had begun to think, because if he believed it, then it would mean that he was an accomplice to a murder—if not solely guilty. No matter how crazy it sounded, he couldn't shake the certainty that if it wasn't for him, Peter Irons would still be alive (and oh so well) behind bars down there in Little Rock. There was blood on Richard's hands now.

But it's true justice *and you know it,* a voice inside his mind stated bluntly. To Richard, the voice sounded foreign yet recognizable—Jerry's voice. That thought somehow brought with it a queer sort of relief to his guilt, and it made the blood on his hands seem a little less visible.

But what, or who, *had* killed Peter Irons? Richard knew (or believed so, anyway) that he had somehow helped, but what had really happened in that prison cell? What had Peter Irons seen before he was killed? How did it happen? Surely it wasn't rats, as some of the other prisoners speculated in the papers. These thoughts pressed at him now, but he had no straightforward answer for any of the nagging questions.

And in a moment of sudden clarity, he thought perhaps it would be better if he *didn't* know the answers. Because he had the precarious feeling that the police, and the authorities, and whoever else was in charge, were never going to have the answers to any of those questions, either. If he *did* know the answers, he thought he would go insane trying to keep such a dreadful variety of information bottled up.

So he found it easier to think that justice—*true* justice—had been served. It was easier to live with that, and he thought if he tried to figure out some of these things he *would* go crazy, because right now, with what had happened over the last several days, he felt he was already edging dangerously close to that fabled state.

Then there was what happened yesterday to think about. It was something minor—so small—compared to everything else, but it gnawed at his mind nonetheless.

Yesterday, as he did this morning, Richard had talked to Jerry for a little while before going to work and, also as this morning, he left the TV on. He was pretty sure he had, anyway. But when he'd gotten home yesterday, the television set was not on. And this was strange, because Jerry had told him only yesterday morning that if he would leave the set on while he was not at home, he would be able to watch the apartment for him. A sort of built-in security system. Richard had balked at Jerry's idea at first, but had soon realized that it could do no harm. Of course, Jerry had reminded him that 'one in every four homes will experience a break-in this year,' and that had sort of figured into the equation. So, he had left the set on.

Or, maybe he hadn't.

Yesterday afternoon he had walked into the apartment after work, and the set had been off. He had immediately turned it on, and it had seemed like a long time before Jerry's smiling face appeared on the screen.

"Hello, Richard."

"I thought I left you on," Richard had immediately told him.

Jerry waived an impatient hand at him. "I have more important things to discuss with you than power failures."

A power failure, he had thought. *I never even thought about that happening.*

"Of course, you didn't," Jerry said. "Now, I'm afraid I don't have much time to talk to you right now, but I just wanted you to know that the business we discussed last night has been taken care of."

"You mean—"

"Yes. Peter Irons. But I'm afraid it won't be in the papers until tomorrow morning. Just thought I'd let you know." Jerry had smiled at him and disappeared from the screen.

Richard had started drinking and wondering about Jerry's words. He waited the rest of the evening for Jerry to come back on the screen and tell him more, but he never did until this morning, when they'd had only a brief chat before he left for work.

The small, minor thing that bugged him now was not so much the set being off yesterday afternoon, but Jerry's elusive excuse for it. A power failure? The more he thought about it, the less likely it seemed. Whenever there was a power outage—or even a flicker—in his apartment, the digital clock in the kitchen under the cabinets automatically lost time and began flashing twelve o'clock.

That hadn't happened. The clock in his bedroom had a battery backup, of course, but both of those clocks were keeping time just fine yesterday afternoon, and as far as he knew, they still were. He had gotten up for work by the clock in his bedroom just this morning, and finished his breakfast—hot coffee and toast (all his thumping head could handle)—in front of the one under the cabinets.

Jerry told him that there had been a power failure, so he *must* have left the set on.

Then why had it been off? And why hadn't it come back on when the power returned? It was an old set, and therefore did not remain off when power to it failed and the returned.

He didn't have an answer for that right now, but there was one thing that seemed certain, although he could not think of a reason why.

Jerry had lied to him.

And if he had lied to him about that, about what else had he lied?

6

September 10, 1997

Paul Frazier looked across his desk at Richard, who had finished reading the morning paper and now seemed to be in deep thought.

Now's the time, Paul. Just go right up and ask him what's bothering him.

But he couldn't. Not yet. He had to think about something else first.

Five minutes ago, Tina Raines had called the office asking for Richard. Paul had taken the call on his phone, and when he covered the mouthpiece and told Richard that she wanted to speak to him, Richard had glared at him as if he were some kind of idiot, and told him to tell her that he hadn't made it in yet.

Paul had relayed the message to Tina, who didn't sound very pleased about it (she had called the day before, also, while Richard was downstairs going over some layouts with Patrick Garnell). This was all fine and dandy with Paul—he didn't care much for her, anyway—but what wasn't setting too well with him was the look that Richard gave him when she'd called minutes ago. That look had a message behind it. One that was very clear to Paul: *Stay out of this, it isn't any of your business.*

That look was what now caused Paul to refrain from asking Richard what was on his mind. Right now, he didn't think he could get up enough courage to ask him if he'd like some more coffee.

And then there was the other call that Paul had gotten while Richard was downstairs yesterday. It had been a man—an older one by the sound of his voice—and although he had asked several questions that were centered primarily around Richard, he preferred not to speak to Richard directly. Paul smelled a fish right away, and when he asked the man his name, the man would only say that Richard probably wouldn't remember him because the two of them had only met once.

The man had a friendly enough voice, but Paul had been able to detect an urgency in it. He asked three questions about Richard, and Paul had only answered one of them for him. That had been the first one: "How long has Richard been working at JAC?" Paul had proceeded from there to tell the man that if he wanted to know anything else then he would *have* to speak with Richard personally. The man then explained to Paul that it was extremely important that he have this information, although he wouldn't say why.

Paul had given a few cordialities, and then he'd hung up, for some reason troubled by the call.

He still had not told Richard about that call, and the reason he hadn't was because of the third question that the man on the phone had asked him.

The *second* question had been: "What hours does Richard work?" That was something else that Paul noticed right off. The man referred to Richard by his first name, as though he knew him on a personal level. Yet he claimed he'd only met Richard once.

Paul had come very close to answering the third question, because it *did* seem the type of question that someone who knew Richard on a personal level might ask: "Has Richard been acting abnormally lately in any way that you can tell? This is *very* important."

Paul had almost said yes, because 'yes' was, in his book, the right answer for that question. But then he remembered he was talking to a stranger who had yet to even offer his name, and he told the man that he would have to talk to Richard himself.

Paul had trouble going to sleep last night because of the phone call, and he felt ashamed of himself for not telling Richard about it. But the truth was, the man's questions had hit the stone right on the head, because Richard *had* been acting different lately. He still was. Throughout the entire day at work yesterday, he didn't say much to Paul, and today Paul had done nothing but relay a message to him for Tina when she'd called, and had gotten that seemingly hateful look for his trouble.

He decided now that he wouldn't tell Richard about the personal call he'd gotten yesterday. He knew that something was bothering Richard, and evidently so did some stranger whom Paul didn't even know—and Paul knew nearly everyone that his friend knew. Perhaps Richard would eventually see for himself how he was behaving. He knew he would have to give him time for that, but Richard would have to see it soon because, to Paul, the change in him was crystal clear, and he knew his friend should be able to see it himself.

At least talk to him, Paul told himself. *You don't have to bring up any of his problems, just* talk *to him.*

What could be so hard about that? They had been friends for too long not to. The weekend fishing trips in the summertime, drinking beer after beer in a boat out in the middle of Lake Norfork, swapping lies and fantasies that were never going to happen. The two trips to St. Louis each year to watch the Cardinals play. Paul could remember the time two summers ago when Richard had been hit in the head by a foul ball while paying a vendor for two hotdogs and a beer. He'd had light dizzy spells the rest of the afternoon, but refused help from the Cardinal's trainer, who had offered to look at it for him. He had a small bump on his head for two days, and when they'd returned home that evening Tina had taken one look at the bump—after hearing how he'd acquired it—and told him that was what he deserved for not getting seats behind the backstop. The two men had just laughed, and Richard told her that she just didn't understand what pains some people would go to in order to get a foul ball at a Major League game. There was also the little get-together every year on New Year's Eve. To Paul, the new year was not the new year unless it was brought in by celebrating with Richard, getting inebriated, singing songs from the seventies, and saying 'happy-fucking-new-year' to everyone in sight.

They'd had spats before, sure, but not anything major, and things always turned out all right one way or the other. But now Paul thought that if he didn't take the proper measures and break the ice with Richard—ice that was steadily getting thicker—this might be one time when things *didn't* turn out all right. And he couldn't take a chance on that happening. He felt already that Richard was drifting inexorably away from the friendship, and if that happened there was too much that might be lost.

He took a deep breath and walked nonchalantly across the aisle to Richard's desk. "Anything happening in the world today?" he said, nodding at the folded paper on the desk.

Richard glanced up at him as if shaken out of his thoughts. "I'm sorry. What?"

"The newspaper. Anything happening?"

"Oh. Not much," Richard said. He tossed him the copy of the *Arkansas Times*. "There's a story on page two that's pretty interesting, though. At least more interesting than your horoscope for today, and mine too." He smiled.

Paul smiled back, and some of his uneasiness passed. The air between them felt a little warmer. A little. "Usually, *anything* is more interesting than my horoscope." He opened the paper and scanned the article on Peter Irons' murder. "I remember this guy. Isn't he the psycho who murdered his whole family a few years back over in West Memphis?"

"That's him," Richard said.

"I thought so. Funny that the police have no leads, and it

happened right there in the state pen. I guess they'll end up blaming it on some other con, regardless of whether he did it or not.

"Probably so," Richard said. After a moment he said: "So, what do you think?" He was looking intensely at Paul.

"What do I think? I think the son-of-a-bitch got exactly what he deserved. I mean, he killed his *family.*"

Richard's smile widened at that, and Paul felt some relief. "That's precisely what I think."

Paul folded the newspaper and dropped it back onto the desk. "What are you doing after work?"

"Why?" The pleasant smile had disappeared. In its place was a guarded look.

"I don't know…I just thought that maybe we could get together over at my place, drink a few beers, watch the redbirds on the tube."

"I'd really like to," Richard said, "but I'm going to take some of this crap home with me tonight and see if I can't catch up on some of it. I'm getting a little behind, and you know how Pat is."

"If you need help with anything…"

"I appreciate that, I really do, but I think I can handle it by myself. It will only take a couple of hours once I get going."

"Well…okay. You can always call if you need any help."

"I know," Richard said. "Tell you what, maybe we'll get together this weekend and do something."

"That would be great," Paul said.

"But right now, how about us going downstairs and getting some coffee and donuts?"

"That sounds good, too."

As they went down the hall to the stairs, and down the short flight to the second floor, Paul wondered to himself just how sincere Richard was being about the two of them getting together on the weekend. He wanted desperately to believe what Richard said—wanted to believe that more than anything at the moment—because his offer sounded so much like that Richard he'd always known. And yet, he had the somehow depressing feeling that Richard knew he wanted to talk to him, and also what he wanted to talk about, and that the offer had been made only to delay the inevitable conversation.

But why?

He could think of no answer for that question, just as he could not think of an answer as to why the old man had called about Richard yesterday.

The only thing he knew to do right now was to play the whole situation by ear. He was beginning to make a little headway with Richard now, and any questions Paul asked him might very well put their relationship in jeopardy.

Paul had a feeling, despite the coffee break and Richard's gesture for the upcoming weekend, that their relationship was already in peril.

That frightened him, because he didn't know how—or why—it had gotten that way.

But he planned to find out, one way or another.

7

George Morrison sat at his desk in his small office, reading the article on Peter Irons' death from the *Arkansas Times* for the third time. For the past two days, he had been scanning all the major papers for articles such as this one, and now that he had found one, he wasn't at all sure that it had anything to do with Richard Raines *or* the television set. The only thing that was noteworthy for now was that fact that the cause of death—even if it *was* in Little Rock—was *unknown*.

Of course, people died—or were killed—from unknown causes more often than one would suspect, and the main reason George was interested in this fact was because nearly every one of the people to whom he had sold that damned black and white TV had died of *unknown* causes. Sure, something had killed them; mutilation, stabbed, and a number of other ways that the body ceased to function. But it was always, initially, *unknown*.

And that wasn't all. In four of eight cases, several people with ties or relations to the TV's owners had *also* died within the same time span that the TV's owners had. It was a strange thing, and it had taken George a lot of telephone calls and plenty of research to link the people's deaths, and their relationships to each other.

In 1989, Donald Forrester's wife and brother had been murdered just two days before Mr. Forrester's own death. Articles in the newspapers had made it easy to make the connection there.

In 1990, Phil Clayton had purchased the television from George, and four days later his housekeeper, an unfortunate woman by the name of Sandra Windham, was found toasted to a crisp, the victim of electrocution due to faulty wiring in—you guessed it—the television set. Two days after that, Phil Clayton was also found dead, and this time the cause was not known. The housekeeper's mishap was the only time George could find where the cause of death was related *directly* to the TV.

The rest was only…what? Speculation? Coincidence?

George suspected neither. What he suspected was that it was the truth. The deaths—all of them—*were* somehow linked to the television set.

In 1995—just two years ago—Martha Stonewall purchased the TV from George's shop. She had died—or was killed—eight days later from an *unknown* cause. What was ironic in this case was that the police linked a murder that had happened two days prior to Miss Stonewall's death to her own murder. This had come about nearly a week after poor Martha was found dead and mutilated in her clapboard house on the outskirts of Jonesboro. It turned out that the man who was murdered—and this had happened over two-hundred miles away, just south of St. Louis—was Martha Stonewall's lover. At least, he had been. Friends of hers told the police that he and Martha had a bad fight less than a week before she was murdered, and that he (his name had been Joseph Hallard) had left town. According to the friends, Martha had been a nervous wreck after that.

This case had been the first one to come to George's mind when he first read the article on Peter Irons' death down at LRSP. It seemed that similar things had happened before, so why not?

He picked up his copy of the *Jonesboro Daily Journal*—he'd been getting both papers for years—and read the article inside. Near the end it stated that Peter Irons had been a native of Jacksonville, Florida. Maybe he should call down there. It would put a dent in his phone bill, he knew that, but he also knew that it might be the only way to find out if Peter Irons and Richard Raines had ever crossed each other's paths.

He would like to call Richard's office at the Jonesboro Advertising Corporation again (it might save him the long-distance bill), but he didn't feel like it would be a good idea at the moment to talk to the man directly. And if that guy Paul Frazier answered the phone again...well, George didn't want to contemplate that right now. That young man hadn't been the nicest person he had ever talked to, but George had sensed—even over the phone—that he had wanted to talk about Richard. There were just enough pauses in the right places, and George's instincts were thrumming.

He had put the phone back in its cradle on his desk, wondering if the man who said his name was Paul Frazier might be closer to Richard than just an associate. A quick call to

Larry Vincent over at the Federal Building had supplied him with Mr. Frazier's address. He had been rather surprised to see both men lived on the same street, and that only two digits differentiated their homes (Paul's 2902, Richard's 2900). They were next-door neighbors and, most likely, friends.

So maybe he *should* call Paul Frazier again.

He mulled it over, finally deciding if he were to call Mr. Frazier, he would need an excuse to do so.

He would call Jacksonville first, and find out anything he could about Peter Irons. If he found something—anything— that could be linked to Richard, he would definitely call the young man again.

What if you don't *find out anything?* he asked himself.

He thought about it and decided that, even if the call to Jacksonville didn't turn up anything, he would likely resort to calling Paul Frazier, anyway. If the men were friends, as George felt they were, then Paul might be the only person who could help him—and help Richard.

For he knew that time was slipping away, and if he didn't do something soon, Richard Raines was going to die. He knew this as sure as his name was George.

8

Saturday, September 12, 1997

Richard sat on the sofa in the sunny warmth of his living room, sipping on a bourbon and coke. It was a little after nine, and cheerful outdoor sounds filtered in through the screen in the open window behind him; birds chirruping lazily in the oak trees, cars passing slow on the street, their drivers mindful of the children who laughed and frolicked while playing a Saturday morning game of kickball on the wide tarmac. A cool breeze blew in irregular gusts through the window, cooling the back of his neck, which was damp with perspiration although it wasn't uncomfortably hot in the apartment.

He whistled an amusing tune in between sips on his drink. A tune he was familiar with. Yesterday he had even made up his own variation of the lyrics and had sung them to himself on and off that night while he got blitzed on whiskey and cola. Actually, it was only the last line he had changed.

> Jimmy crack corn and I don't care.
> Jimmy crack corn and I don't care.
> Jimmy crack corn and I don't care.
> I've lost my fuckin' nuts...

Of course, he *hadn't* lost his nuts—*Jerry had said so!*—but he liked his version of the nursery rhyme, anyway. And as far as Jerry was concerned right now, screw him if he couldn't take a joke.

Richard would never consider thinking such things if the television set was on, but at the moment it wasn't. He hadn't turned it on yet this morning. He had a few things to think about first, and he knew all too well that thinking was next to impossible when the TV was on. When it was on, anything he said *or* thought was picked up by not only Jerry, but by his unseen audience as well.

What *was* it about that 'audience'?

After what Jerry had shown him on the TV screen two nights ago, Richard was forming an idea in his mind of the people who made up that audience.

He had been drunk—again—on the night of the tenth, and had finally succumbed to his curiosity about Peter Irons' death, asking Jerry how it had happened. He hadn't expected what happened next. Jerry had *shown* him Peter's death. Impossible as it seemed, he had watched—in gruesome detail, as though he were watching a movie—as three pairs of blood-streaked hands covered Peter Irons' face and body. Four of the hands were small, as if those of children, and one of the larger ones had struck Peter with some object. A knife? He didn't know. Just as he didn't know to whom the hands belonged. Peter Irons had been murdered—in front of his eyes—and although he felt no remorse over Peter's death (hadn't he wanted it—*agreed* for it—to happen?), the gory, brutal murder nonetheless left him feeling a little nauseous.

But who had done it?

Richard had missed work yesterday, and had spent most of the day drinking and brooding over that very question (while the TV was off, anyway). He hadn't been able to come up with a logical answer, yet he was beginning to think that Jerry's unseen audience might have something to do with it.

But what?

He didn't know.

Paul had dropped by the apartment around six, checking on him since he'd missed him at work. Richard made up an excuse and asked Paul in for a drink. After finishing his drink, he left, although Richard sensed that he had something on his mind.

"What about Saturday?" Paul had asked as he walked out the door. "Still want to do something?" There had been no real hope in his voice.

"I don't know," Richard had said. He had been drunk for hours and could barely focus his eyes, let alone his voice. "I'll let you know, good buddy."

But so far, he hadn't let Paul know anything.

And why is that? he asked himself. *Paul is your best friend. Matter of fact, why don't you let him know* everything?

Jimmy crack corn...

But he couldn't do that

and I don't care,

because even though he *was* his best friend, he would think

I've lost my fuckin' nuts.

that he was crazy, insane, and who was to say he wouldn't be correct?

Jerry, that's who.

Ah, yes...Jerry. From the Thought Network, channel 94 (the network that shows you more!). And *wasn't* it a thought network? Jerry had explained to him that by 'tuning in' to his train—or network—of thoughts, he could help Richard with things—could help him *do* anything at all. Weren't two heads better than one?

But it wasn't just two heads, which to him was the most amazing thing. Not only was Jerry 'tuned in' to his thoughts, but so was his unseen audience. And how many of *them* were there? Twenty? Fifty? A hundred?

Richard didn't know. He knew when he talked to Jerry he felt more comfortable, more at ease, with his thoughts. It was as though his unconscious mind had come alive and taken on an identity of its own. Jerry seemed to always have a different perspective on whatever he was thinking. He seemed intelligent and full of wisdom; a type of wisdom Richard had never seen or heard before. The man seemed *almost* like a father.

Was he beginning to like Jerry?

He thought he might be, yet there was a part of him that was repulsed at the idea of having anything to do with someone who could read his mind; someone who had lied to him, could have someone murdered, and who could *show* him that murder, while the police down in Little Rock were scratching their heads and wondering what the hell had happened. This was also the part of Richard which still insisted he was losing his mind—perhaps all of this was in his head.

When this voice began its mutterings, all he had to do to get rid of it was turn on the television. This simple act seemed to take care of a lot of things. He rose from the sofa on unsteady legs and made his way to the bar, leaning to his left, as if the floor was tilted.

He mixed another drink and weaved his way over to the silent television. What would Jerry tell him today? What would he *show* him?

Jimmy crack corn

There was only one way to find out.

and I don't care.

The volume control clicked as he turned the set on, and snowy white static filled the screen, as it always did. Two days ago, the set had quit broadcasting regular TV, even though the cable was still hooked up to it.

Eyes on the TV, Richard back-stepped to the sofa and plopped onto it.

A few seconds later Jerry appeared on the screen. "Good morning."

Richard lit a cigarette and nodded at the screen. "Morning."

"I see you're already hitting that damn bottle again." There was a touch of scorn in his voice.

"Yeah, well, it helps me cope."

"But that's one of the things *I'm* here to do," Jerry said. "To help you think straight, to help you cope."

Richard laughed dryly. "I know that. The whiskey helps me cope with you, Jerry."

"What do you mean?"

"Hell, you sit there behind your desk and talk to me, and you *know* everything about me, what I'm going to say, what's on my mind. But I don't know anything at all about you except—"

"Except I'm your friend and you like me," Jerry finished for him. His face looked filled with pride.

"Yeah…right," Richard said. "But it's about *all* I know."

"Well, I like you too, Richard. However, maybe we can get into this subject a little later. Right now, I want to tell you a few things…and then I have something to show you."

9

"How do you feel about your divorce from Tina?"

"What do you mean, 'how do I feel?'"

"Just what I said. Are you happy? Are you angry? Do you feel cheated? What?"

Richard was caught off-guard. "I don't know…it's over. It's just over."

"Let me rephrase my question, then. How do you feel about Tina?"

Richard thought about it. After what she had done, he sure as hell wasn't happy. Hell, he had walked in on her and Kerry Jorgensen—who had been one of her old boyfriends—while they were having sex on Richard and Tina's bed. And there had been Billy before that (he had found this out after the fact), not to mention Patrick Garnell. His *boss*, for crying out loud. Richard hadn't blamed Pat for Tina's infidelity on that occasion. By then he was getting to the point where he no longer cared. The marriage was ruined and it was Tina, and her alone, who had ruined it. As far as Richard was concerned, it had been over the minute he walked in on her and Jorgensen, their bodies locked together in a sexual position he had never heard of—or seen—before.

He'd been hurt at first, hurt terribly, but when he found out about her and Billy, he managed to shake the deep pain and betrayal that he felt in his heart.

From that point, all he wanted was out.

Now, after brief consideration, he felt he could describe how he felt about her with just five words, and he spoke them now: "I think she's a bitch."

"A bitch."

"Correct, a bitch. I could think of several other choice names which would fit her like a glove, including whore and slut, but 'bitch' pretty much sums it up." Richard considered this for a moment. "Why do you ask?"

Jerry looked pleased. A smile formed at the corners of his thin-lipped mouth. "I just wanted to make sure that we both feel the same way about her."

"And do we?"

"Oh, yes. Definitely so. But…doesn't it make you angry? What she did?"

"Well…"

Jerry's voice rose. "Doesn't it make you angry how she slept around on you, played you for a fool?"

Richard could say nothing.

"She *laughed* at you behind your back, Richard. *Laughed!*" Now Jerry's face was stern.

Drunk, and dumbstruck for the right words, Richard was reminded of the dream he'd had several nights ago; Tina laughing at him, and the fangs mutilating her mouth as she talked. Maybe Jerry had picked up on those images. Now, he could only repeat what he'd already said: "It's over…It's just…over."

"Like *hell* it is," Jerry said, leaning back in his chair and lighting a cigarette. "She's *still* laughing at you. She's sleeping with anyone who will look at her." He paused, and his eyes bore into Richard's. "Doesn't that bother you the slightest bit?"

Richard had to admit that it did, although he was reluctant to say so.

Jerry continued. "Well, she's got her a boyfriend now, a *big* boyfriend, and all she ever talks about is how big and strong he is, and what a wimp you are."

"How do you know this?" Richard demanded.

"How do I know *anything?*" Jerry said. "Furthermore, does it really matter in the grand scheme of things?"

Richard shook his head. "No. I guess it doesn't."

Outside, the sky had begun to cloud over and the kickball game in the street ceased, the children scattering in different directions.

"I want to show you something now," Jerry said, and Richard felt a small stab of dread come over him. The gruesome details of Peter Irons' death were still fresh in his mind. "Don't worry. This isn't as...messy...as what I showed you the other day."

Richard knocked back the rest of his drink. "Thank God for that."

"Were you not happy with the way Mr. Irons was handled?"

"Sure, I was," Richard said. "Extremely happy. That bastard. It was just a little gross."

"Such a weak stomach," Jerry mused aloud. Then his voice rose a notch as he said, "But don't you worry about that right now. In time, we will fix that little problem of yours."

Richard just looked at him.

"Now," Jerry said. "Getting back to what I'm going to show you. I don't think you truly feel Tina is a bitch. Jerry held up one hand. "But that's okay. Anything that *can* be changed, *will* be changed. Take a look, Richard."

Jerry disappeared from the screen. In his place appeared a shot of Tina and a rather tall young man in gym shorts and a muscle shirt. The two were sitting on a drab sofa, sipping drinks, and talking. Two things disillusioned Richard right away. As with the scene of Peter Irons' death, he felt as though he was watching a movie—the picture was that clear. The second thing—and *unlike* the Peter Irons 'video'—was that the picture on the screen now was in *color,* and he had never seen anything in color on his black and white TV, except Jerry. Yet, even the fact that Jerry was always in color had never computed to Richard's mind until now; the black suit, red tie, and different colored shirts—usually white or yellow—the man always wore had been taken for granted by a now-appalled Richard, who had been too caught up in the fact Jerry existed at all to notice what color he or his clothes were. Later, he would kick around the idea—and not in impossible one—that perhaps it simply took a broader picture (such as the one he was seeing now) instead of just a close-up of Jerry, for him to discover what he should have noticed from the first time Jerry appeared on the screen—*color.*

Now, his sudden clarity about the color faded away as the action before him on the screen began to command his full attention. Tina and the tall man in the gym shorts (who Richard supposed was the *big boyfriend* Jerry had mentioned minutes ago) had placed their drinks on the small table in front of the sofa and were engaged in a long, passionate kiss, arms locked around one another. Tina's left hand seemed to waste no time leaving its perch on the man's shoulders and finding its way down to the elastic waist of the blue shorts, and a few seconds later it disappeared inside of them, only to emerge more seconds later pulling and fondling something that was growing quite visibly on the screen.

Richard felt the first hot flash of jealous anger. It crackled through him like a thunderstorm at the end of a long dry spell. His ears were hot, burning. He began to get an erection and felt embarrassment and shame, which enraged him more.

The picture changed, and Tina and the man were in another room, in bed, where they were performing sexual acts of a varying nature. Richard was reminded of the X-rated films that Tina had occasionally borrowed from her girlfriends. He hadn't liked watching them, and he would usually read a book in a different room while Tina indulged herself. He had sat through one such movie with her (feeling embarrassed the whole time— he hadn't watched another after that), and what he was seeing now seemed to parallel the way the movie had been made. The only thing missing was the funky background music.

This thought passed through his mind in microseconds, pushed forcefully aside by the anger which now invaded his entire being. He shut his eyes and clenched his fists. "Turn it off!" he yelled. His voice seemed to echo in the nearly empty living room. "Turn it off, or I will! Get it off there *now!*"

He opened his eyes and saw Jerry staring serenely at him with a face that reflected no emotion.

Richard took a deep breath and exhaled slowly. "I'll kill them," he said calmly. "I'll kill them both. Myself." His voice rose several decibels: "That fucking *bitch!*"

Jerry's voice was smooth and calm. "That wouldn't be a very good idea."

Richard looked at him. The anger and hate on his face dissolved into mild bewilderment. "And why not?"

Jerry sighed and folded his hands together. "Because if you went to that extreme it would not be in the best interest of either of us. For one thing, the police would be here before you could say 'boo.' You would be a prime suspect in the murder of your ex-wife and her boyfriend, and in your current condition, which is constantly drunk and angry, you'd no doubt be their number one suspect. Don't get me wrong," he continued, holding up his right hand slightly before resting it in the folds of his left. "You have every right in the world to be angry. But if the police ended up suspecting even half of the truth…which they more than likely would…they would think along the same line. In other words, you had every right to be angry, so you took care of the problem and killed them both." Jerry stopped and looked gravely into Richard's thinking eyes.

"You're right," Richard said after a moment. *Of course, he's right,* he told his frustrated mind. *How stupid can I be to think I can pull something like that off and get away with it? Jeez.*

"Not stupid," Jerry said. "Your reaction is what I would expect from anyone in your situation. All I want to do is show you what is not in your best interest...and what is.

Richard leaned forward. "And what *is* in my best interest?"

"What I propose is that Tina's boyfriend...his name is Biff Larento, by the way...be eliminated. Neither you nor I need Tina's murder on his hands, and if anyone killed her...anyone at all...the police would look at you first. As I said before, that would not be in your best interest. Or mine. Besides that," Jerry said coolly, "I have some business with Mr. Larento myself. At least, some of my people do."

Richard didn't grasp what Jerry said. He was trying to think coherently, but the anger he had cast momentarily aside was beginning to resurface, and he knew that pretty soon it would swallow him. He remembered the way he had felt after recalling what Peter Irons did to him so many years ago. He had felt as though he would never stop being angry, and was quite taken aback at how easily that anger had been sated when he read about the man's death—and when he had later seen it on his own television set.

He had been angry, yes, but the way he felt now—the savage fury, the black rage that seemed as though it would end nowhere—was stronger than any emotion he had experienced thus far, and that both frightened and disoriented him.

He'd thought that he had been single-handedly responsible for Peter Irons' death—perhaps even was, when you boiled it right down—until Jerry had shown it to him in black and white. What he grasped at now, while early morning became late morning, was the naked knowledge that he had gotten away clean. Well, whoever did it had gotten away with it. But Richard knew if it hadn't been for him, that gruesome murder would have never taken place. He had wanted it. It was that simple. He wanted it to happen—had given Jerry his permission—and it had happened.

And he had been glad.

So why not? He asked himself as he looked at the TV.

"Yes, Richard. Why not?"

Jerry's voice hadn't startled him, but he'd heard it, and he knew what he wanted. His mind repeatedly returned to the scenes Jerry had shown him less than twenty minutes ago: Tina's body entangled passionately with the body of her boyfriend, Biff. Tina fondling his erect penis, and then putting it in her mouth, engulfing the head of it lovingly. Biff humping away at her faster, harder, and longer than Richard *ever* had. Her desperate, satisfied cries when she came.

What he felt now was beyond anger. He'd been enraged at what Peter Irons had done to him, but that had happened years ago—forgotten years that had only been recalled with Jerry's help. What Tina and her boyfriend had done had happened recently.

He looked at Jerry squarely. "Take care of him."

Jerry seemed more than pleased. "Richard, I think you've made the right—" But before he could finish, Richard, in his fit of rage, turned the television set off.

10

It was two hours later before Richard had calmed down enough to turn the set back on and apologize to Jerry.

Jerry took the apology in stride—he said he understood, and didn't blame Richard for his anger-directed actions—and then said he had to leave for a while, as he had things to tend to.

He advised Richard to get some rest, and Richard took the advice. After turning the TV off, he shambled down the hall to his bedroom feeling—aside from drunk—more tranquil than he had in hours. His anger had abated remarkably, because he knew something was being done about Biff Larento.

He lay down on the bedcovers and fell into a peaceful sleep.

11

On that same Saturday, the twelfth, a little after three o'clock, Tina Raines was sitting alone in her apartment, contemplating the telephone call she was about to make. Cars and trucks droned by busily beneath the fourth-floor window.

She knew what she wanted to say to Richard; there was no problem there. All she wanted to do right now was make casual conversation with him. If her plan went as she hoped it would, she would most definitely need to be on good terms with her ex-husband.

What if he knows you were prowling around in his house the other day?

Now *there* was something for her to think about.

Suppose a neighbor, someone other than the Fraziers, had seen her that day? Suppose they had recognized her and told Richard. Suppose even further that he went through the house in that meticulous way of his and discovered she had been in his 'bills and records' box.

What, then?

I would have heard something from either him or the police, by now, she told herself, but that thought didn't bring much comfort. Richard didn't even know where she lived or worked, so it would probably take some time for him to track her down.

Maybe he doesn't know or suspect anything.

There was only one way for her to find out, and she knew it. She wished she could trust Biff enough for him to be here with her now, but knew this was something she would have to do on her own. She couldn't take any chances. Biff had left just over an hour ago, and although she hated to see him leave—knew that she would miss him in bed tonight—she was also relieved.

If Biff knew of her plan, she would lose him. Never mind that the two of them, when together, seemed to flow and join together like a couple of Lego blocks. Forget that their lovemaking was the best either of them had ever experienced—he would be gone. And she couldn't chance that.

She grabbed her purse and went downstairs to the pay phone. She pushed a couple of cigarette butts off the top of the phone, then used a Kleenex from her purse to wipe the handset, and slugged a quarter into the slot.

With a hand that shook minutely, she dialed Richard's number. She let it ring six times and was beginning to think that he wasn't home, when the line was picked up. "H'lo?"

"Richard? It's me," she said.

"Oh…Hi." He had recognized her voice, then. His own was sluggish, slow.

"Did I call at a bad time?" *Here is where you find out if he knows,* she told herself.

He coughed, and Tina recognized the sound of him lighting a cigarette. "I was sleeping. What do you want?" He sounded irritated.

"I just thought I'd call and see how you were. We haven't spoken in a while."

She rambled on before he could respond, anxious to know. He hadn't given her any clues, yet. Hell, she had woke him up. "So," she said, "have you had a chance to refurnish the condo yet?" Her hand tightened painfully on the receiver in anticipation of his answer.

"No, not really." He sounded less irritable. "I got another TV, a few knick-knacks…" he trailed off.

"How are things at the office?" This was another of her carefully planned questions. She had called JAC three different times the past few days, speaking to Paul Frazier, who had told her on those three occasions that Richard was either 'out', or 'hadn't made it in yet.' She didn't know if Paul had given

Richard any messages—she certainly hadn't left any—but hoped he hadn't. Richard had never liked her calling his office for casual small talk. He wouldn't care for it now, either. But she had only called the office those times because he hadn't been home, and she counted herself lucky that she had caught him at home now.

"Things are pretty much the same at work," he told her. "How about you?"

"Well, I guess I'm making out," she said (she heard Richard laugh softly after she said this, but she had no idea why). "I got a job, and an apartment…"

"Where?" Richard asked, and she didn't like the sudden interest in his voice. She didn't know exactly why, but she felt that telling him where she lived and worked might be dangerous—and might possibly screw things up for her, spoil her plan.

"Well, it's not the greatest job in the world, but…hey, listen, I'm gonna go ahead and let you go. I just wanted to see how you were. I've got a girlfriend coming over in a little while, and I really need to straighten the place up a bit." This, of course, was a lie, but Tina thought she had talked enough for now. If her plan was going to work, she would have to go about it gradually.

"Well, okay. Suit yourself," Richard said. Now his voice was groggy again, and she knew he was about to nod off.

"I'll talk to you later," she said, and hung up.

She let out a long breath, and started back up the stairs. He didn't know. He didn't know she had been in the apartment, and he didn't know she had called his office. She felt she knew him well enough to know that if he *had* known, he would have mentioned it.

Now that the call had been made, she wished that she had been able to tell him how she really felt about him; how much she hated him for what he'd done to her. The pansy.

She thought she'd done a good job at keeping her voice casual, her mannerisms tolerable. She wished her mother was alive to see her final revenge when it happened. *And it will happen soon,* she told herself.

When she entered her apartment, she went over to the bed and lay down, going over her plan again and again in her mind, combing it for errors, making sure it was as fool-proof as it seemed.

Later, she slept.

12

Biff Larento turned off the tap over the bathtub and stepped gingerly into the steaming water. He sighed deeply as he submerged his body up to his neck, his arms raised, resting, on either side of the tub. He had just finished working out at The Flex, a fitness and health club over on West Cate Avenue, and his aching muscles seemed to sigh also as they absorbed the hot water like some kind of human sponges. The feeling was sharp, piercing, but pleasant.

His thoughts as he relaxed in his tub on this alluring Saturday evening should have been on his newest girlfriend, Tina Raines. Lately, they *had* been, almost exclusively, and although he *did* think about her to a certain degree, total concentration on her lovely face was difficult tonight because of the three girls who had paid him so much attention at The Flex this afternoon. He was accustomed to garnering attention from the opposite sex, but these girls had been the three sexiest females he had ever seen in his life. It is what he'd come to believe, anyway. And telling himself that is what made his thoughts turn back to Tina, because before today he'd thought *she* was the sexiest girl on the planet.

Now, he wasn't so sure.

Tina was beautiful, yes—often while having sex he would think that he was on top of (or below) a goddess—but he had a precarious feeling her beauty was only skin-deep. He sensed something just below the surface of her smooth, creamy skin, but it was hard for him to see exactly what it was. She was striking, but he didn't really know much about her—other than what she'd shown him in bed. He knew she was single by a recent divorce, but how recent he didn't know. If he ever brought that subject up, or questioned her about it (which had been only twice—Biff was a quick learner), she grew defensive and cold; so cold he thought that if he reached out a hand to touch her it would stick to her skin—the same way it would if he stuck a wet hand into the freezer over his refrigerator and pressed it to one of the walls.

He also knew that she occasionally talked in her sleep. Although this normally wouldn't have bothered him, it had begun to the last couple of days, and he was beginning to believe the two real things he *did* know about her went together somehow.

The first time this thought crossed his mind was on Thursday night. He had awakened around eleven with a painfully full bladder. On his way back from the bathroom he had heard her say, in a wakeful voice which sounded so casual she might have been talking to him, "Richard, you're going to pay, Buckaroo." Biff had felt an unpleasant chill race through his nude body. Tina sounded so *awake*, yet there was no movement from the shape beneath the crumpled sheets where she lay; she was sound asleep. He'd felt relief at that. He crawled beneath the covers, pulling them up to his chin. She was fast asleep, and he didn't think he would want to hear her speak those same words while awake.

But then...that sentence hadn't really been directed at him. It had been for some guy named Richard. Tina's ex-husband?

Biff didn't know, but the satisfaction in her voice was clear, and made him not *want* to know who Richard was. In fact, it made him glad he wasn't in the guy's shoes.

There had also been something else in Tina's sleeping (yet wide awake) voice. It contained a threatening undertone, as if the message held a dark secret. That, more than anything, is what bothered Biff. Tina seemed to him like one big secret. A sexy one, for sure, but he knew so little about her, and didn't dare ask too many personal questions, for he knew how cold she could be.

She had talked again in her sleep last night, and it had startled him awake, causing him to scoot backward and bang his head on the small bookshelf at the head of his waterbed. "What?" he had asked, for once again it sounded as though she was awake and talking to him. She had said two things this time. The first was, "Mother was right, you bastard." He had recoiled—and bumped his head—with something akin to fright. The anger in her voice was so bitter. Worse than that, she *could* have been talking to him this time. No names had been mentioned. "Bastard" could have been for anybody. Tina had not answered his one-word question; she was indeed asleep. Shortly after she spoke the first time she spoke again. This time she said...

She said...

Biff splashed hot water from the tub up into his tanned face, breaking his thoughts. *Don't think about that. Not that.* He splashed more water onto his face and felt his facial muscles first tense, and then relax, as the water soaked into his opened pores.

Today had been the first time since meeting Tina that he'd had a chance to stop by The Flex for a workout. He normally went at least three times a week, and sometimes four, but the only exercise he'd been getting lately was in bed (not to be complaining, of course). His aching joints and muscles were letting him know about it now, although he'd ended up cutting his regular routine in half. And, of course, the reason for that had been the three girls.

They wore A-State visors, so Biff figured they were college students, and he first noticed them while finishing his sets on the rowing machine, the first exercise he had done after a brutal series on the Nautilus. Two of them were blond-haired and one was a dark brunette. The two blondes were about the same height, both of them slightly shorter than the brunette. All three wore florescent red bikinis that left little for the imagination. They looked as though they might have walked right out of the pages of a *Sports Illustrated* swimsuit issue.

No, Biff thought as he lowered his arms into the steamy water. *They were too classy for even* that *rag. Too good for* any *magazine.*

And there was something else about them; they looked familiar. Biff didn't now why, but they did. His first thought on seeing them (after looking them over) was that he was seeing the three girls that had been killed in a car crash he was involved in a year ago. He had been drunk at the time, changing the CD in his stereo as he approached an intersection, and had slammed into the stopped pick-up truck ahead of him. The man and his wife driving that Ford had escaped with no injuries, but the force of Biff's Mustang had thrown the truck into the small sports car ahead of them, killing all three people in that convertible. Biff's father had known some city officials, and had gotten him off with a DWI, instead of a manslaughter charge.

This accident ran briefly through his mind on occasion, so he figured it was only natural that his first thought would be of those three accident victims.

He had stopped rowing on the machine. He couldn't help it. All three girls smiled at him (the sexiest *smiles* he'd ever seen), and he, of course, had been a gentleman and smiled back. He got off the machine and stretched, preparing himself for the weights, and they had *really* smiled then, making 'oohs' and 'aahs' that he could hear thirty feet away, and whispering amongst themselves. Biff had grown used to that reaction to his body since he'd become a member of this club three years ago—had taken it as a matter of course—and had even made a few dates with women he met here (and been laid more than once). But never by three girls at once. Certainly not any as beautiful as these, either.

The three girls stood where they were by the Nautilus while he began his series of workouts with the weights, and soon they were headed in the direction of the pool, glancing back over their shoulders at him and smiling in a manner so sexy it caused goosebumps to crawl up his legs. He decided to cut his workout on the weights short—after all, it had been quite a while since his last workout—and strode ever so casually to the pool. A good swim after a workout might do him some good, help him relax his taxed muscles.

The girls had found a spot on the far side and were sitting in lounge chairs at that end, facing the indoor swimming pool. Biff dove in and swam back and forth near that end of the pool, staring at them whenever he had the chance, unable to keep his eyes off them.

What were they whispering about over there, anyway? Maybe he should go over and talk to them.

For one brief moment he felt absolutely sure that what they were talking about had nothing to do with his body, but about something he felt sure he didn't want to hear or know. Once again, he thought of the college students from the accident. This thought was only a small lapse, and it disappeared as quickly as it had come. Seconds later, he couldn't even remember that it had crossed his mind. Only now, at home in the bathtub, could he remember, his mind reeling the images and feelings as though everything was happening all over again.

After two more laps across the width of the pool, he decided to make his move. He got out of the water, started walking toward them...

...and that is when he'd thought of Tina.

What in the hell was he going to do here, anyway? Return their flirtations? Ask for a date? Perhaps a foursome in the hay?

Guilt engulfed him and he halted in his steps, still a good twenty feet from the stunningly beautiful girls.

No. No, he couldn't do this. He couldn't to it to Tina. Not that he felt anything more for her than he thought she did for him—sexual lust; he didn't—but because she might find out. And for some reason he couldn't put his finger on, he didn't' want that to happen.

So he had turned toward the indoor bath house instead of continuing his way to the girls, had showered, gotten dressed, and made his way to the entrance of The Flex. The girls had been standing a mere five feet from the door when he left, smiling and winking at him. The two blondes had even said hello, in a tone of voice any man would have taken as an invitation to converse. Possibly, even, to things beyond that. Biff had smiled briefly at them and forced himself to exit the building before something *did* happen. All he could think of while he left was that Tina would find out if he stopped and talked (or did things beyond that) to these girls. Although this thought was ridiculous and had no logical bearing to his rational mind—*how the hell is she going to find out?*—an inner voice told him it was *not* ridiculous, and to keep moving.

And so he had...all the way home.

Now, as he relaxed in the stillness of his bathroom, he realized maybe he *did* know why he thought Tina would find out. It was because of what she had said in her sleep last night. The *second* thing she had said. He didn't know exactly why, but what she said made him feel uneasy. And the way she had said it...*had* she been talking to him? To him, instead of someone named Richard who may or may not be her ex-husband?

No. Couldn't have been you, Biff. She loves *you. She loves your body, anyway.*

Still.

He leaned his head against the back of the tub and let the incandescent water continue to sooth his body, which had loosened up steadily and was beginning to feel better. He lay there like that, letting his thoughts drift lazily away.

He was just dozing off when he heard the latch on the front door turn *(click!)*, breaching the silence that lay over the house like a veil.

He sat up quickly, sloshing water about in small tidal waves. The water was the only sound, save for the one of the front door being opened down the hall in the living room, out of Biff's line of vision. There was no cheery or questioning hello. Only the sound of the door opening...and then clicking shut.

"Tina? That you, babe?" His voice boomed through the house, echoing loudly, although he hadn't yelled.

Of course it's her, idiot. She's the only person besides yourself who has a key, and the door is locked.

Was it, though? He couldn't remember, but for some reason he cursed himself for giving her a key.

Silence.

"Tina?" This time he *did* yell.

He heard giggles coming from the living room; female, flirty, and teasing. He stood up then, fast, and grabbed the towel from the lid of the commode, where he always placed one before bathing. That wasn't Tina in there.

Unless she's brought a girlfriend over.

Biff wasn't sure. It *could* be Tina...but those giggles didn't sound like her, and they had come from more than one person. He was uneasy now, and he wrapped the towel around his midsection.

A few seconds later a thought came to him. A thought that

rang so true in his mind that he knew it was so, although he didn't know how that could be: *it's the girls from the fitness center.*

But it can't be., how…?

And then they were there, at the door to the bathroom, and he let out a startled, silent scream in his mind: *It's them!* And then, embarrassingly: *All I have on is a towel.*

There they stood, the two blonde-haired girls and the brunette, side by side in the bathroom doorway, all but blocking the view of the hallway.

"Hi, Biff," the blonde on the left said.

"Hi," said the blonde on the right.

"Hello," the brunette said, and winked.

Biff stumbled backward and nearly tripped on the side of the tub and into the water. He was flabbergasted. The girls had evidently chunked their A-State visors, but they still wore those little florescent red bikinis—which wasn't wearing much.

"H-how did you know my name?" Biff croaked. "How did you know where I live?"

"From your mailbox," the blonde on the left said.

"We followed you," said the blonde on the right.

The brunette said nothing, only pursed her lips at him and gyrated her tan, slender body sensually.

He felt a stirring beneath the towel, and for a moment was paralyzed with fear. Tina would know now for sure. They said they had followed him, and if these mistakes for swimwear were all they'd had on, they must have drawn a lot of attention when they strolled up the sidewalk to his front door. It wasn't quite dusk, and there was plenty of daylight left. If someone told Tina they'd seen these three girls walking into the house…

Biff inhaled deeply. The blonde on the left had walked up to him while he was momentarily lost in his thoughts. Without any advance warning, her hand had escaped beneath the towel and was now fondling him. Her had was warm, vibrant.

"Don't worry, Biff," she said in a pouty voice. "We weren't seen by anyone."

"Only you," the other blonde said, moving forward. She went to the girl in front of him and untied her bikini top. It fell to the carpet with a soft sigh. She then untied her own, and Biff was left gaping at four upturned breasts.

The brunette moved up to him and slowly removed the towel from around his waist. He felt it brush is buttocks on its way to the floor. Two hands moved at his groin now, one blonde joining the other, and he tilted his head up toward the ceiling. Every sense and nerve in his body was now alive with sexual excitement, and thoughts about Tina—or her finding out—were gone entirely. His father had told him years ago while Biff was going through the stages of puberty that a stiff penis had no conscience, and at this moment he couldn't have said whether that was true or not because it currently felt as though his whole *body* was without a conscience.

There *was* enough left, however, for him to see to fondle one of each blonde's breasts as they stood on either side of him and, of course, they let him. He was in a swoon of ecstasy now, and when the brunette knelt in front of him and exchanged the pair of hands for her mouth, Biff's body broke out in a sweat and he thought he would explode with the sensation it caused.

After only a minute or so, he felt his climax coming, heedless to be held back, and beyond going back, anyway. And even as he began to expend himself, he felt the breast he held in each hand wither and dry up as he squeezed them, tearing them away from each girl's body—bodies which had begun to age and decompose in front of his eyes. He was terrified, but still he could not stop the sexual activity south of his stomach; it was just too late.

For one second there was a burst of pain down there, mixing with the sensation of orgasm, and he looked down, mindless of the living corpses on either side of him, and gawked in horror at what he saw. It was blood—*his* blood—and it was spurting out of him right along with the semen he was releasing. Only something was wrong, because there was a lot more blood coming out of him than there was semen. It splashed all over the floor in front of the decomposing body of the brunette, who had backed away. But she was no longer a brunette; her hair had turned gray and old, and some of it drifted in tufts off her rotting scalp onto the floor, where it was swallowed by the massive amount of blood flowing from his penis.

He didn't understand fully what had happened until he saw the corpse that had been the brunette spit a chunk of pink flesh out of her mouth—a mouth whose lips, so pouty and beautiful moments, now folded inward to reveal gray, vacated gums. Two of her teeth lay in the floor with that pink piece of flesh, and one was embedded in it, slanting toward the ceiling like a crooked stop sign.

He finally managed a scream. It was terrifying, but weak. He couldn't find the voice for one any louder.

He watched the three corpses walk quietly out of the bathroom, backs to him, and as they walked they began to fade. For just a second Biff could see through them, to the paneled wall of the hallway…and then they were gone.

He continued to scream, but silently now. The room was spinning, and so was his head. He fell to his knees, sitting in his own hot blood, and put his hands over what was left of his penis, trying but failing to stop the flow of blood. It was useless; it just kept coming.

Oh, God, please make it stop, make it stop!

He thought of what his mother used to say over and over whenever he got in trouble at school—either for fighting, cutting classes, or both—the triviality of it ringing in his mind: *what did I ever do to deserve this?*

As he thought it, the answer appeared—at least part of it. This was what Tina was talking about last night in her sleep.

This was what she had meant. She *had* been talking to him...but *why?* "Coming for you, you son-of-a-bitch." That is what she had said. But *why* had she said it? What had he done to her? Why had...*this* happened? Biff closed his eyes. Maybe the room would stop spinning if he did that.

But when he opened them again, there *was* no room, only a deep, dark abyss that seemed to fill his entire mind—his entire soul. There was a pinpoint of light at the end of that abyss. It looked like hundreds, *thousands* of miles away, but closer to him were dozens of outstretched hands, reaching for him. He took comfort in the almost certain knowledge that the hands were friendly hands, soft and pink, smooth—untouched by decomposition—detached from unseen bodies in the darkness.

The hands beckoned him.

He stepped (only it wasn't really stepping because he seemed to have lost his legs—it was more like floated) toward that dark abyss, welcoming it, somehow unafraid, and his last thought before entering it was that all of this was Tina's fault. *She* had done this somehow. *She* had done this to him.

And for no reason.

No reason at all.

13

Saturday evening, September 12, Richard sat at his small kitchen table, thinking. Although he had a beer resting in front of him, it was only his second since he'd awakened this afternoon around three.

Actually, he had been awakened by the phone ringing. Which is why he now found himself on only his second beer. At a time like this, with his head fogged by alcohol, he needed all the concentration he could muster. Yet total sobriety was unthinkable, unattainable, because of the residue of his drinking binge earlier in the day.

That the telephone woke him from his slumber was of no consequence to him, as it had been earlier in the week when Paul had called to let him know that he was late for work. What bothered him was the fact the caller had been Tina.

That little slut!

She had sounded strange—too nice, perhaps? Richard felt as though she had wanted to ask him something important and hadn't. But what? And why? And why did he think that, anyway?

He didn't know the answer to any of these questions but something about her call troubled him. She had sounded so innocent, so sweet, as though the two of them were still happily married.

As if she was calling to check up on him.

Now *there* was a thought.

The more he thought about it, the more he realized there had really been no reason for her to call in the first place. She hadn't asked for anything—and he felt that if Tina ever called him, it would be because she wanted or needed something, most likely, money—and she certainly hadn't called to start a fight with him.

So...what?

She called to see how I was doing.

And why should she care how you're doing? an inner voice spoke up at once. *That little bitch only cares about who she's fucking.*

The television was not on, but Richard thought the interior voice sounded a little like Jerry. Maybe a *lot* like Jerry's. On a more frightening level, he realized the voice could belong to himself...and probably did.

He lit a cigarette and took a sip of his beer. He craved a glass of strong bourbon, and the beer tasted flat, but he knew that once he started on the hard stuff all thoughts of Tina's phone call would be forgotten, and he might or might not be able to remember it later.

He didn't want that at all. That call *meant* something, by God. But *what?*

Jerry. Ask Jerry. Maybe he can tell you.

Richard pushed that voice aside. He knew it was his own this time, and that made him angry. He was already depending on Jerry enough as it was, and if he depended upon him for every little thing that cropped up, what kind of a man was he?

He was accustomed to working out his problems on his own. At least he had been before he'd purchased the TV.

No, you mean before the divorce.

Now, whenever there was a problem, Jerry had a solution for it, which had its attractions. Lately, he often felt as though he had a true friend in Jerry; someone he could confide in about anything. It was almost as if Jerry was a part of his conscience, a mental part of his physical being.

He thought of the 'film' Jerry had shown him just this morning of Tina and her boyfriend, and the anger returned like a dropped weight on a naked toe. That she could do something like that and then have the gall to call him and ask how he was doing was beyond him—and suspicious as hell. *What did the bitch want?*

He didn't know. *Couldn't* know now, since he was good and angry again. He couldn't keep thoughts about the phone call together long enough to make any coherent sense of them.

And what about her boyfriend? Buff, Biff, whatever his name was. What had been done about him?

He had forgotten all about his order for Jerry to take care of Mr. Larento. He picked up his beer and headed for the living room, to the television set, thinking he would kill two birds with one stone. Jerry would tell him—or at least give him an idea—why Tina called, and he might also update him on her boyfriend. Perhaps ex-boyfriend, if things had gone the way he hoped they had. He was angry, yes, but as he reached forward to turn on the set the anger abated somewhat, because he knew that whatever he was angry about, Jerry would have a remedy for it.

He turned the volume to the right. The set came on as it clicked. On the screen, white staticky snow.

His heart sank, but only a little. This happened sometimes, but he knew if he left the set on Jerry would eventually appear; usually in a matter of minutes.

This time the wait lasted a little under thirty seconds. He picked up his beer and had just put it to his mouth when Jerry said, "Hello, Richard."

Startled, he jerked the can away and cold beer spilled down his chin. He swiped at it absently. "Shit."

"I see you're drinking again," Jerry said conversationally. He was dressed today in what looked like the same black suit he always word, but appeared to have changed shirts. The one he wore now was blood-red.

"It's only my second one."

"At least you aren't on the hard stuff," Jerry said. "I'm impressed."

"I bet. Listen, Jerry. I got a ph—"

"Phone call. Yes, I know. Tina, was it?"

"Yeah," Richard said, almost in a sigh. At times like this he was glad Jerry could read his thoughts. It cut through a lot of the bullshit. "What do you think she wanted?"

"It's hard to say, but I don't think it was to see how you were doing."

"That's what *I* thought."

"If it was, she most assuredly had an underlying motive," Jerry said.

"Like what?"

"Perhaps she's already heard the terrible news about what

befell her boyfriend. I doubt it, though I could tell you for sure if by chance…"

"I wanted to ask you about that," Richard broke in.

Jerry looked agitated at this interruption, but seemed to take it in stride. "I know," he said. "As a matter of fact, I was going to say you turned me on just in the nick of time."

"What do you mean?"

"You can probably be sure that she knows nothing yet about her boyfriend. Throw that idea for a motive out the window if you want. You see, what happened to your ex-wife's sexy boyfriend happened less than ten minutes ago." Jerry looked at him with eyes that were flat, regarding.

Richard was caught off guard, flabbergasted. "Really?"

"Really. Want to see it?"

Jerry's tone was so business-like, so to the point, that Richard was almost startled into laughter. Then he thought about Peter Irons. That had nearly made him sick. The laugh died before he could release it.

"I can tell you," Jerry said, "that it is not funny. Be happy about it, yes. Be glad, yes. But don't laugh about it."

Immediately on the screen, Jerry's firm yet gentle face left, and in its place was a replay of the scene he had shown Richard this morning—Tina and her boyfriend Biff, romping it up and having a blast.

Richard became so outraged he thought his ears were going to fall off. They were that hot.

"Okay, okay," he yelled. *"Okay!"*

Jerry's face returned to the screen. He was calm, unsmiling.

"That was a rotten trick," Richard told him.

"No trick. I only did it to let you know I mean business, and that you had better mean business, too. We'll be lucky if the police don't question you about Mr. Larento's death. I don't think they will, but the possibility is there. It all depends on how your ex-wife takes it."

156

"Meaning…?"

"Meaning, how *will* she take it?"

"I-I don't know," Richard stumbled. "Were they close?"

"Hardly."

"Did she love him?"

"I doubt it," Jerry said. He sat back and lit a cigarette, never taking his eyes off Richard. "The point is this: Biff Larento is dead. You got what you wanted, and I think you're relatively safe from the police." Jerry leaned forward again. "Now, the *question* was, before you thought I'd tricked you, do you want to see it?"

The image of what he'd just seen on the TV was still fresh in Richard's mind. He didn't think he'd be able to just cast it aside. The more he thought about it, the angrier he became.

Through clenched teeth he said, "Show me."

14

Two minutes later it was over.

Richard's first thought when the three beautiful girls—two blondes and a brunette—walked in on a surprised, towel-clothed Biff Larento, had been, *this looks like one of the X-rated films Tina and her girlfriends enjoyed watching.* He had expected that funky, bass-clad music to start up at any time.

Things took a turn, however, and before long Biff no longer looked surprised. He looked as though he was enjoying himself immensely. *What could possibly happen to him,* he'd thought. *What could kill him besides over-indulgence?* The three girls weren't wearing enough clothing to hide a weapon of any kind, and they, too, looked as though they were having a good time. He thought Jerry must be showing him how Biff spent his time away from Tina, perhaps to illustrate that the death was justified. His anger turned down a new channel then, and he'd thought: *How could he do this to her?* Richard had been surprised at that feeling. Did he still care so much about Tina that he worried about the way she was treated by her boyfriend? It was hard to let that thought go once it was out there, and he mentally filed it away for future consideration because the thought caught him off-guard. It seemed foolish to let himself feel anything for the tramp he'd married a million years ago. He somehow managed to maneuver his anger back onto its previous course.

In spite of the fact that Tina's boyfriend was now on his TV with three beautiful women, Richard had become increasingly aroused by the action on the screen.

Biff had a hand on each of the blonde's breasts, and the brunette was now on the floor in front of him, back to Richard, her head bobbing back and forth. He was embarrassed by his erection, but could not pull his eyes away from the screen.

He was shown a close-up of Biff's face, twisted in ecstasy, and then it twisted downward in a grimace of pain, followed by a whimpering scream from his vocal cords. There was a shot of Biff with both hands cupped over his genitals. Richard could see nothing but blood, and knew beyond a shadow of a doubt what had happened.

He winced inwardly, and was surprised his stomach didn't threaten to make him sick.

The last shot was of Biff lying on the floor in front of his bathtub in what looked like *gallons* of blood, his body silent and still.

Now Jerry was back on the screen, and he seemed to be waiting patiently while Richard played all of this back in his mind.

"Well?" he finally said. "What do you think?"

Richard lit a cigarette and took a pull from his beer. He looked at Jerry...and then started to laugh. "What do I think? I think that's a really ironic question, Jerry, but I'll answer it for you." The smile left his face and he looked at Jerry soberly. "I think I like it. I feel sorry for the guy, because that had to hurt, but imagine what it will do to Tina when she finds out!"

"My sentiments exactly," Jerry said. "That's who we were trying to hurt in the first place, am I right?"

Biff's death *had* been nothing but an effort to get back at Tina, and to his credit Richard knew it. "You're *very* right," he said. And because it somehow seemed necessary, he added. "Thank you, Jerry."

"Don't mention it, Richard." He perked up in his chair a little and lit another *Demptus*. "Now. About that phone call from Tina. I only have one question to ask."

"Ask away."

"Do you think she will call back say, in the next day or two?"

"I'm not sure," Richard said. "She has pretty much stayed clear of me since the divorce was finalized, but I kind of got a feeling she was wanting something when she called, so I guess there is a chance she might call again."

"Good," Jerry said. "I was going to explain this earlier, before you had to see the gory stuff, but I was afraid you wouldn't stand for it. I understand, though. You were anxious to find out what happened to her boyfriend."

"Explain what?" Richard asked, honestly puzzled.

"There is a way," Jerry said, "that I can find out what Tina wanted today."

The puzzled look melted away and now Richard's face held nothing but acute interest. "How's that?"

"Well, first and most importantly, she has to call back. I agree with you that it is possible she will. In fact, probable. You could call *her* and it would work also, but…" Jerry held up his hands. "I don't think you want to do that."

"Yeah," Richard said. "She would smell a fish right away. Especially if I called after she learns what happened to Biff.

"Exactly."

"So, what's the idea behind me talking to her on the phone?"

"You see," Jerry said with a cold smile. "I can tune in to *her* network of thoughts over the phone almost as easily as I can tune into *yours* right here. The idea is, you have to talk to her while this television set is on. I'll take care of the rest. Does that sound easy enough?"

Richard sighed. "It does sound good. But she'll have to call first."

"Yes, she will have to call."

"So, until then we…"

"Until then, we wait," Jerry said.

"Yes," Richard said, looking out the living room window at the dwindling sun. "We'll wait." He thought the waiting wouldn't last long with Jerry there to keep him company. They would pass the time together like old friends.

He was right.

Less than two days later they got the phone call they were waiting for.

15

Tina sat at the small table next to the window in her fourth-floor apartment, looking out at the night. In her right hand was a freshly lit cigarette. In her left was a martini. It was 10:45 Saturday evening, and the two police officers had just left her small dwelling.

The officers, one named Lacey the other named Stone, had questioned her for about five minutes before deducting that she must be innocent. She had been at work, and a quick call to Maurice's by Lacey had confirmed her alibi. The two men had thanked her for her time and told her they would be in touch if anything came up. What they meant by that, Tina had no idea. She dismissed it as formality, similar to what she'd seen on many modern-day television dramas and shows.

Inside, she was shaken, but she also felt it was no problem that Biff was now dead. *Murdered!* her mind screamed at her. She hadn't been deeply in love with him, so the hurt she did feel was minimal.

What bothered her the most was the fact that she had been on the *verge* of being head-over-heels in love with him, and now that he was dead, she feared his death might somehow interfere with her plans of getting back at Richard.

Relax, girl. You didn't tell the police what you thought. Quit worrying about it.

What she hadn't told the police officers is that she thought her ex-husband might have something to do with it, and maybe they should question him, instead of her. She didn't know why she thought that (as far as she knew, Richard had never seen, nor heard of, Biff Larento), but her mind insisted anyway that he was somehow responsible. If she had told the officers that, they might have suspected him on the grounds of 'insane jealousy' or something like it, whether they had anything on him or not.

If that happened, her plan wouldn't work.

Her plan was simple.

She planned to kill Richard.

Somehow, some way, she aimed to see him dead.

If she told the police what she thought, and proceeded to carry out her plans, she would be the prime suspect if Richard turned up missing or dead. And of what use was her idea if he ended up eating worms (the thought made her smile) and she ended up in a cell?

She sipped the martini and congratulated herself on keeping her mouth shut.

She planned to kill Richard, but there was one small hitch.

She hadn't figured out *how* she was going to do it.

For the past few days that small problem had gnawed at her like a sore tooth. She was constantly thinking of ways to kill the man she had once loved and now loathed. She thought of poison first, but knew she didn't possess the means to acquire a type that would not show up in an autopsy. She thought of running him down in the road as he crossed a street—no good, as there would undoubtedly be too many witnesses. She thought of shooting him—a possibility that intrigued her—yet she had no gun, nor money for one, and wasn't sure how to acquire one without it tracing her to the crime. And now, since Biff's murder, she had thought of the way that would give her the most pleasure—castration. She didn't think there would be a chance to get so close to him, but boy, it would sure be satisfying.

These thoughts went through her head relentlessly at work, at home—she had even been haunted by these thoughts in her sleep the past two nights. And although she wished that the reason for these reckless thoughts was because of the way Richard had caused her to have to live, she knew inside that the bottom line was the money.

The money she would receive from the insurance policy if he ceased to exist.

She crushed out her cigarette, lit another, and thought about the third factor in all of this—Paul Frazier.

She had tried calling Richard at his office three different times Friday morning and afternoon, and on each occasion Paul either answered the phone, or his secretary had put her in touch with him. Tina thought that could mean one of several things; Richard wasn't at work that day (a possibility she considered remote—he *never* missed work), he was having Paul screen his calls, or he had been fired.

She wanted to believe that Paul was simply screening his calls for him. It would more than explain her third call.

Paul had asked her, rather calmly, if she would please not call Richard at work anymore because he didn't want her to call him there. Tina, playing every bit the fool, had then feigned surprise that Paul didn't know she and Richard had been talking and were thinking seriously about a reconciliation. The lie had been out of her mouth before she could stop it, the thought going through her mind being that she had to give Paul an excuse for why she was calling the office so frequently. She had recognized her mistake immediately, and knew if Paul *was* screening calls for Richard, he would know she had lied.

So, she had played it a little further.

She had proceeded to curse and swear bitterly at Paul, and told him to stay away from Richard. Paul had protested that, and had sworn at *her*, calling her a few choice names that did nothing but make her angrier. She said three more words to Paul, and then she hung up on him.

She knew that Paul likely didn't believe her lie about the reconciliation, but what she told him after that would make him step back and think about things before he opened his mouth to Richard about her call. Perhaps he wouldn't say anything to him. At any rate, he would stay away from telling him until he figured out a way around what she had told him, and that would give her some time to *think*.

What she had told Paul was this: "Remember Garnell's party."

Yes, she thought, *Paul will be out of the way for a while.*

But would he? Only time would tell, and she hoped now that she had bought enough time to carry out her plans before Paul could alert Richard to her phone call and raise his suspicion.

*****

16

Sunday, September 13, 1997

A warm, late summer sun rode high in the early afternoon sky outside George Morrison's small repair shop. The weather had been fabulous all morning, and the bright sun promised mild, pleasant weather for the remainder of the day. There were more people than usual strolling about town and bicyclists were also plentiful. It looked like a picture-perfect day.

Inside his shop, however, the atmosphere was less cheerful. He sat in his small office behind his desk, which was heaped with newspapers, notebooks, scribbled notes on rattily torn off swatches of paper, and two or three telephone books. If someone walked in on him at this particular moment in time, and saw the untidy heaps of papers on the desk, they would think he had let his business slide, to the point where he was behind on everything.

In spite of what the scene looked like, George Morrison was behind on only one thing, but inside he felt he had a faint hope of catching up to it. That one thing, of course, was his 'puzzle.'

He now had—at least he felt pretty sure of it—several more pieces in place, concerning Richard Raines anyway, and felt he just might have a tenacious grip on the whole thing, although most of it lay just beyond his reach. Possibly, even, beyond his understanding.

He had called the Department of Records in Jacksonville, Florida, after studying the articles on Peter Irons, getting the phone number for the Federal Building located there from Larry Vincent. Larry told George that his effort at any information from that office would be futile, but he had made the call anyway, thinking that no effort at all would bear even less fruit. It was better to try. And so he had...with no luck. The

Department of Records was not going to give up information of any kind to a civilian.

George had expected as much, but he wasn't through yet.

After conning Larry over for a few games of cribbage and more than a few drinks, he had persuaded Larry to make a call. Because he worked in Records in the Jonesboro Federal Building, he would have access to the type of information he was after, and by the time the two of them had gotten in four hands of cribbage and downed an equal number of strong bourbon-rocks, he had talked Larry into the chore.

Larry had agreed to do it the next day at work, and give him a call when he had something.

He had needed Larry to find out two things, and at ten-thirty the following morning Larry delivered, expending the information on George's word that he would tell him what he was up to sometime before he got any older and died.

What George had wanted to know first and foremost was if Richard Raines had ever had an address in Jacksonville, either under his own name or his parents' name. He had, indeed—for a good chunk of his childhood—and when George heard that he could almost *hear* a piece of his 'puzzle,' although small, clunk neatly into place.

The second thing he'd wanted was the address, or addresses, of Peter Irons while he resided in that city. There had been only two, but the first one was located only blocks from the house where Richard spent the first nine years of his life. The small piece which had fit snugly only moments before had now turned into a large piece that *thumped* into place like a leaden weight.

But...hadn't he *expected* the information relating to Richard Raines and Peter Irons to fit? It only confirmed the sneaking suspicion he had felt after first reading of the man's death down at Little Rock State Penitentiary in the newspapers a few days back.

There was something going on, but what?

George had managed to successfully link the deceased Peter Irons to the new owner of the television set, *but what did it mean?* He had wracked his brain trying to see the big picture (no pun intended) but nothing came. He had finally resorted to more waiting, scanning, in the meantime, all the notes and clippings he possessed, searching for something he might have overlooked—some clue that would lead him to the final truth.

Now, as he sat behind the mounds of miscellaneous paper covering his desk, he had a glimmer of an idea lurking in the back of his mind, now that he had made yet another link between Richard Raines and another recently deceased person. That person was one Biff Larento, and his death had been splashed all over the front page this morning.

This particular murder had happened right here in Jonesboro and he had scanned the article closely. Near the end of it he found what he was looking for, what he had been expecting with a morbid sense of both excitement and dread. There would be no need for Larry's help on this one, for he could see the connection immediately: Richard's ex-wife, Tina Raines, had been questioned by the police, along with several other of Mr. Larento's close friends.

George suspected almost faithfully that Tina had been seeing Mr. Larento. If he took it further, wouldn't it be safe to think that Richard had been jealous of the relationship? Perhaps so jealous that he would take the life of his ex-wife's lover? That sounded right, but the police would have undoubtedly thought of that. Besides, Richard was mentioned nowhere in the article.

Which led George to think that maybe Richard really *didn't* have anything to do with the murder, that there had to be some outside force involved. He also thought he knew what that outside force was—the television set. The television...or whatever possessed it.

And in a flash, the idea that had been forming in his mind

gelled *almost* to solidification. The solution to his 'puzzle' was in sight now—it was just a little blurry.

His idea was silly.

His idea was absurd

His idea was damned near incomprehensible, which was probably partly responsible for the leagues of time if had taken to think of it.

Yet his idea could save Richard's life, if he could only see it better. It could save his life and countless others; he was certain of it.

The answer to everything about the television was not plainly seen, but it was *there*, and George knew almost without thinking what his next step would have to be; he would have to call Richard's friend, Paul Frazier. He would have to tell Mr. Frazier everything and, more importantly, he would have to make him believe it.

Although he loathed the idea of bringing anyone else into this mess, he knew he couldn't do it alone. There wasn't enough time. He estimated two days at the outside—and probably less—before Richard Raines ended up with the same fate as the past TV owners—dead, of a mysterious cause. An *unknown* cause.

And so George took a large step toward the solution that was just beyond his field of vision. He picked up the Jonesboro phone book, found Paul Frazier's home phone number, and called him.

17

Later, after the call from George Morrison, Paul Frazier would think their brief conversation earlier in the week had been lurking in his mind ever since. He just hadn't put much thought to it. He would also think later maybe he *should* have been thinking about the call. He should have been thinking a *lot*.

And so, when the phone began ringing just as Paul was finishing his Sunday dinner of roast beef, potatoes, and carrots Margie had slowly cooked in the crock pot all morning, he didn't put much thought into who it could be. He just answered it.

"Hello. May I speak to Paul Frazier, please?" a male voice greeted him. The first thing he thought upon hearing this voice was it must be a telephone salesman; these types of people never failed to call right when you were busy doing something important—like eating your Sunday dinner.

"Speaking," he sighed into the mouthpiece, preparing himself mentally to kindly listen to the sales pitch…and just as kindly turn it down.

"Listen to me carefully," the man on the other end said. "I called you a few days ago at your office."

Paul was thrown off guard because it *wasn't* some sales person, but that voice…it sounded vaguely familiar, yet he couldn't put a face to it. He talked to *a lot* of people at work in the course of a week. "I'm afraid you've caught me with my mind temporarily stumped," he told the caller. "I can't seem to…"

"I called about your friend."

And of course, he remembered that—how could he have forgotten the peculiar call he'd received from this man? "Richard," he said.

"Yes, Richard," the man said. "Mr. Frazier, if you will listen to me carefully, I have something important to tell you concerning your friend."

Paul registered the words, but before the man could go any further, he asked the question to which he wanted an answer. "Who *are* you? And how do you know Richard?"

"My name is Morrison. George Morrison."

Paul went through his mental files and couldn't recall having heard the name before. At least now he had a name to give the voice on the other end of the line. "Mr. Morrison, I've never heard Richard mention you before."

"I told you the other day that he and I had only met once."

"Yes, I remember now," Paul said. "That still doesn't explain how you know—"

"Do you remember me asking if your friend has been acting out of character lately?"

"Y-yes," Paul said. "I do recall you asked me that." Boy, did he ever. That had been one of the questions the then-nameless caller had asked him. It was *the* one he had wanted to answer, because Richard *had* been acting out of sorts recently. He still was. Had he, Paul, really been so concerned with Richard's behavior he would confide in anyone about it—even a total stranger whose name he hadn't even known? "Is he in trouble?" he asked now. Is it the d—" He stopped before that question came out. There was no way this man, who had met Richard only once, could know about he and Tina's divorce.

"It's not about the divorce," Mr. Morrison said, "although I guess it probably figures in somewhere."

How could he know? Paul thought fleetingly. *How could he possibly know?*

"How do you—?"

"Listen to me!" The man's voice was crackling thunder in the earpiece. "Listen to me *carefully* if you want any chance at all of helping your friend. Will you do that?"

"Okay," Paul said. The tone of the man's voice was dead serious, and he guessed the situation, whatever it was, must be as well. He wondered briefly if Richard had been kidnapped or something and then discarded the idea. He had seen Richard just this morning through his living room window. He had come outside, picked up his Sunday paper, and gone back in.

"No more interruptions? Please?"

"Okay," Paul agreed. "No more interruptions."

Margie stuck her head in from the kitchen, where she was rinsing off the dishes. "Who is it, honey?"

Paul waved her away impatiently with one hand. "It's for me." She retreated back into the kitchen, a small frown on her face.

"No more interruptions," Paul repeated. He heard a heavy sigh on the other end.

"Richard is in terrible danger. I know that may be hard to believe, but you have *got* to believe me. I can't explain everything over the phone, there's just too much, but if you care about your friend at all then you'll agree to hear everything. And to help me." Mr. Morrison's voice sounded tired yet frantic to Paul.

"Everything started when he bought that TV from my shop. Are you all right, Mr. Frazier?"

Paul had sucked in a deep breath when he heard that. "I-I'm okay," he said. "It's just...the TV is when I noticed the first change in Richard. That TV set was so out of character for him, and he hasn't been the same since."

"It started with the TV, yes, but everything really started long before that," Mr. Morrison said.

"What do you mean?"

"I can't explain the rest over the phone. Number one, it's too complicated, and number two, you might not believe it. You're going to have to see everything for yourself...and believe in what you see, and I know you can't do that over the phone."

"What do I have to do?" Paul asked. If Richard was in trouble, if his *life* was in danger, he intended to help any way he could. He realized that George Morrison might be able to provide him with answers about Richard's recent behavior. The current state of their relationship was touchy at the moment, and he wasn't sure at all how to safely approach Richard about it. Maybe he would know how after listening to what Mr. Morrison had to tell him, and had seen what he had to show him.

"Do you think you could make it over to my repair shop, say, tomorrow evening about five-thirty? I hate to wait even that long, but I think tomorrow will be okay. I'm a block over from Main, on the corner of Third and Chestnut. Can you make it?"

Paul found himself wanting to check his calendar (his work habits seemed to follow him everywhere), and decided no matter what occupied that space tomorrow, it wasn't as important as this. "Yeah," he said. "I can make it."

"Good," Mr. Morrison said. Paul could hear the relief in his voice, and that reaffirmed what he thought to be true; this man was serious.

"Come by yourself, and in the meantime try to remember everything peculiar you've noticed about your friend lately. It could be useful. *Anything* could be at this point."

"Okay," was all Paul could say.

"And one other thing," Mr. Morrison said. "Stay away from him as much as possible until our meeting tomorrow. Stay away especially from his home. At least the inside of it."

"Any reason for that?"

"Yes. Until we meet."

"Alright," Paul said. "I'll dodge him until tomorrow evening as best I can." *Which won't be too hard since we hardly ever speak anymore,* he thought to himself.

"And Mr. Frazier."

"Yes?"

"Thank you."

"I hope you have something to thank me *for.*"

"Yes. Me, too." Mr. Morrison clicked off the line. The resultant silence felt unsettling.

He hung up the phone, and Margie stuck her head in again. "Is everything okay?"

"Everything's fine, babe" he told her.

But he wondered. He knew he would be avoiding Richard. Would have been, anyway, even if a stranger named George Morrison hadn't called him with what seemed like such urgency this afternoon.

Because of what Tina had said.

He knew damn well the two of them—Tina and Richard—weren't getting back together. He was as certain of that as he had ever been of anything in his life. She'd had another reason for calling. But what was it?

He didn't know, but what he *did* know was, as shaky as his relationship with Richard was at this point, he couldn't risk Tina jeopardizing what was left of it by telling Richard something he was better off not knowing.

And what Paul *also* knew, what he felt to be true (although he would be hard-put to say why), was the sense that Richard *was* in some sort of danger. For some reason it seemed to fit with the way he had been acting for the better part of a week.

The kicker was that he didn't know what to do about what he knew.

He only hoped George Morrison, who he would meet face-to-face tomorrow, would be able to help him find a way to get to the bottom of everything going on…

…and everything that wasn't.

*****

Part Three

On the Verge of Madness

There are two kinds of women—
one who wants to correct a man's
mistakes, and the other who
wants to be one.

—*anonymous*

1

September 14, 1997

Richard laid the phone down in its cradle, a sigh escaping his lips. What was going through his mind right now, as a light drizzle tapped against the north windows, was he was glad he hadn't turned the TV off.

He had been conversing with Jerry for most of the morning and afternoon. They had talked mainly of Richard's past, but also of the deaths of Peter Irons and Biff Larento (had even watched a rerun of each, and he found that Jerry was right—his stomach seemed stronger this time around). Less than five minutes ago he had said his 'good-by-for-now' to Jerry and had actually been walking to the TV set to turn it off when the phone rang.

It had been Tina; the call he and Jerry had been waiting for.

She had again asked him how he was doing, and then asked him if he had seen Paul lately. Richard told her no, he hadn't, just at work. She had then rambled on in a very casual tone about everything *but* the death of her lover, and everything *but* the divorce.

He had peeked over at the TV, where Jerry had his hands folded in front of him, his head bowed, nodding.

Richard, taking that as a cue that Jerry knew what they were wanting to know, excused himself abruptly from the phone, telling Tina he had some things to take care of, but it was nice of her to call. They had said their good-byes and he had hung up, feeling relieved and a little uptight. It was sort of like sitting in a small room in a hospital ward, expecting—and preparing to hear—bad news.

"Well," Richard said now, looking at Jerry and lighting a cigarette. His smoking had nearly doubled since he'd bought the television. "It was Tina."

"Yes," Jerry agreed. "It was."

"Were you able to find out anything?"

Jerry laughed lightly. *"Oh,* yeah." He shook his head, still smiling. "and it all fits so well. I should have known it was something like this. I should have been able to figure it out." He laughed quietly.

"What fits?" Richard asked. "What are you talking about?" His frustration at not knowing showed clearly.

"Do you remember," Jerry said, "the day you came home and found this television set off?"

"Yes, I remember," Richard said. "You said something about...oh...a power failure or something he fulminated. "Why?"

"That's not what happened," Jerry said.

"What? You mean—"

"No, I didn't lie to you, Richard. All I said was I had 'more important things to discuss with you than power failures,' if my memory serves me right. And it does. I never told you a power failure actually occurred, and you never asked me anything more about it."

"Then what *happened?"* Richard asked, flabbergasted. He remembered thinking, at the time, he had been lied to about the power outage, but had since forgotten about it.

"Tina did it," Jerry said matter-of-factly.

"Tina?" Now he was furious. "What was *she* doing here? How did she get *in,* for Chrissakes?"

"She has a key, doesn't she?"

Richard thought a minute. Tina *did* still have a key to the apartment. He had forgotten to get it from her when she moved

176

out, and she had never offered to return it. "Yes, she does. But that doesn't mean she can just waltz in here any time she pleases. She's not my wife anymore."

"I know, I know," Jerry said soothingly. "That's just one little mistake you made, not getting the key from her, but I don't think it's really going to matter much in the long run. If she didn't have a key she would have gotten in some other way."

Richard stared squarely at his TV set. "Talk straight to me, Jerry. What was she doing here?"

"I didn't know that day. All I knew is that she was here. She turned off the set shortly after she came through the door. All I could pick up from her was that she was looking for something. What, I don't know. Or, at least I didn't at the time."

"But you do now?"

"Yes," Jerry said after a slight pause. "Thanks to the call she just made."

"So? Tell me."

"It appears she was looking for a life insurance policy of which she previously knew nothing. She was very bitter when she found it, to say the least."

Richard was at a loss for words. "I'll be right back," he said, rising from the sofa. "I want to check and see if she took it."

He got up and walked quickly toward the bedroom. He was back a few minutes later, a frown on his anger-reddened face. He held the policy in one hand. "She didn't take it. It's still here."

"Of course it is," Jerry said. "She didn't need to steal it, only discover what was in it and then leave. She wasn't disappointed, either."

"But she never knew about this," Richard said, his anger growing. "Who could have told her?"

"Does the name Thomas Harrington ring a bell?"

"That *little* weasel," Richard said, sitting down hard on the sofa.

"She was looking for something, *anything*, you might have left out of the divorce papers. Anything you may have overlooked. This Mr. Harrington evidently provided it for her."

"But he's not supposed to give out that kind of information. It's confidential, and he's my attorney!"

"A woman such as Tina has the ability to persuade men fairly easily, wouldn't you say? Mr. Harrington was a push-over. All she had to do was hike her skirt up enough to give him a good look at her thighs and promise him that they would get together for drinks sometime."

"That slutty *bitch!*" He felt his head swim. He had forgotten all about the life insurance policy during the divorce proceedings. Hell, the damned thing had been paid off for quite some time. Tina might not have known about it, but he had forgotten it completely. "What is she planning to do?" he asked now.

Jerry smiled and laughed that low chuckling laugh again, shaking his head ruefully. "It's all so simple, really. She aims to see you dead, Richard. She doesn't plan on waiting around for you to die, either. She plans on killing you herself."

"You've got to be joking," Richard said. It was all he could think to say. What Jerry told him couldn't possibly be true. Tina might be a bitch, and a slut, but she wasn't a murderer. He felt he knew her enough to know that.

"I'm not joking," Jerry said.

"But...but she was so *nice* to me on the phone," he said, trying to keep his voice level, his mind calm. "She talked to me like...like nothing bad had ever happened between us."

"Exactly," Jerry said.

"Then why?"

"To her, you have made her life intolerable. She has a shitty job, a shittier apartment, man-trouble, and last but not least she has no *money*. Nor does she possess the means to earn it legitimately. By that I mean, a way other than on her back. You see, she blames you for every little trifle she has run into since the divorce—and believe me, there have been plenty of them. The death of her boyfriend was just the icing on the cake, and although she knows you never saw Biff Larento before, she blames you for his death, anyway. I think her basic reason for the belief is that she subconsciously needs it to feed her hatred for you, in order to possess the confidence to carry out her plan," Jerry finished.

"Why the false pretenses on the phone?" Richard asked. "I mean, why so innocent?"

"In order to explain that," Jerry said, "let me tell you what has happened. You see, the police have questioned her in the murder investigation of her boyfriend. She had a legitimate alibi, of course. What she failed to tell them was that she suspected maybe *you* had something to do with it. Her reason being—and it fits in well with her behavior on the phone—that if she *did* tell them, it would draw unwanted attention to you, and if something happened to *you*, it would draw attention to *her,* and that would spoil everything. She wouldn't be able to get away with murdering you, and she would *definitely* not get away with the money that would befall her from the policy—and that is her goal.

"So, what is she going to do?" Richard still found the whole thing hard to believe—he and Tina had *loved* each other once, even if it *had* fallen apart at the last—but felt he wore an invisible cloak of protection with Jerry on his side. It was easier to handle. He believed whole-heartedly there was no way in hell she could pull off something like this.

"She doesn't know yet," Jerry said. "If she did I would be able to tell you, and we could do something about it. Being cordial to you is simply a part of her overall plan."

"Why don't we just kill her, too?" The words were out of his mouth before the thought cleared his mind.

I believe we've already discussed the reasons why we can't,

Richard. I know by what I could pick up from her that she has to get close to you to carry out her plans, so I suggest we do something else."

"Like what?"

"We wait," Jerry said. "I think she will likely call again in a day or so. She plans for it to happen within the next few days, if possible."

She plans for it to happen within the next few days, if possible. Those words chilled Richard. It struck home to him just how real the situation was. She was going to *kill* him. Or at least try to. How was he to defend himself when he didn't know how she was going to do it? He began whistling and made himself stop. "I think I need a drink," he said.

"Go ahead," Jerry said. "You deserve it."

He got up on rubbery legs that felt full of water, and threatened to buckle. When he had made his drink, he returned to the sofa. "So, what now?"

Jerry said, "If she calls back—and I think she will—then she will probably have the 'how' all figured out. I should be able to pick it up, and we'll decide on a course of action. Until then, we play the waiting game again. What do you think about that?"

He opened his mouth to respond, but before he could utter a word a wild cheer rose up from Jerry's unseen audience. It made Richard jump a little. He had not heard them in the background in nearly two days, and had almost forgotten about them.

Just as abruptly, the unseen audience stopped cheering. There was only Jerry's voice on the screen. "Have a few drinks, but not too many, Richard. I can't stress how important it is that you keep a clear, sharp head for the next few days. I have to go for now. I'll talk to you a little later." With that, the TV went blank, followed by snowy static that filled the screen.

Richard was reminded absurdly of the first night Jerry had appeared on the screen; *we'll talk more later, perhaps as soon as this evening. My people will be here then.*

Again, he wondered just who Jerry's 'people' were, but before he could think on it very hard his mind filled with the situation and its recent developments. He lit a cigarette, lay back on the sofa, sipped his drink, and thought about the things Jerry had told him today.

If Jerry wanted him to wait, he would wait, but while he was waiting, he would also *think*. He could do it now. He found he was beginning to enjoy the times the television was off as much as when it was on. When the set was off, his mind wasn't a mirror through which Jerry could see.

Thinking he had forgotten to do something, Richard sat up. It took a few seconds before he remembered what it was and he walked over to the television set and turned it off.

If the phone rang, he would turn it back on, but for now he wanted to be by himself.

He had found that was a rare thing these days.

2

As Paul Frazier pulled off Third Street into the small back lot behind George Morrison's repair shop, he marveled at the fact he had not been to this particular fix-it shop before. As a child he had been the type of kid who took his toys apart to see how they worked. He would wind up fixing more than half the toys he accidentally—or purposefully—broke. The innards of toys and (later) transistor radios, small engines, and clocks fascinated him from an early age, but his hobby had never developed into an obsession. Nevertheless, he still enjoyed visiting such shops when the inspiration hit him, and when he had time. Repair shops and Pawn shops were high on his list of interesting places to browse.

But he had never stepped foot inside this particular shop.

He turned off his parking lights, got out of the car, and walked up to the back door of the building. A small, cracked sidewalk with wild grass and weeds growing in every nook led to it, flanked on either side by gray, dented garbage cans. There was a sign tacked up crookedly on the metal door. It said:

Not an Entrance
Please Use Other Door

As an advertiser, Paul wished every American would do what an ad (especially one he had authored) told them to do. Likewise with an ordinary sign. Under normal circumstances he would have gone around to the front of the building before entering. Instead, he rapped hard three times on the flat metal surface of the rear entrance door to the shop.

He waited thirty seconds or so, knocked again, and then heard a voice on the other side: "I'm coming."

He heard several locks turn and a deadbolt thrown back, and then a small, round man was bidding him inside. "Come in, Mr. Frazier, please. I'm glad you could make it." He held his hand out.

"Mr. Morrison?" Paul said, shaking the welcoming hand. "Paul Frazier."

"Please. Just call me George."

"Fair enough, George. Call me Paul. I would like to say I'm pleased to meet you," Paul said with some trepidation in his voice, "but…"

"Yeah, I know," George said. "Come on back. I've got a pot of coffee on." He shuffled with a limp down a small darkened hall lit dimly on the other end by a room bathed in yellow light from a bare, sixty-watt bulb on a cord, hanging from a high rafter. Paul followed him.

When they entered the large room, Paul saw that three sides

of it were piled high with shelves full of broken toasters, coffee makers, waffle-irons, small radios that were mostly disassembled, and rolls of electrical wiring. He guessed this was where George did his repairs. The display and sales room would be in front. Paul had seen many such rooms before; appliances and other household gadgets—mostly used—polished and cleaned for the best look, sitting sentinel on wood or corrugated metal shelves with price tags dangling from them like broken arms and legs.

He followed George into another room and wasn't surprised to see this room and the other connected to it were the man's living quarters.

"Have a seat over here," George said, shuffling to a small kitchen table whose top was almost completely covered with newspapers, notebooks, and untidy stacks of other miscellaneous papers.

Paul sat down in the chair opposite George and got directly to what was on his mind. "What do you need to show me?"

"In a minute," George said. "How about a cup of coffee first?"

"Sure," Paul said, letting out a deep breath. He didn't feel awkward talking to a man he hardly knew—in his line of business it was basically a requirement—but, because of the circumstances of the phone call that led to this meeting, he didn't feel totally comfortable, either. "Those afternoon showers really cooled things down out there today."

"That they did," George said. He moved slowly to a bare well-varnished kitchen counter and poured two cups of steaming coffee, returning to the table slowly to prevent spilling it on his liver-spotted hands. "Here you are," he said, handing Paul a cup.

Paul sipped it, decided it was good (certainly better than his wife's coffee) and took another sip before setting it down. "What kind of danger is Richard in, Mr. M—George? I've been a nervous wreck all day waiting to find out."

Instead of answering, George asked a question of his own. "Was Richard at work today?"

"No, he wasn't," Paul said. "And today isn't the first day he's missed in the past week. That's rare for him." He took another sip of coffee. "Why do you want to know?" Paul found it odd to be talking to a nearly total stranger about his work. However, since walking through the back door into the shop owned by this round, jolly-looking man, his ordinary mannerisms seemed to have eluded him. It happened primarily because he felt this small man posed no threat to him.

"I was just verifying my suspicions," George said. "I'll explain later. When I get to it." He let out a deep sigh, folded his hands in front of him, and said, "Do you remember reading in the paper last week about a murder down at the pen in Little Rock? Fellow by the name of Peter Irons."

"I remember," Paul said, and then another thought struck him. "In fact, Richard and I discussed it at work the next day."

Interest dawned like a bright light on George's face. "And do you remember how Richard reacted to it?"

Paul's brow crinkled in thought. "Not really. Only that it seemed a little odd that he took a lot of interest in the article."

"How so?" George asked.

"He seemed—happy about it. I can get behind that, I guess. I mean, the man murdered his family in cold blood. But for it to be someone he didn't even know, I guess his reaction to the murder...puzzled me. I haven't really thought about it that much."

George shuffled through a notebook which was crammed full of newspaper clippings and finally pulled one out. It was one reporting on Peter Irons' death. He shuffled some more and came out with another, facing this one toward Paul so he could see it. "I suppose you know about Mr. Larento's death, as well?" George asked.

"Only what I saw on the news," Paul said. "Why?"

"You mean you didn't read the front page of the local paper yesterday?"

"I saw the headlines, sure," Paul said. "I just haven't read the write-up yet. The Sunday papers are so thick it usually takes me until Tuesday or so to read all the features."

"Then you don't know that Mr. Larento was seeing Richard's ex-wife, Tina, at the time he was killed." It was not a question.

Paul's mouth dropped open in an 'o' of surprise. His mind was racing, trying to think of why he was here tonight. This seemed to be the reason. He voiced his worse fears: "You don't mean Richard—"

"Murdered him? No," George said. "Paul, I know you must be anxious about your friend, and just as anxious to know why I asked you here tonight. But I'm an old man, and if you'll just bear with me and not get too excited, I'll get to everything. I just have to do it my way, because there *is* no other way. Because you *have* to believe what I'm going to tell you. And by jumping to conclusions, and not listening, you're going to make it extremely difficult for me to make you see what is happening to your friend."

Paul was stung by the words. Partly because he felt now like he did when he was a child and had just received one of his father's famous lectures, but mostly because the stern, serious face of the man reminded him that this was serious business. He wouldn't find out anything if he didn't get his act together and *listen*.

"I apologize," he said. "Go on."

"Richard didn't murder Tina's boyfriend," George said, "but the two deaths *are* linked to him."

Paul's stomach turned queasily. "How?"

"Peter Irons lived just two miles from Richard when he was growing up in Jacksonville, Florida. At least for a while. That's the only connection there. You might be thinking that is nothing more than mere coincidence, but I don't take to that notion, myself. Tina connects him with the other murder, but there is one thing that connects with everything, including Richard himself."

"The TV?" Paul asked incredulously.

"The TV," George said.

"But how? I mean, it's just a TV, isn't it?"

"See for yourself," George said. "Let me show you something." He pulled another notebook from the three or four laying on the table. He opened it, and after a minute lay it in front of Paul. It was a list of some kind:

NAME	OCCUPATION	CAUSE OF DEATH
Victor Haynes	Factory Supervisor	Heart Attack
Merv Calhoun	Farmer	UNKNOWN
Donald Forrester	Business Executive	UNKNOWN
Phil Clayton	Restaurant Owner	UNKNOWN
Gary Grisham	Business Executive	Stabbing*
Wade Crosset	Attorney	Mutilation*
Martha Stonewall	Police Officer	UNKNOWN
Louis Griffin	Hdwr. Store Owner	UNKNOWN
Richard Raines	Advert. Executive	

Paul looked closely at the list. The first thing that caught his attention was the number of 'UNKNOWNs' under the list headed CAUSE OF DEATH. The second thing, which caused a flash of fear while further enhancing his puzzlement, was the last name on the list; Richard.

He handed it back to George. "I don't get it. Are you trying to tell me that Richard is going to die from an unknown cause, like most of the people on this list?"

Instead of answering him, George pulled another sheet of

paper from the notebook, put the notebook back in front of Paul, and laid this culled sheet next to the first list:

NAME	DATE BOUGHT TV	DATE DECEASED
Victor Haynes	7/21/89 (sold TV)	7/22/89
Merv Calhoun	7/27/89	7/30/89
Donald Forrester	8/21/89	8/25/89
Phil Clayton	7/24/90	7/30/90
Gary Grisham	8/27/92	9/06/92
Wade Crosset	8/16/93	8/26/93
Martha Stonewall	9/14/95	9/22/95
Louis Griffin	8/18/96	8/26/96
Richard Raines	9/06/97	

Paul was shocked after reading this second list. What the two lists suggested—that the owners of the television Richard had bought *died* shortly thereafter—happened only in horror movies and novels. George Morrison seemed to be presenting it as hard facts.

"How do I know you didn't just make this list up?" Paul asked. He knew George might get irritated at his doubt, but this was utterly ridiculous and, after all, enough was enough.

"I have documentation right on this very table to back that list up, including sales receipts for the TV," George said.

"You mean you *sold* the TV to all these people?"

"Yes, I did," George said candidly.

"And you knew they were going to die after they bought it, yet you sold it to them *anyway?*"

George lowered his head slightly. "I'm not the best guy in the world, Paul. I'll admit that much. When I sold that television the first two or three times, I was out for nothing but a quick buck or two. This shop is, after all, how I make my living. I knew people were dying but I didn't know why. That all of them were owners of the same TV set seemed like nothing but a rare coincidence at the time—in the front of my mind, anyway. In the *back* of my mind, where the real thinking takes place, I knew better. I *knew* it was the television—I just didn't know how, or why."

He rose from his chair and went to a kitchen cupboard, pulling out a bottle of whiskey. He took a glass off the drainboard next to the sink where some dishes were drying and brought it and the whiskey back to the table, where he poured two fingers worth in the glass. He took a drink and grimaced.

"I began a small scrapbook after the first two deaths. They say that inexplicable things hold a curious fascination for some people, and I guess it's true for me. I didn't know *how* these people were dying—or why—but it all seemed to me to be so *interesting*. I made a game out of it…well, I hate to call it a game. It was more like a puzzle. I wanted to see if I could figure out the 'why' and the 'how.'

"I never thought I had any purpose in life after my wife died right after our wedding—within two months, anyway. I never remarried, never fathered any children—oh, I wanted to—but I loved that woman too much to ever even *think* about falling for someone else. I began to think, and I guess I still do, that if I could figure out this puzzle of mine it would give me some sort of purpose in life other than just running this worthless business and growing old and dying all alone, with no children to carry on my name, no grandchildren to spend time with on the weekends."

He pulled a hanky from his rear pocket and honked into it before stuffing it back, leaning to one side as he did so.

"After nearly eight years of one unexplained death after another, and no answer to my 'puzzle' in sight, I finally began to get my priorities straight and to realize that, even if *I* didn't have a purpose in life, the people who were dying because of the television might have, and probably did.

"Living with the guilt of all these people's deaths, their lost *lives*, has gotten to me lately. This thing has got to end. I know that saving one person's life won't make up for the others who have died, but it will be all the purpose I need in life.

"And I guess that's why I called you. I can't do it alone. I need your help. I'm old, and I'm tired, and I just can't do this by myself. I'll understand if you think all of this is a bunch of hogwash, because it sounds so ridiculous. But if you decide to walk out that door, please go with the knowledge that I will do all I can for your friend, even if it means my own life—which I'm certain it might. If you decide to help me, there's a chance it could cost *your* life, as well. If we sit back on our heels, Richard will die. I *know* this, and I need your help to stop it. *This has got to end!*"

George stopped and looked at him.

Paul felt a mixture of emotions. What George had told him sounded beyond belief, yet he was becoming increasingly inclined to believe it. He felt disgust—even anger—when George said that he knew these people were dying. He felt sympathy when he heard why he hadn't done anything about it. He was fascinated with this surreal story in spite of himself.

But what made him decide was instinct: he *felt* what George said was true. No matter how silly the whole thing sounded, it was the way he felt. Something was going to happen to Richard. Something bad. If there was even the slightest chance of it being stopped, he felt he *should* help the old man. It was more than a test of the friendship he and Richard shared—it was his *spirit*. The way he felt inside now, it could have been the life of a total stranger at stake—he would still do all he could. And he saw that, to George Morrison at least, that's exactly what it was.

You didn't turn your back on instinct.

"I'll help you," Paul said evenly. "What do we need to do?"

George let out a sigh full of relief. He finished his drink in one huge gulp. "I want to go over what I know with you in a little while," he said. "Maybe if we put our heads together, we can come up with something I've overlooked. For right now, I have a pretty good idea what is going to happen. Richard is in danger, but so is his ex-wife. I suspect she may be the next person killed. I think Richard is safe for a day or so, but certainly no longer than that. As you can see on this list, no one who has bought that damned thing has lived more than ten days after the fact."

Paul looked again at the second list and felt a chill spread down his spine, cold fingers tickling his nerves. "That's not much time."

"No, it's not," George said. "What I'm going to suggest right now is that you keep an eye on Richard. Visit him, find out what he's up to, see how he's behaving. I've already got his ex-wife's address, and I'll keep an eye on her."

"She's been calling the office a lot lately," Paul said. "Asking for Richard. I think she's up to something."

"What?" George asked.

"I'm not sure, but she told me the other day that she and Richard were seeing each other again, and were thinking seriously about a reconciliation."

"Do you believe this to be true?"

"I don't believe one word of it," Paul said. "I know Richard better than that. He can't stand her after what she did to him."

George clearly wanted to ask about that, but instead he said, "Let's go over my scrap-books, Paul. You need to see the scope of this whole thing, and then we can add whatever details you might have."

"Okay."

They bent over the notebooks and piles of paper together.

"This man, Victor Haynes, was the first person to bring the television into my shop..."

3

Nearly three hours later, Paul was walking to his parked car at the rear of the shop. His eyes felt fuzzy from straining to read dozens of faded and yellowing newspaper clippings and George Morrison's slanted, handwritten notes. It was warm and breezy outside. The skies had cleared, and groups of stars twinkled in the night sky between patches of scattering clouds.

He looked up at the bright stars—as much a mystery to him as the television set his friend had purchased from this shop—and, as he had done when he was small, wished upon the brightest one he could see. He didn't believe in wishes coming true, but tonight…tonight he wished that he could.

He got into his car and drove home.

4

Tuesday, September 15, 1997

The sun broke through a partly cloudy sky as Paul left his apartment and made his way next door to Richard's place. Although it was a work day, he had taken off just before lunch. He thought he needed to, for that was less than an hour after Patrick had fired Richard. He had not shown up again today and Patrick, whose anger had reached a stairstep type of build each day Richard was absent, had dismissed him over the phone.

Paul thought Richard might like some company and, more importantly, he wanted to see first-hand how he was doing, and how he was handling the loss of his job.

He won't show a care in the world about much of anything, is my guess. The television is all he cares about now. These words, spoken from the mouth of George Morrison last night, echoed in Paul's mind as he rang the doorbell to Richard's condo.

He waited thirty seconds, knocked, and was just beginning to think that Richard was either not home or asleep, when the door opened and Richard peered out at him sheepishly.

"Oh, hey Paul. Hang on. Would you give me a minute?"

"Sure," Paul said. Richard left, and although the door was only open a crack, Paul could hear a minute click. The TV. But was he turning it off, or on?

Richard returned and opened the door for him to come inside.

The first thing he noticed about Richard, as he got a better look at him, was his unshaven face, and how sunken his eyes appeared to be. He looked as though he hadn't been sleeping well. He held a bottle of whiskey in one hand, a half-finished cigarette in the other.

"C'mon in," he said. "Get you a fuggin' seat anywhere you want."

"Thanks," Paul said. He chose to sit in the recliner. It was the only piece of furniture not covered with empty beer cans and whiskey bottles, full ash trays, and clothing. The place looked as if it hadn't been cleaned in a week.

Richard took a seat on the sofa, pushing clothes, cans, and newspapers to the side, spilling most of them onto the carpet.

Silence hung on the air for an awkward moment. The TV was off, and Paul wondered briefly why Richard didn't have it on if he was so obsessed with it, as George had said. The quiet in the room was oppressing, and Paul began to feel uncomfortable.

Richard drank from his bottle and stared at Paul with piercing eyes that seemed to belong to someone else.

The moment felt like an eternity.

"I'm sorry about your job, Richie." It was the only thing he could think of to say, and the only way he knew to say it. He felt a surrealness at the change in his friend. Richard always kept a clean house. He was probably the most structured and organized person Paul knew. The contrast was sharp, jarring. Because he felt something else was needed, he said: "It really bites the big one."

Richard laughed—more of a chuckle, actually—and tilted the bottle up. He grimaced before he spoke. "Thanks for being concerned, Pauly boy, but if you want the truth, I simply don't give a rip. Patrick can kiss my ass. There's more important things going on in my life right now than busting my ass for *that* prick."

"Well, if there's anything I can do—"

"The only thing I want anyone to do right now," Richard interrupted, "is to just leave me the hell alone." He took another drink from the bottle, rose from the cluttered sofa, and half walked, half stumbled toward the kitchen.

Thinking that he definitely didn't want to stay on the subject of work, Paul decided to change the conversation to something *he* wanted to talk about. He hated to see his best friend like this—half drunk, and angry at the world—but there were a few things he had to find out.

"So," he said. "How's your TV holding out on you?"

Richard's eyes seemed to brighten. "Great," he said. "Just great. I never really got into watching TV much until I got this set." He laughed softly, as though to himself. To Paul it sounded like a secret laugh.

"You want to watch something?" Richard asked suddenly. He walked quickly to the television.

"No, no," Paul said. To him, the television, sitting next to the book shelves, looked like a closed green eye. For some reason, he thought if Richard turned it on, the eye would open. And what that eye would see, or what *Paul* might see, was something he wasn't sure he wanted to know. "I just came by to see how you were, how you were getting along by yourself, see if you needed anything. You know..."

Richard lit another cigarette. "I'm doing just fine now that the *bitch* is out of my life." He laughed again, looking at his cigarette as though there was something interesting about it. It was just an ordinary cigarette.

Paul groped for something to say—the *right* thing to say. He hoped that Richard might finally open up to him about the divorce and the effects it had on him. The divorce had not caused such drastic changes in him, as far as he knew, and in fact he thought Richard had been handling that part of things pretty well over the past few months. "I'm sorry about the way she did you," he said now.

"The way she did *me?*" Richard said. "Hell, she did everyone *but* me, the little slut." He put his cigarette out in an ash tray already overflowing with butts, most of them only half-smoked. "She's the only one who has something to be sorry about. Not you, not me. Not anybody." He laughed that same, secretive laugh again.

It sent chills through Paul to hear his friend laugh like that. He had heard other people laugh that same way, but only in the movies; those people had been crazy, usually locked up in some institution.

"I never like her much, myself," Paul fumbled.

Richard looked at him, and his eyes seemed to soften. A little. "You were about the only one who didn't. Hell, even my boss—excuse me, *ex*-boss—screwed her."

Paul turned his gaze away from Richard. "I'm sorry things couldn't have been different," he said lamely. "I guess some things just aren't meant to be."

"Yeah, I guess they aren't."

Paul didn't like his friend's tone of voice. It sounded like the desperate voice of a man who has long given up hope for anything good to happen in his life.

Silence once again hung in the air between them. It was almost visible this time, thick and full of tension.

Paul decided to leave.

"Well, I'd better get back home before Margie comes looking for me," he said. "If you need anything, you know where I am."

"Okay," Richard said absently. He wasn't looking at Paul. Instead, he was looking at the TV, which sat silent at the far side of the room. To Paul, regardless of the warmth of a full bookcase, that corner of the room looked colder than any place in the messy apartment.

He let himself out and walked home, wondering just how Richard could have changed so quickly.

And also wondering what he—and George Morrison—were going to do about it.

5

Around 3:15 Tina picked up the phone at Maurice's Café and dialed Richard's home phone. She felt some trepidation as she did this. She had just called JAC and he had not been there. She'd talked to Patrick Garnell, and he told her he'd had to fire Richard this morning. He'd been missing too many days, including three consecutive without calling in.

In light of this new development, she supposed Richard must be pretty angry right now, but she couldn't let the loss of his job get in the way of things, considering how nicely they were finally moving. Besides, as far as she was concerned, his job wouldn't mean anything to him after tomorrow. Nothing would.

At least, if her plan worked as she intended for it to.

She listened to the phone on the other end ring four times and then Richard, his voice slurred, picked it up. "H'lo?"

"Richard? It's me, Tina. Are you all right?"

"Sure," he said. "Fine as a fiddle. How you been?"

"I'm okay," she said.

There was a brief pause on the line, as if neither of them knew what to say to the other.

Tina knew what she wanted to say to him, but what made the mutual silence so ominous to her was a feeling that he was doing nothing but being patient with her, putting up with her phone calls, because he knew what she was up to.

She didn't know why she felt that for the brief second or two, when neither of them said anything. By the time she got off the phone later, she had forgotten all about it.

"Did you call for something?"

"A couple of things," Tina said. "I tried calling you at work. I figured that's where you would be about now, but—"

"I guess you got the news, then."

"Yes. Patrick told me. He sounded pretty upset, Richard. I think he regrets going to that extreme."

"Patrick doesn't regret anything," Richard said pointedly. "He just doesn't want to look like the asshole he is."

"Anyway," she said. "I'm sorry to hear about it. Got anything else lined up yet?"

"I'm not in any hurry to do anything right now as far as work goes. Maybe I'll start looking next week."

Here goes, Tina thought to herself. "Well, since you're not busy with work, how about going out to dinner with me?"

Before he could answer she plunged ahead.

"It wouldn't be anything serious," she promised. "I just thought we could get together and talk for a while. We can talk about your old job if you want, I don't know. I just feel as though we've come through some sort of terrible watershed lately, and even if we aren't coming out of it together, maybe we can at least come out of it on speaking terms. Maybe we can be friends."

The silence on the other end was long, palpable, and she felt her hopes drop. "What do you say?" she asked. "My white flag is out here."

She heard him lighting a cigarette. "I'll have to think about it. What did you have in mind?"

"I was thinking about tomorrow," she said. "I know that's short notice but please consider it, Richard. I know what I did to you was wrong, but I don't think it's going to help anything if we're enemies for the rest of our lives."

Richard said, "I need to check and see if I don't already have something planned for tomorrow night. I don't think I do, but I want to be sure."

"That's fine," she said.

"Do you have a number where I can reach you say, around five o'clock? I should be able to let you know something by then."

"Sure. I'll be on shift until five-thirty." She gave him the number of the pay phone. "And Richard?"

"Yes, Tina?"

"Please call me back."

"I will. Good-bye."

He clicked off the line and Tina put the phone back onto its mount, a smile playing at the corners of her mouth. She felt certain that he would accept her proposed date, and that made her smile even wider.

It would be a night to remember.

Dinner.

Dinner…and then death.

Yes, things were definitely looking up, and if they continued the way they were, she planned to be able to quit this shitty job and live the life she'd been accustomed to before October's leaves fell.

She put on her apron and went back to work, the smile still glued to her face. "Waitresses are expected to smile all the time," she was told when she took this job, and tonight there would be nothing forced in her smile. She would give her customers nothing but the genuine thing.

6

Richard hung up the phone, a thoughtful expression on his whiskey-reddened face, wondering if he had done the right thing; that right thing being not turning the TV on as soon as the phone rang. After picking up and discovering Tina on the other end he had almost turned the set on. The urge was there, but he had found himself fighting that urge, and had thus decided to leave it off.

He had been enjoying himself in the silence of his home since Paul left earlier, and today he felt he needed a dose of silent tranquility. He had just lost his job, and he still wasn't sure how it had happened. So he had missed a few days. Big deal. Was a guy supposed to spend most of nearly every day slaving for some asshole he cared nothing about? Some guy who had unselfishly screwed his wife, to boot?

Things were getting out of control. And although he knew Jerry would know what he'd been thinking as soon as he turned the TV on—what he was thinking *now,* even—Richard couldn't help it. A part of him—some hidden part—realized things had begun spiraling out of control ever since he'd bought the television. Perhaps even before that. But that part of him was out of sight of his conscious thinking; a thing he dared to contemplate and look at only when the TV was off—and he could only peek at it then.

With the TV on—and often when it was not—he didn't

seem to have much control of his life, or what happened around him.

Tina, for instance.

The whole idea, the very *thought*, of her plotting to kill him was just *crazy*. Yet he felt compelled to believe it. And why? Because *Jerry* had told him she was. And what if Richard had never bought the TV? What if he had no idea what Tina was or wasn't planning? Would she have ever called? Even once?

Then she would kill you, and you'd never know why or what to do about it, a voice spoke up immediately. *True.*

But *Tina?* He never would have thought her capable of murdering *anyone.*

And after you married her, you never thought she'd sleep with anyone but you.

This was also true.

Perhaps it was only her phone call. Maybe it instilled some sort of false hope inside him for something which could never be again; something that had slipped away from him almost as easily as his job had.

He thought of the *other* images Jerry had shown him: Tina with other men besides the late Biff Larento. Tina and Patrick, Tina and Rob, Tina and Billy, Tina and Kerry. Even Tina with the two men she'd claimed she'd slept with at the same time—one screwing her from behind, one in her mouth, her enjoying every minute of it. Richard didn't even know who they were.

Jerry had shown him these things, and Richard believed them to be true. He *knew* they were true.

He realized with a sense of sadness that Jerry was probably right about this, also.

Tina *was* planning to kill him. He didn't know how, or why, and although he wished things different in his heart, he believed Jerry.

That was the bottom line.

He believed him.

He decided to turn on the set and tell Jerry about the phone call he'd just received. And if he was upset for not turning him on when the phone rang, then so be it. It wasn't a perfect world.

Besides, he hadn't been too upset when Richard told him about getting fired.

He turned the TV on and sat down on the sofa, lighting a cigarette and smoking it while he waited for the snowy static to leave the screen.

A few minutes later, Jerry appeared. "Hello, Richard," he said.

"Jerry," Richard nodded.

"So, what's new?"

"As if you didn't already know," he said humorlessly. "Tina just called, and I didn't have the TV on." He paused a moment as his scalp began to tingle and then went on. "Jerry, sometimes I just feel—"

"I know, I know," Jerry said in a fatherly tone. "And I sympathize. You have to have some amount of control over your life. That's good. You deserve that. But understand one thing."

"What's that?"

"Tina *is* planning to kill you. No matter what kind of doubts you may be entertaining, it's the truth."

"I know that now. I just wish I'd turned the set on. I guess I caught up in a bunch of sentimental bullshit while I was talking to her. I wanted to believe nothing bad had ever happened between us. I guess I was wrong, but…"

"No harm done," Jerry said. "That's exactly the way she *wants* you to feel. You can't let on to anything different."

"Yeah."

"Do you plan on calling her back at five o'clock?"

"I thought I'd ask you what you think."

"Oh, I think you should. Definitely. The only way we're

going to find out exactly what she plans to do is for you to play along with the silly game she's playing with you."

"I don't think her killing me is just a little game," Richard said angrily. "At least to me, it isn't."

"I wasn't referring to *that,*" Jerry said sternly. "I'm talking about the way she's playing with you, like a cat does with a mouse before devouring it. That's what she's doing, and you *have* to play along. If you don't it will put her guard up. In order to stop her from killing you, you *must* have the element of surprise on your side. Without it you might as well kill yourself, because *she* will."

"So, what should I do," Richard said, feeling helpless. That feeling of not being in control was there again, but he ignored it.

Jerry said: "By now she most assuredly knows how she is going to kill you. Or at least how she's going to *try*. When you call her back at five, be sure you leave me on. I should be able to tell you what exactly it is she has planned, and when. After that, we'll decide what to do about it."

"It's that simple?"

"Yes. It's that simple. But remember—the less she thinks you know, the better. By playing into *her* hands, we can make her play into *ours.* And that, my friend, is the only way we can pull this off." Jerry folded his hands in front of him and looked at him squarely. "Do you understand what I'm talking about now?"

"Yeah," Richard said. "I just can't get over the extremes she's going to, that's all. But I will," he added.

"Why do you not want to believe that she is serious about killing you? To her, her life is hell. Poverty sucks. You've told me how her mother was, and of the relationship she had with Tina." Jerry paused and shook his head in exasperation. "I just don't see what's so hard to believe about it."

Richard squirmed on the sofa. "I'm not saying I don't believe it," he said. "You told me it was so, and I don't think you would lie to me about something like that." And, after a pause: "Would you?"

"No," Jerry said. "I don't see what I could gain from it."

"I believe you're right," Richard continued. "It's just that I thought I *knew* her. I would never have dreamed she would even *think* of something like this. I guess some people don't know each other as well as they think—even if they've been married for years. There can be too many secrets—and this is an ugly one. I think I'm beginning to finally accept it, though."

"You will have to before long," Jerry said. "Before she carries out her plans you must see and accept her true motives, no matter how much your mind—or your heart, for that matter—doesn't want to. If you don't, you will die. I can't put it any simpler than that."

Richard nodded.

The two of them said nothing for perhaps two minutes, but he could *feel* Jerry picking his brain, reading his thoughts, sharing the same feelings he was experiencing. His scalp tingled like massaging fingers.

He finally broke the not unpleasant silence. "What makes a person commit murder, anyway?" It was a question which had been on his mind lately, although he had never voiced it. "What leads a person to it?"

"I guess that all depends," Jerry said. "You know as well as I do there are many factors involved. I guess most scholars believe a good deal goes into how a person is raised. Personally, I think that's bullshit, Freudian crap. It has *something* to do with it, I'm sure, but not as much as some people think.

"Scholars, doctors, psychologists—they have to find a reason behind these things. Hell, it's their job. They say it's genes, it's the parents. It's the code of ethics the parents did, or didn't, impose. And all it boils down to is that the scholars and head shrinks know no more about what makes a person commit murder than the next guy. They just believe there is a rational reason for it—that there *must* be—and a rational reason for everything else, as well. And really all they are doing is laying blame. To top it off, people pay them to do it. They're making a living rationalizing something that they don't understand themselves—and that's dangerous."

Jerry took a pack of cigarettes from the inside of his jacket and lit one, inhaling deeply.

Richard was nodding. "I never thought of that before."

"A man like myself acquires a lot of knowledge and different viewpoints over time. I see a lot from this side."

That side of what? Richard wondered.

He expected Jerry to answer him—although he'd only thought it—but if Jerry had heard it, he wasn't showing that he had. His eyes held a reflective look. "I guess it's just humanity's way of coping with things that frighten them. I suppose it's always been that way.

"The only thing I'm concerned with," he continued. "The only thing important in *my* eyes, is whether or not the person who commits murder does so out of justification. *That* is the key which turns the lock. A murderer's motivation is not treated the way it should be. It is used to convict him or her of the crime, and afterwards it is tossed away almost in the same fashion the person is. Most murders are *not* justified—but a few are.

"Which leads me to—not the answer to your question, but to the answer of why you asked it in the first place. You asked it because you want to know *why* your ex-wife is going to do this. The type of revenge she is seeking, and the *reason* for her revenge is, in my book, *not* justified.

"If there is one thing I can tell you to relieve some of your anxieties, it is this: if she *does* succeed with her plan, you will have the rare opportunity for your *own* revenge. And if that is the case, it *will* be justified. She will lose any way it goes."

Richard looked hard at Jerry. He had laid off the alcohol for the past forty minutes or so, but it still took some effort to participate in the conversation. It sounded as though Jerry was suggesting that, even if Tina killed him he would still be able to get even with her. He couldn't see how that could be. On the other hand, if Jerry said it was so, then most likely it was. "What do you mean by that?"

"I don't want to get into explaining things of that nature," Jerry said. "at least, not right now. Besides, you wouldn't be able to conceive of it in the first place." The latter he said in a lower voice, as though to himself. "What's important right now, Richard, no matter how curious you are about why people commit murder, is that they do. And your ex-wife is trying desperately to get into that particular group. As long as we keep that in mind, we should be able to mount a defense against it. And that will start with the call you make to her in an hour or so."

"Okay," he agreed. Jerry's voice was soothing, and somehow —even through the whiskey-haze—he understood what he was talking about. He thought that if anyone but Jerry said these things, he would no more believe or trust them, than if that person told him the earth was flat and all the history, science, and physics books were full of shit.

"After you call," Jerry said. "we'll be in much better shape in this matter. You've got to trust me on that. I should be able to ascertain when she plans to do this, and maybe even how."

"That's a relief to know," Richard sighed.

Jerry spread his hands before him. "Nothing to it, my man. Nothing to it."

The two men talked some more. To Richard, it was amazing how much Jerry knew about things—from cartoons (he said with a smile that his favorite was Tom and Jerry) to baseball and most other sports, to science, to English authors.

As they talked, waning away the late afternoon, they both

waited patiently for five o'clock to roll around, and for the answer to a major question to show itself.

7

George Morrison pulled away from the curb in his battered pickup truck and was soon two cars back from the vehicle he was following. The vehicle was a '92 Caprice Classic which belonged to Tina Raines. Last night after Paul Frazier left his shop, he had called Larry Vincent (at home, where he was connected via modem to the computers at his office) and had coaxed out of him Tina's address and the type of vehicle she drove. Larry had sounded reluctant, but in the end obliged, telling him that whatever he was doing had better be good, and had better not get him—Larry—in any kind of trouble. George assured him it wouldn't, and he hoped to be able to tell him everything in the near future, perhaps when he came over and serviced all of his household appliances next week at no charge. Larry hadn't minded at all, then, to swap a little harmless information.

George kept his eye on the car, following it discreetly. Morning traffic was fairly heavy—the sun was young and bright, and there always seemed to be more people out and about on a nice, sunny morning, and he almost lost sight of her once. But as he turned onto Matthews Street, he caught a glimpse of her car pulling off to the right, into the parking lot of Maurice's Café. Tina had been dressed in the attire of a waitress when she'd left her apartment, and he guessed this was where she worked.

Maurice's Café was just six blocks over from George's own shop, and he'd eaten there on more than a few occasions since the place opened eleven years ago. It had been an attractive restaurant back then, serving breakfast and lunch to most of the working class on the north and west ends of town. Their special at the time had been, in the mornings, egg-and-cheese omelets, with two pieces of toast and three pieces of bacon on the side. Now, weeds threatened to choke the granite bricks (painted a light shade of baby-shit yellow), and the short sidewalk in from the parking lot was cracked and raised, and infected with grass and weeds. The only attractive thing about the place now was the parking lot itself, which had recently been resurfaced.

George pulled in four slots down from where Tina had parked and limped amply to the door. The fresh morning smell of eggs and bacon greeted him as he entered, making his stomach rumble. He went to a booth in the corner and sat down, looking around the small room.

The cafe was fairly crowded with people scarfing their breakfasts, reading the morning paper, or smoking cigarettes and talking. The constant babble was comforting. Three or four women walked briskly between tables, stopping every now and then to take an order, or deliver one, before hustling back to the counter, where the five stools along it were occupied by more patrons who ate the house special (ham and eggs, with rye toast) and washed it all down with steaming mugs of Maurice's legendary coffee.

George spotted Tina three tables over, holding a pad in one hand, jotting down a burly man's order. The man was looking her over as she did this, and George could see why as he got his first really good look at her. Her long, wavy hair made her high cheekbones stand out, as did her sensual eyes against the yellow of that mane. Her lips were full, puffy, and George thought she could grace the cover of any magazine in the country.

She finished taking the man's order, and as George watched her half-run over to the counter, a different girl appeared at his own table.

"What'll it be today, pops?" The girl was chewing gum, and

playing with her hair with one hand. The other hand held an order pad. She looked like every waitress in every 1950's movie he had ever seen.

"Three eggs, over easy, bacon, toast, and coffee," he told her. Whether at home or at a café such as this one, George consumed the same things for breakfast, as he had nearly every day for the past twenty-five years. He knew the cholesterol would probably help stop his heart and kill him one day, but he also knew there were things worse than a heart attack which could do the same thing.

As he waited on his food, he spent his time sipping the water the young waitress had brought with his menu, and watching Tina Raines. She seemed to get as many lookers as she did orders, and he supposed she probably got tipped better than some of her homely-looking (by comparison) co-workers. With her looks, she seemed totally out of place in a joint like this. She bustled back and forth in a never-ending hurry—as most waitresses do—but aside from her looks, he thought there was something else different about her, as well.

He just couldn't put his finger on what it was.

A few minutes later, his waitress brought his food and laid the check down on the table next to his plate.

"Looks good," he told her. Her blonde hair was styled almost the same as Tina's and her eyes were also identical in color, but beyond that she was as homely as they came.

"Tastes even better," she said, chomping her gum with a fervor. "Hope ya enjoy it." She started toward the counter.

"Just a second," George said.

The waitress turned back around. "Did I forget something?"

"No, no," he said. "I just wanted to ask you about that girl over there." He looked at Tina, who was taking an order a few tables over.

"You mean Tina?"

"Yes. I haven't seen her before. New girl?" he asked.

"Yeah, I guess you could say that. She's been here a few weeks, maybe a month." The waitress, whose name tag said 'Gayle,' looked at him and said, in a voice laced with venom: "Maurice gave her two of my tables this week. I'm having a hard enough time getting decent tips without losing two of my best tables to *her*. Seems like everyone who comes in wants her to wait on them. You'd think she'd hate all the extra work, but it doesn't seem to bother her. All she does is bitch about her ex-husband, and what a miserable wreck he's made of her life. You ask me, she's making some pretty good money." After a slight pause she said: "And if you ask me, I don't think I blame her husband for getting out." She cast daggers with her eyes in Tina's direction, seeming to go through some conflict with herself. She blew a bubble with her gum, and it popped loudly as she turned back to George. "Can I get you anything else, pops?"

"No, this is fine," George told her. "Thank you."

"Don't mention it," she said. She left and went to wait on a couple who had seated themselves at one of her tables.

George ate his breakfast, thinking about what the girl had said, and keeping one eye on Tina Raines. He had just finished mopping up his last egg with a piece of toast when he realized what else about Tina was different from the other girls working the establishment.

She was smiling.

Some of the other waitresses were smiling, sure, but the smiles looked forced, as if they would rather be anywhere else in the world but here. Perhaps they all felt the same way about Tina as the girl named Gayle. Yet the waitress had said all Tina did was bitch about her ex-husband—Richard.

So why the smile? She seemed almost *too* happy. About what, George didn't know, but there was an energy of nervous excitement in her smile he didn't care for.

He didn't care for it one bit.

He finished his coffee, paid his bill (leaving a three-dollar tip for his waitress—almost as much as his meal cost, but he felt sorry for her), and went out to his truck. He pulled it into an empty slot in the back corner of the lot, facing it toward the entrance door. He would keep an eye out for Tina on the off chance she might leave the café before her shift ended.

She probably wouldn't, but he was content to wait anyway. He didn't want to take a chance of losing knowledge of her whereabouts, even if she *was* only working.

He would go in again at noon for lunch, and observe her further. He might, he thought, even be able to pump additional information from that waitress, Gayle.

In the meantime, he had brought along a solar-powered calculator and a small stack of bills and invoices from his shop. Although he'd hung the tattered 'closed' sign on the front of his place, he would do his book-keeping while he watched the door to the café. It would pass the time as well as anything.

He'd tossed and turned last night until the early hours of the morning, thinking about the television set and trying to ascertain through what he knew about it how he could stop the inevitable from happening to Richard Raines and his ex-wife. Mental exhaustion had claimed him sometime after two-thirty, and he had finally fallen asleep.

This morning, over his first cup of coffee, he had decided to take along some of the paperwork which had gotten backed up in the last week or so, just in case a situation arouse like the one he was in now, where he was required to wait for an extended period of time.

He knew thinking about his puzzle would make the hours ahead of him stretch into what would feel like days, and so he sifted through his papers, punching the calculator and jotting down figures on a yellow legal pad.

As he did so, he kept one watchful eye on the entrance to the café.

8

At quarter to twelve, George glanced up from the invoice he was tallying (wincing mentally at the small margin of profit he would realize from these particular high-priced repair parts) and then laid it on the seat next to him as Tina Raines came out of the café.

His stomach rumbled at the thought of the meal he'd had planned in about fifteen minutes, and it turned over again as Tina got into her car. He guessed she was on her lunch break and also guessed he would miss his.

He started his truck as she backed out of her slot near the building, and followed her as she turned onto Matthews in the direction of downtown.

She turned onto Main Street five blocks down, and George followed her down the one-way street, pulling his truck over to a curbside parking space when he saw her park in front of a pawn shop, one of three located along Main.

Main Street was the home of most of the oldest buildings in the city, crumbling brick monoliths which looked for the most part like they could be toppled by the slightest breeze. A few of them had been demolished by the city recently, and new buildings had been erected in their places, most of them housing different business. Standing among old red-brick buildings, these new structures looked like shiny new teeth in a mouthful of cavities.

The pawn shop Tina had just entered was not one of the new buildings. In fact, it was one of the oldest, with a red-brick façade and dirty, curtainless windows looking onto the street from the top four floors through cracked panes of glass opaque with age and sunshine. The ground floor of the building housed the pawn shop. Two large display windows faced the sidewalk, and they were bare except for the many signs advertising the bargains you could find if you went through the door conveniently located between the two windows. There was a three-way sign above the canopy shading the front walk. It could be read from anywhere on the street, although a lot of the high blue letters had faded with the sun and many seasons of rain, and George read the sign from his truck, even though he already knew what it said:

MILO'S PAWN
Guns, Gold
Loans of all Types
COME ON IN!

He had known the shop's owner, Milo McPherson, for more than fifteen years. Although they had been close friend in years past, their relationship had become, over the last five years, not much more than a business one—helping each other out in a field where their businesses intersected quite often. Milo often got appliances (mostly small ones like radios and VCR's) that had one thing or another wrong with them, from people who were strapped for cash. He never bitched about broken items, for he paid accordingly. George would fix whatever needed fixed, and Milo would have a sale tag on it two days later, usually with an outrageous price attached, and the words 'Like New' right above that price.

George thought about going into the shop and seeing what Tina was up to, but Milo was a talker, and if she happened to leave while they were talking, he might miss the opportunity to follow her further. After all, she might not only be on her lunch break; she might have taken the rest of the day off, and he didn't like the idea of spending the rest of the afternoon looking for her if she didn't go home. Jonesboro was a large city.

He decided to wait in the truck. He could find out what he

needed to know from Milo, later. *No later than today, though,* he thought.

He totaled up the last of the bills he had with him, and about twenty minutes later Tina walked out of the pawn shop, stepping briskly to her car.

She carried only her purse, which was the only thing she had taken into the place, and George thought maybe she was supplementing her income some other way. He tossed the idea away quickly; a girl with her looks, even if she *was* pressed for cash, wouldn't fool around with an old coot like Milo McPherson.

No. She had gone into Milo's shop looking for something (who didn't, when they entered a pawn shop?) and evidently, she hadn't found it.

So, she'll go to another one, he thought. *If she's looking for something, she's sure to find it on this street.*

But Tina turned left a block up and headed back towards Matthews Street. He followed her—this time he was the sole vehicle behind her—and it was soon apparent she was going back to the café.

He looked at his watch. Almost thirty minutes had passed since she'd left the café. He realized she was probably not allowed more time than that for lunch. Additionally, whatever she was doing must be important for her to take her lunch break during one of the busiest times of the day. He imagined the other waitresses on shift wouldn't complain about it, though.

He pulled into the parking lot behind her and parked in the same spot he had been in earlier, whispering his thanks none of the growing crowd had taken it. He waited until Tina went inside, and started that way himself.

He was going to get his lunch after all. His stomach grumbled happily at that prospect.

Lunch first, and when he was sure Tina was staying on-shift,

212

he would make the short drive back to Milo's Pawn.

She might have been in there just taking a casual look around, but he didn't think so. There seemed to be nothing casual about that girl. His thinking was that a woman like her would probably not be found dead in a place like Milo's. Or any other pawn shop, for that matter.

But this isn't just any normal situation, George, a voice spoke up in his head. *Not normal at all. Something is going on, and I think you know what it is.*

I don't, he countered to the voice. But that inner voice was stronger.

You know what's going on, George. At least more than you admit. You're just too afraid to come to terms with what you know is true.

But *I* don't *know.*

What about when you broke your ankle? Huh? Explain that. The voice was teasing, playful.

"It was an accident, that's all," he said aloud, before he was even aware he had done it.

"Excuse me?" A waitress had come over to his table.

"Oh…nothing. Just talking to myself." He meant it, too. The voice was gone.

"What can I get you?" the girl asked. He hadn't been able to get the same table he'd had this morning. He had been hoping to get the same waitress. This girl's name tag said 'Melanie.'

George ordered his lunch (double-hamburger, large fries, and a diet Coke) and kept his eye on Tina, whose tables were on the other side of the crowded room.

When the waitress brought him the check, he asked her what time the waitresses went off shift.

"Are you flirting with me?" she asked. Her pale cheeks were flushed with red high up, near her nose, and a lock of coal black hair hung limply over her left eye.

"No, no," he laughed. "My niece is looking for a job in the

afternoons after classes. She's a junior in high school," he added smoothly to the lie.

"I see," the girl said. "Well, most of us who came in this morning usually get off around five. Unless it's busy, of course. We get the option for some overtime if we want it, but there's usually enough help by five o'clock for all of us to go home if we want. Most of the girls that come in after five are in high school, same as your niece."

"That's great!" he said, with more enthusiasm than he felt. "I'll be sure to let her know. Thank you so much."

"Any time." The girl headed back toward the counter.

Five o'clock.

He took a peek at his watch. It was going on one-thirty now. He should have plenty of time to visit Milo and get back here before Tina left work.

If I can keep the old bastard from jawing my head off, he thought.

He put two dollars under the salt shaker, picked up his check, paid it at the counter, and made his way out to his truck.

He didn't figure to get anything useful from Milo McPherson, but it would kill some time, if nothing else.

George had no idea how wrong he was.

9

Bells jingled as George opened the door to Milo's Pawn and went inside.

Milo was over behind a glass case of jewelry, some of it undoubtedly fake, junk. He was a burly man at six-feet-two, with dark bushy eyebrows which made him appear to be frowning although he was constantly smiling. He was fifty-five, but his reddish-brown hair, thick and combed back neatly, made him look younger.

Although George was his senior by more than a few years, he had never thought of Milo McPherson as being anything less—or more—than himself, and he nodded to him as he closed the door.

"George!" Milo said, smiling. "Be right with you." He was dickering with a young boy of about twenty over one of the rings in the glass case. It lay between them on the counter.

"Take your time," George told him. "No hurry here." Of course, there was *some* hurry on his part, but he wouldn't tell Milo that. Milo hated to be rushed, and he worked a slow deal with anyone, no matter if he was buying or selling.

George walked across the aisle to a shelf full of radios and boom-boxes of all makes. He looked some of them over, mentally comparing the price tags to those on his own shelves, and waited for Milo to finish cutting his deal with the young man.

"But my fiancé will know it's a used one," the boy said.

"I tell you she won't know the different between this one and one from the store in the mall uptown," Milo countered. "All she's gonna care about is the size of that rock, and *it* ain't the smallest I've ever seen."

"Well, I don't know," the boy said. "Couldn't you come down on it?"

"Five-eighty's as low as I can go," Milo said. "I just got it in and I haven't had time to really study it and put a price tag to her. But you can see for yourself it's worth a helluva lot more than that. Besides, just think of the look on your girl's face when she gets a gander at it. That will be priceless." He smiled down at the boy.

"Okay," the boy said, reaching around for his wallet. He had blonde hair and a red mole on his left cheek. I hope you're right."

"Course I am," Milo said. He swapped the ring for money, filled out a receipt for the boy and the kid left, holding the small velvet box protectively in both hands.

George had stepped over for a glance at the ring while Milo and the boy were working out the deal, and he looked at Milo now with a big, toothy smile. The ring had been a gem all right, a diamond of the size and weight he knew Milo didn't carry because it was one which might get a guy held up.

"Just about gave that one away, didn't you?" George said.

Milo reached across the glass counter and shook his hand firmly. "How are you, George? You know, I was just thinking about you today. I got a radio in this morning that's gonna need a little fixing up."

"I'm fine," George said. "and I'll be happy to work on it for you."

"Good, good," Milo said. "He looked at the front door, as if the boy was still standing there. "Yep, I guess I did give her away. Prettiest one I've seen come through here in years, too. But you know how it is. Some thug would come in here to look around, see if there was anything worth stealing, and decide that ring was worth more than my life. No thank *you*."

George nodded.

"I guess I could have gotten more for it, but I made a pretty good penny off it, and I've still got the matching gold band from the set. Almost as pretty as the woman who sold it to me."

George's eyebrows raised in interest. "This afternoon?"

Now it was Milo's turn to look interested. "Sure. Why? Did you see her, too? My goodness, what a woman!"

"Yeah, I saw her," George said. Milo had all but pushed him into what he'd come here to find out. "What'd she do? Sell them?"

Milo's eyes narrowed in suspicion, and although he looked to be angry, George knew the frown was only exaggerated by the man's eyebrows. "You know I can't tell you that, George."

He sighed. Milo was a good man, and he always dealt him right (more than he could say for some of the other people who came in here), but he was stern when it came to the confidentiality of his customers. He guessed Milo suspected him of trying to steal one of them. Preposterous, of course, and not the type of business he had intended here. He decided he was going to have to be straight with Milo; at least partly.

"Look, Milo," he said. "I know you're going to find this hard to believe, but I've been following that girl who was in here. Not because I want to steal any business from you—I think you know better than that, after all these years—but because whatever she is up to may be important in saving someone's life. Maybe even hers."

There. It was out.

Milo's expression changed, but not by much. "That's still not—"

"Milo," George interrupted him. He glanced around, but there was no one in the shop but the two of them. "I'm telling you as a friend that you've got to trust me on this. I don't care where the rings from, or how much you made on them. I just want to know how you *got* them. Did she sell them to you, or what?"

Milo wore a hurt expression on his tanned face, but George knew that look to be one of understanding. Milo's train ran a little slow sometimes, but he was smart when it came to most things, and telling the difference between a lie and the truth was one of them; especially when it came from an old friend.

He ran a hand through his hair and sighed heavily. "No, I didn't buy 'em from her. She didn't pawn 'em, either."

"Then what did she do?"

"She swapped them. She swapped the diamond *and* the gold bank.

"Swapped them for what?" George asked. But he thought he already knew the answer to that, and felt his stomach tighten.

"For a gun," Milo McPherson said. "A .357 Magnum."

10

As George drove back to Maurice's Café, the thought going through his head was: *What is she going to do with it? What is she going to do with it?*

But he knew the answer to that, didn't he?

According to Milo, when he'd asked what a pretty girl like her wanted with a big gun like that, Tina told him that she lived alone in a bad neighborhood (which, George supposed, was true), and she wanted the gun to guard against intruders.

She'd had a clean police record, Milo said, a perfect driving record, a perfect body...why not let her have the gun if she wanted it? He thought it had been a normal deal.

Milo also said he had shown her how to load, unload, and fire the gun (dry-firing it several times, and having her do the same), and how to break it down for cleaning. She had wanted bullets, but he had directed her across town to a hunting and fishing store. The law didn't allow him to sell ammo.

That was all fine and dandy to George, and he'd told Milo so, thanking and reassuring him he had done nothing wrong.

But there was two other things Milo said which troubled George, as he pulled into the parking lot of Maurice's and spotted Tina's Caprice.

The first thing was that she had asked Milo if he knew of a place where she could go to practice firing the gun, where the gunshots wouldn't bother anyone. Milo had told her about a place five miles outside of town, to the north. It was the old Miller Homestead, an abandoned, run-down farm practically in the middle of nowhere. It had always been a popular place for hunters to sharpen their skills before deer season.

George thought nothing about this at first. Going down Greensway Road past the farm in early Autumn, you would hear nothing *but* gunshots. Plenty of them.

Although this wasn't early Autumn, it was close, but that was okay, too.

He thought nothing of Tina taking target practice at the old Miller Homestead until what Milo had said just as he was leaving.

George had been opening the door to leave, having said his good-byes to Milo, and he had muttered to himself: "I sure hope Tina knows what she's doing."

"What was that, George?" Milo asked. He had been less than ten feet away.

"I said, I sure hope Tina knows what she's doing. You know, the woman who got the gun from you."

"You must be mistaken," Milo had said. "Wasn't no Tina in here that swapped those rings for that gun. That pretty thing's name was Gayle. Gayle Lombard."

11

At ten minutes of five, Tina went to the back room at Maurice's Café to wait on the call from Richard.

He had promised to call back at five, like she'd asked him, and as she waited, she was filled with the same nervous excitement she'd felt most of the day. She had no doubts he would call. One thing she'd always admired about Richard was, when he said he was going to do something, he did it. He believed strongly in committing himself to his word, and regardless of how things had turned out, she still admired him for that.

But that was virtually the *only* thing she admired about the man, and even *that* admiration was tempered with hate—hate because he *was* like that. She was not inclined to believe these feelings could be caused by her guilt of what she had done to him, and to their marriage.

She went over to the small row of lockers, unlocked the one belonging to her, and felt the hard bulge in her purse.

It was still there.

Nearly five hours after she had acquired the gun, she still found it difficult to believe how easily that missing piece of her plan had fallen into place.

She had been in the Ladies restroom this morning before the shift started, along with Melanie, Gayle, and another waitress named Lorna. The four of them were touching up their makeup and swapping jokes, and preparing themselves for the vigorous breakfast crowd that would soon file in through the front door of the café. Tina hadn't participated much in the general conversation. She didn't like the other girls and knew they felt likewise about her. But when Gayle Lombard had spilled the contents of her purse all over the floor, she had nevertheless bent down to help her and the other girls pick things up. Regardless of how Tina felt about her co-workers (or they about her), they were accustomed to working with each other, and to Tina this team effort came instinctively.

Her hand had just happened upon Gayle's driver's license.

She had not thought much about it at first, only noticing the similarities between Gayle's photo and the one on her own license. Both girls had the same color of hair and eyes, but Tina thought if they stood side-by-side, there was really no comparison between them. Gayle was much uglier. On the other hand, the photo on Gayle's license *was* worth comparing to her own. Tina had last gotten her license renewed three years ago. The picture on it showed a much younger Tina, closer to Gayle's own age.

She didn't really *think* about the similarities until this

morning around nine o'clock. She had been figuring up a customer's bill on the one register at the counter, and thinking while she did this about the problem she was having coming up with a way to get Richard out of the way, and her hands on the insurance money. She was adding in the sales tax when it clicked home for her.

She could use Gayle's driver's license to purchase a gun. If she took all her makeup off, someone who didn't know her or Gayle would have a hard time saying the girl on Gayle's driver's license wasn't Tina.

Immediately, another problem presented itself.

How would she pay for a gun? She didn't think she would have any trouble swiping Gayle's license—and she hadn't; Gayle was one of the trusting types who left her locker unlocked while she worked, and Tina had merely taken it out of her purse before she went on her lunch break—but where would she get the money to pay for a gun?

She had thought about it, feeling her hopes sink like so many gray pebbles, and then remembered that her set of wedding rings were somewhere in the bottom of her purse.

And just like that, the solution to her problem was there.

The man at the pawn shop had been extremely nice, and even though he had looked at the license while filling out the forms for her to sign, he evidently hadn't been able to tell any difference between her and the photo on the license.

She had asked to be shown how to load, unload, clean, and fire the .357 Magnum She had let the pawnbroker pick it out for her, telling him it didn't matter to her which one he chose because she only wanted it for protection, and he had eagerly obliged (men were always eager to oblige her, she had long ago discovered).

When she'd offered the rings in exchange for the pistol, he had insisted that the diamond ring was sufficient enough to cover the cost of the gun. Tina then insisted herself that he take both of them—she didn't want to answer any questions down the road about why she only had one of her wedding rings—because she didn't want to separate the set. The pawnbroker had offered her fifty-dollars for the gold band and she had taken it. She'd go to Walmart for ammo later, with the cash.

So, the gun in her purse was registered in the name of Gayle Lombard, and even though she knew she would be questioned after she carried out her plans, she didn't see any way she could be linked to Richard's death, by the police or anyone else.

At least, if she played her cards right the rest of the way out.

She had returned the license to Gayle's purse after returning to the café, reapplied makeup to her face, and when those acts were completed, she'd felt a mixture of triumph and relief.

She thought about these things, and when the phone rang shrilly behind her it made her jump.

She calmed herself, letting the phone ring three times before picking it up. "Hello?"

"Tina?" It was Richard. He had made good on his promise. She felt more relief surge through her.

"Yes," she said. "I'm glad you called."

"I told you I would."

"I know. I was just thinking maybe you wouldn't. That you wanted to get rid of me."

"Now, why would I want to do that?" he asked. The icy sarcasm in his voice did not escape her.

Gritting her teeth, clamping down on what she really wanted to say—why do you have to be such a smart-ass?—she pressed on. "Did you decided what you wanted to do …about tomorrow night?"

"Yes, I have," Richard said. "What, exactly, did you have in mind?"

"Well, I thought we could get together for dinner, drinks, talk a little…you know. Just chew the fat, I guess." She paused a moment before continuing as her scalp began to tingle lightly.

It had done this yesterday, also, and she figured it had something to do with the cheap payphone.

"I don't hate you, Richard. Do you still hate me?"

There was a brief silence, and she could almost *hear* him deciding on an answer. She wished she had used a different approach. Then his voice came over the line, thin and flat. "No. I don't."

"I'm glad," she said.

"So, where do you want to meet?"

"Nowhere," she said.

"What?"

"What I mean is, we don't have to meet anywhere. I'll pick you up, if that's all right."

She could almost feel him thinking again. "That will be fine with me, Tina. If that's what you really want."

His voice sounded odd, detached...*cold*. For just a second she was frightened. *He knows! He* knows!

But of course he didn't. It was ridiculous to even think it.

Instead of voicing her fright, she said: "Does seven-thirty tomorrow night sound okay to you?"

A shorter pause this time. "Seven-thirty is okay."

She had gotten all she wanted, and could think of nothing more to say. "I guess I'll see you tomorrow, then."

"Tomorrow," he agreed.

"Good-bye, Richard."

"Bye, Tina." She heard a click as he hung up.

She put the receiver on the hook and let a smile play at the corners of her mouth. It had been almost too easy.

Yes, but can you really do it? Can you pull the trigger?

She thought—not for the first time that day—about the money she would soon receive from the insurance policy and decided that, yes, she *could*. Not only could she, but she *would*, and gladly.

This one act could get her out of the hole her life had

become, and it could do it more quickly than anything else.

Just one little pull on a small piece of curved metal.

There were alternate ways to attain a better lifestyle, but they required more work and dedication than just killing someone for it. Tina, however, did not comprehend such things. All she could see, now that all parts of her plans were in place, was a chance to regain the lifestyle she'd always been accustomed to.

As far as *she* could see, this was the only way.

After all…it wasn't her fault.

12

6:15p.m.

Dusk had already settled outside George Morrison's repair shot; a deep purple and violet line on the western horizon that capped off what was, to George, a very unsettling day.

He had left Maurice's Café a few minutes past five o'clock when he saw Tina exit the building. He had spent the time since lunch brooding over her purchase of the gun. He'd found the remainder of his bookkeeping would have to wait.

Tina had gone straight home.

He had sat in his truck, which he'd parked across the street, for about thirty minutes before finally going home himself. He at a light supper (the two meals at Maurice's had filled him up and he honestly didn't feel like eating, anyway), and had then called Paul Frazier.

Now, as dusk gathered itself into night, the two of them sat at the table in George's small kitchen, each with a glass of bourbon in front of him, going over the events of the day. Paul told him about Richard getting fired, and how he had shown an odd mixture of anger and lack of concern about it all.

"This wasn't typical behavior for Richard?"

"Not even close," Paul said. "He has always cared about his job as much as he has everything else in his life. I *still* can't believe he let it get away from him like that." Paul looked both disgusted and frightened, as though some part of him could see *exactly* how that could happen.

"I take it he cared about his marriage quite a bit, also," George said. "Am I right?"

"Yeah, you're right, there," Paul said reflectively. He and Richard had talked on several occasions, as most men will when there are two of them together—friends, anyway—about the ups and downs of marriage. Paul had always taken the pragmatic view that marriage was like a job; you had to work hard to keep it. Of course, it also helped if you liked it. Paul was a man who liked it, and he knew Richard had been, as well. He could remember a time, only three months ago, when he and Richard had carried on such a discussion.

They had been fishing together one bright Saturday morning out at Kelpner's Pond on the east side of town. A light breeze was rippling the water and the fish weren't biting particularly well. Each of them had caught two fish apiece by this time, but they normally would have had considerably more. They'd been sitting on the bank, sipping beer, and partaking in the age-old ritual of male companionship—'shooting the shit.' Although they did this often, and talked about work, baseball, music, and such, it was the first time he had asked Richard if he was happy in his marriage. Because Paul knew a little more than him about the infidelity Tina had progressed into (he'd heard talk and rumors at work, and he was around the couple enough to begin having his own suspicions about her), it was only fitting he ask his friend this question. Later, in retrospect, he would entertain the possibility that Richard *did* suspect a little of what was happening—but not enough, and too late.

"Paul," he had answered him. "I don't think there are words

enough to describe how happy I am right now in my life. I mean, I've got a wife I still love as much as the day I met her, a secure job, a condo in one of the nicest neighborhoods in town." He had paused for a minute and looked Paul straight in the eyes. "And, I also have the best neighbor and friend anyone could ask for." He had tilted his beer and looked out over the water.

"Thanks, man," was all Paul had time to say, for in the next seconds Richard's fishing rod jumped jerkily off the stick it was propped up with, and it began sliding toward the water's edge.

Richard grabbed the rod before it became totally submerged and had given it a hard yank, straight up. As he fought the fish to the bank, a fierce concentration in his eyes, he had said: "But if God himself came down right now and told me I could only have one thing in my life, there would be no question what it would be. It would be Tina." He had then finished reeling in the line, a six-pound catfish on the other end.

"The loss of the marriage was her fault, not his," Paul said now. "I don't think his recent behavior is his fault, either."

"Maybe. Maybe not," George said. "If I didn't know better myself I could say this: he lost his wife and was so shaken by it he slipped up and let everything else go to hell. Yet I can't, because I *do* know better. But I'm sure that sort of thing has happened before. At least on TV it does," he added.

"The TV," Paul said in a voice filled with sudden interest. "You know, ever since you showed me those clippings, I've had a battle going on in my head about whether or not it's the truth. I mean, I *know* that it is...hell, I've seen proof...no matter how small an amount, and I don't think you would just make something like that up."

"I don't see what I could possibly gain from it," George said conversationally.

"But part of me," Paul continued, "is still yelling that it's so insane. So utterly *insane!"* Does that make any sense?

George, who planned on telling Paul something tonight that would either quiet that voice or spur it on, said: "It's hard for me to say I understand how you could doubt something like this, but it's only because I know it to be true. You might feel the same way if, say, someone you knew told you they really didn't believe your name was Paul Frazier."

Paul looked at him levelly.

"Let me tell you something which happened today. I've got a bad feeling about it, but I want to know what *you* think it might mean."

"Okay," Paul said.

George sighed heavily. "Tina bought a gun today."

Paul's mouth dropped open. "A *what?*"

"A gun. A .357 Magnum." George spread his hand's out in front of him. "Now. What do you think it means?"

Paul composed himself. "Well...I don't know...offhand, I'd say she bought it for home defense."

"That's what she told the pawnbroker," George said.

"You mean she bought it at a *pawn* shop?"

"Yes. Not only that, but she purchased the gun with the driver's license and background information of a co-worker. A girl who doesn't like her." George looked at Paul and raised his eyebrows a notch. *"Now* what do you think it might mean?"

Paul's head swam with this new information, but he was finally able to answer. "If I had to guess, I'd say she plans on killing someone, and used another person's ID so she couldn't be traced to the murder weapon."

"Then we think alike," George said. "That kind of shit has happened before." He leaned across the table toward Paul. "And do you know who I think she plans on killing with that gun?"

"Who?"

"Your friend Richard," he said flatly.

"Tina?" Paul chuckled. "No way. If you only knew her."

George didn't respond right away, just spread his hands in

front of him, palms up, and shrugged his shoulders. "It makes the most sense to me."

"But, why?"

"My guess is, it's not because of something Richard has done, but because she is being influenced by someone or something else. Of course, I could be wrong. But I think it's probably some *one* who is influencing her."

"A boyfriend?"

"No."

"Then, who?" Paul asked. The idea that Tina might be planning to kill Richard was progressively frightening him.

"Before I tell you that, let me remind you that I *could* be wrong, although I'm beginning to think more and more that I'm not. You've seen the newspaper clippings, and you've seen the charts I've made from them in these notebooks."

"Yes," Paul said.

"You've also noticed, I'm sure, my limp."

Paul nodded.

"The newspaper clippings are in black and white, right in front of you, and so they are believable. And this," George backed his chair away from the table and hiked his right let up onto it with some effort. Then he pulled his pants leg up to his knee. "This is *also* believable because you can see it."

Paul whistled deeply. He couldn't help it. George's white leg was a roadmap of varicose veins that crisscrossed each other like busy highways, some of them standing out farther than others, overpasses on the thin and twisty road. These veins led down to a red, swollen, inflamed ankle which jutted outward at an awkward angle from the rest of his leg. "That really looks bad," Paul said, making an effort not to say what he really wanted to: that the ankle looked as though it had been caught in a grinder.

"I never had it set," George said. "In fact, I never even went to a doctor about it until weeks after the fact—and then it was only to get something stronger than aspirin for the pain."

"How come you didn't go after it happened? Why did you wait so long? That must have been painful."

"It was, it was," George said. "But at the time I couldn't. Not after the way it had happened, although I knew I could probably make up some story to tell the doctor. I was frightened, you see. Afraid that if I told someone, I'd end up like the others."

"Others?"

"Of course, in a few weeks I was able to tell myself that what happened couldn't have been real, that it *was* an accident. But now I have to stop telling myself that awful lie, because it *wasn't* an accident. Not in the ordinary sense of the word. And I have to tell you about it now, no matter if it seems even more unbelievable than these news clippings and charts. I have to tell you about that day...and about the man.

Paul could only sit and listen to George. He felt as if something of utter importance was about to be unveiled before him, and although he dreaded hearing it, he also *wanted* to hear it.

"It was near the end of August of 1990 when it happened," George began. "I had just purchased the television set roughly a month after it had claimed its fourth victim, a restaurant owner named Phil Clayton. You've seen the article on his death."

Paul nodded, and George paused to pour more bourbon into his empty glass. He tasted it and made a slight face as he set it down. "Anyway, the day this happened (he gestured to his lame ankle) a young man of about twenty brought that TV into my shop, looking to sell it. At that time, I was still trying to convince myself the TV wasn't related to its owners' deaths, and it was just one big coincidence. But part of me knew better, and so I wasn't really surprised when that the television had found its way back to my shop. After all, I'd had it and sold it on four different occasions. This time would make the fifth.

"But I felt something different for the first time. The boy who brought it in was fidgety, nervous, and it was only later that I found out he was Phil Clayton's younger brother, Ronnie. I don't know if he was in the process of liquidating his brother's estate, or what, but he unloaded the TV on me for a twenty-dollar bill, and he looked relieved when the two of us finally had that set off his truck and in my shop."

George stopped and drained the bourbon from his glass and then poured it full again. He looked at Paul. "Need some more?"

Paul raised one hand from the table. "I'm fine."

George set the bottle on the table. "I got to thinking about things that night. The death of Donald Forrester was still on my mind, and the TV was back in my shop again, but what bothered me the most and caused the greatest loss of sleep that night was remembering how that kid Clayton had acted when he brought the set into my place. He'd looked almost like a murderer getting rid of the last piece of evidence, perhaps the weapon itself. I got to wondering, first, if maybe *he* had killed his brother. Through a little digging early the next day I was able to find out he had been over thirty miles away at the time of Phil Clayton's death.

"When I found that out a new thought struck me, and when it did I for some reason believed it to be true. I believed—I was about seventy-five percent sure, anyway—the TV was somehow relevant to Mr. Clayton's death...and I think his kid brother believed it, too. It explained why he behaved like he did. My idea about the TV being linked somehow to four separate deaths didn't seem so foolish to me, anymore. Clayton's younger brother felt something about it, also. Maybe not as much as I did, but I was convinced he knew *something*.

"I spent most of that day looking for this kid, and was able to find out through a friend of mine—a man who has helped me indirectly over the years with this thing—that Ronnie Clayton had lived thirty miles away, in Paragould, but had moved out of state about a week after his brother's death, which had been on the thirtieth of June of that year. He left a forwarding address at the post office for some small burg down in Texas. So that was a dead end. He'd evidently sold me the set on his way out of town."

George took another drink from his glass, wiped a hand across his mouth, and continued. "It was about an hour after the young man left when I decided to take a look—I mean, a good *long* look—at that TV. Business had been slow, so I closed up shop a little earlier than usual.

"He and I had set the TV in a far corner of the front room of the shop, and after I put the 'closed' sign up in the front window I turned around to find it staring at me stupidly. Yes, *staring* at me. I know how odd that sounds, but it felt as though that old black and white had *eyes,* and it was *looking* at me. I mixed my first drink of the afternoon and sat drinking it in front of that set, debating with myself about whether or not to turn the damned thing on. After all, I hadn't even turned it on to see if it worked when the boy brought it in.

"I finished my drink, and walked over to it. My first impulse, bad as it may sound, was to slap a price tag on the damned thing, reopen the shop, and sell it to the first sucker who walked through the door. Because I was almost certain that the TV had somehow caused the deaths of its previous owners, I became so scared of it that none of that mattered to me. I just wanted it out of my shop.

"My *second* impulse, and the one I finally decided to act on, was to grab a sledgehammer and destroy it, beat it to pieces. Enough sense came into my head to make me realize people were dying because of this TV—I knew they were; that they had—and if I could destroy it, then it would all end. And I couldn't believe I had not thought of it before now.

"But before I destroyed it, I would turn it on. For some reason I still wanted to do that. With more than a little effort, I scooted it over near an electrical outlet—that sucker's heavy—and I plugged it in. Before I turned it on, I got the sledge from the back room. I was going to do the thing in one way or the other. A quick peek to see if it worked and then I'd ram that hammer through the picture tube.

When I turned it on there was nothing but white static on the screen, so I knew the thing worked. There wasn't a picture of any kind, but I hadn't expected one. I hadn't put any rabbit ears on it, and besides, I wasn't planning on watching anything, anyway. I was reaching down to turn it off when the man appeared on the screen."

George stopped and emptied the remainder of his drink. He rose from his chair and made another and returned, talking while he did this. "Even though I now realize what I saw that day was real, it was years before I could convince myself to accept it as the truth. I have always passed it off as old age setting in, or on my mind playing tricks on me...a number of various excuses and reasons. But, in the end, I guess my mind finally tired of denying the truth and hiding behind false asssumptions. It was real then, and it's real now, but in between, the incident wore a mask inside my mind so I couldn't see it. But it was there."

He stopped again and looked at him, and Paul, who thought George had aged twenty years over the past ten minutes or so, could only look back, unable to speak. He was fascinated with the story thus far. He could picture George in his mind, one hand resting on a sledgehammer, the other reaching out to turn the dial on the TV to 'off.'

But what happened after that? What had George seen?

As if in answer to his thoughts, George continued. "The man on the screen looked like a news announcer or something. He was sitting behind this big desk and looking straight at me, his face filled with hard lines of concentration. At first, I thought the set had picked up some station by accident. Except, to be announcing news, the guy was dressed funny. He wore a light purple suit over a white shirt and a bright pink tie. It wouldn't strike me until later that the man had been in color on a black and white set.

"I paid the whole thing no mind, only reached farther for the dial to turn it off...and that is when the man spoke to me."

He stopped and took another drink of bourbon.

"What did he say?" Paul asked, leaning forward in his chair.

"His exact words were: 'I wouldn't do that if *I* were you, Mr. Morrison. You would regret it forever.'" George shuddered as he said this.

Paul could only sit there, his mouth hanging open like a broken hinge.

"I was scared then," George said after a moment. "Scared plenty. Not only had the man *talked* to me, he knew what I was planning to do to the TV set. I jumped back several feet when he spoke, and after a few scared seconds I mustered up all the courage I could and turned the damned thing off. The man on the screen started to say something else, but I cut him off, picture and all, before he could. He had been looking right at me, Paul. *Right at me!*

"I was still jumpy and frightened after I'd turned the set off, but at least I couldn't feel his eyes on me. I could, you know... before. It made my scalp tingle. I was scared, but I still had enough of my wits left to know that the TV was still plugged into the wall. And so, when I picked up the sledge, I braced myself in front of the TV, intent on bashing the top of it instead of putting the hammer through the tube like I had planned." George paused here and once again hiked his bad leg up onto the table, rolling back the material of his pants. *"This* is what I got in return for not taking one small precaution; for not pulling the plug from the socket."

Paul looked once again at the roadmap of varicose veins and the lumpy, misshapen ankle. "You missed the TV and did that with the *sledgehammer?*"

"No, no," George said, and chuckled. "But believe me, I

would have preferred that over what happened."

"What *did* happen?"

"Well, I'm left-handed, and so when I reared back with the hammer, my right foot was slightly in front of me. What I failed to realize was that it was under the front of the television also, and before I could bring the hammer down from over my head the two front legs of that set fell away just as neatly as you please, pinning most of the weight of it on my ankle."

Paul, who remembered how heavy the TV was when he'd helped Richard unload it, breathed in deeply. "My God!"

"That's what *I* said. That, and a few other choice words. Needless to say, the hammer fell from my hands, and it took the last of my strength to move the TV off my foot. And *that,*" he finished, "is how my ankle got broken."

"And you think—?"

"I think that man inside the TV did it to me," George said. "To keep me from destroying the set and, ultimately, *him.*"

Paul had a slew of questions, but he chose the one he most wanted answered: "How do you think this guy…knew your name and was able to talk directly to you?"

George sighed and shook his head. "I know how it sounds, but if I knew how he did it, this whole mess would be a whole lot easier to straighten out. All I can do is make a few suggestions and theories about it, but of course it's nothing but speculation."

"Go on," Paul said, but inside he was thinking: *What is this?*

"The man is the key," George said. "That is one of the things I am almost sure of. The man is the key, and the TV set is, not the lock that the key fits…but the door." He looked at Paul. "Do you follow me?"

Paul nodded and said, "Then the lock would be…Richard?"

George shrugged. "Richard, or whoever owns the television for a while. Except, I don't think a person would even have to own it for the same thing to happened to them that happened to the people in these notebooks. It could have happened to *me,* and probably would have if I'd kept the thing turned on long enough."

"You mean—"

"I mean I think that man can somehow take control of the person who watches the TV. Not just control of his mind, but of his body, as well."

"Possession?"

"Not necessarily. He must manipulate them somehow, cause them to do things. Maybe he even causes them to kill, or to commit suicide. Hell, I just don't *know* for sure," he said loudly. "But it's got to be *something* like that. He knew my *name,* for Chrissakes!" He walked over to the kitchen counter, and instead of pouring another drink, he poured a cup of strong black coffee.

"It's more than just that, though," he said as he made his slow way back to the table. "That man doesn't kill people all by himself. He...manifests...somehow, in the TV set, and I believe that's as far as he goes, physically. I think he has someone else do the killing. Someone who *can* appear in the flesh, even though maybe they shouldn't be able to."

"But who could *that* be, other than the person watching the TV?" Paul asked.

What he saw in George Morrison's eyes was a knowledge much deeper than he had shown before, and for one fleeting moment he thought—was, in fact, *sure*—George hadn't told him everything that had happened the day his ankle had been broken. His belief was confirmed when George answered his question.

"Who? Why, people who are already dead," he said.

*****

13

Paul was on his way home, late-summer bugs spattering the car's windshield in the new moon's dark light.

Going through his mind were memories of what George had told him.

I think he has someone else do the killing. Someone who can appear in the flesh, even though maybe they shouldn't be able to.

People who are already dead.

What, exactly, did *that* mean?

It was the one question which raced repeatedly through his head, but it was one to which he didn't know the answer—and which George had not answered, shaking his head, and saying, "I don't know. I don't know."

And so Paul asked himself two more questions, and these also traveled through his mind relentlessly.

What has Richard gotten himself into?

What have I gotten *myself* into?

14

While two men in a small repair shop in downtown Jonesboro, were talking and exchanging ideas about a certain television set, two other men were *also* carrying on an interesting conversation.

Richard Raines, and the man in that certain television set.

Richard had called Tina a little over an hour ago, accepting her date. Now, the two men talked—Richard sitting on the sofa (without a drink for a change), and Jerry behind his desk—about what would transpire the next evening. They were going over everything for the third time, for Jerry had said he feared Richard would forget something if they didn't.

For Richard's part, his head had been reeling since he'd hung up the phone and Jerry told him Tina had a gun. That one thing opened wide the doors of reality for Richard. He felt a mixture of emotions: at first a fleeting terror that began in his stomach, then surprise *(how could she?)*, and regret *(she never loved me, not really)*.

But what he felt most, what he had been trying to keep under control since he'd hung up, was a blind, hateful anger that rose to the top of his mountain of feelings and crushed all others flat. The bitch really meant to go through with it.

Jerry told him she had a gun in her possession and planned on using it, but he wasn't sure exactly how. When Richard pressed him, Jerry said: "What I mean it, I'm not sure whether she plans to shoot you, or use the gun to make you do something that will get you killed. It could be either one."

"So, she's not sure herself?"

"Oh, she's sure, all right. I just couldn't pick up which one she was sure *of.*"

"Why not?"

"Sometimes," Jerry said. "it's very difficult to pick up the right network of thoughts. The person is thinking and concentrating so hard on one thought that it's often hard to see the thoughts and images that particular thought is hiding. That's what happened when you called her. She was concentrating hard on keeping her voice steady and innocent …and to keep from laughing. It was all she could think of."

"But why did she want to laugh?" For some reason, this bugged Richard to no end.

237

"Because," Jerry said. "Inside she is celebrating. She believes she can get away with it, that she *will* get away with it."

Those words had chilled Richard. It also angered him even more, if that was possible. She was so sure of herself, and it made him want to puke, if you wanted to call a spade a spade. It was a jealous feeling; she was sure of herself, but he didn't know what the fuck *he* was going to do. At that moment he had felt vulnerable and helpless.

But now it seemed as if Jerry had once again taken care of things. Above all, he had boosted Richard's confidence.

Now they were going over again what bothered him the most—the gun.

"You see," Jerry said, "you're covered either way it goes just as long as you carry a gun of your own."

"I already told you, I'm not taking a gun." This is the one thing Richard couldn't bring himself to do; he was so mad that a gun wouldn't do the job any justice. He wanted to strangle Tina with his bare hands. "I'll kill her with these!" He held up his hands in front of the TV.

"What about hand prints around her neck? Jerry said. "You'd never get away with it."

"I don't care about that, anymore," Richard said. "I just want the bitch dead, and I want to do it myself."

Jerry held out his hands. "Okay, Richard. Okay, you win. You don't have to take a gun."

Richard sighed, and felt his anger abate somewhat.

"I can only tell you this much for sure," Jerry said, "because it's about all I was able to pick up clearly; if she takes you to an unpopulated area, if she drives toward the city limits, she only plans to take you away from where there might be people and shoot you like a dog. If she doesn't, then I guess you're on your own, because she could do anything."

"So what you're saying is—"

"What I'm saying is, if you feel nervous about what she may

be planning while you're at dinner, then *you* suggest the two of you go somewhere secluded. That would be your best move." He paused and looked at Richard, who thought at the moment Jerry's eyes might contain the fires of hell itself. They were so blazing and red that the fury they held was nearly incomprehensible to Richard. Jerry spoke again: "And when you get there you *kill* her! You do it any way you *want!* But *don't* let her catch you with your guard down. Be smarter than that. The gun she's toting is a .357 Magnum, loaded with hollow-point bullets, and you can only screw up once. That baby will leave an exit hole the size of a regulation frisbee."

"I understand," Richard said. "And I'll be careful." He lit a cigarette and inhaled, then let the smoke shoot out of his lungs in a thick jet.

"And while you're being careful," Jerry said, "remember to show no knowledge of what she's up to. Play along with her lead through dinner, but after that play it by instinct. The element of surprise is your best weapon—gun or no gun—so try to keep it in mind."

"Okay," Richard said. He butted his cigarette in the overflowing ashtray next to the sofa.

Jerry eyed the ashtray ruefully. "Don't forget to take care of preparations before you leave for dinner tomorrow evening."

"I won't," Richard said. "In fact, I plan to do it all tonight, so..." He rose from his spot on the cluttered sofa.

"Yes," Jerry said, taking the hint. "Go ahead and turn me off so you can get started." He looked to the left of his desk as if he saw something interesting there. "I have plenty to do myself, so I'll talk to you later."

"Okay," Richard said, reaching for the volume control. "Good night, Jerry."

"Good night, Richard."

White, snowy static filled the screen and Richard turned the set off. Silence set in like a dead weight, and he felt his head clear dramatically. That happened a lot whenever he turned the TV off, and it was still something he enjoyed. He usually missed Jerry's company, also. He felt nakedly alone when the television was off. The condo might have been empty entirely, and he a ghost that haunted it until the next time he turned on the set.

He surveyed the living room. Beer cans and whiskey bottles, all empty, covered every available surface, and the sofa and chair were cloaked with dirty clothes, soiled wrappers from TV dinners and other food, and potato chip bags—most of them half-full or better, uneaten remnants of half-forgotten meals.

Had Paul been in here when the place was such a mess? Richard guessed so, since he had been by just this morning. And just what did *he* suspect was going on?

Divorce lag, that's what. He probably thinks I'm depressed about the divorce. In fact, knowing Paul, I'm sure that's what he thinks.

No matter, he thought now. *I'm making preparations.*

He began by lifting the ashtray from the occasional table and taking it into the kitchen to dump in the trashcan. But the can was already full, and even more trash had spilled over its sides onto the floor. There was a ripe, unpleasant odor in the confines of the kitchen.

Richard sighed. "I'm in for a long night," he said out loud. His voice sounded eerie in the quiet apartment.

He went to the cabinet under the sink and pulled out a box of garbage bags. Then he went methodically about, first the kitchen and then the living room, picking up trash, cans, and bottles and depositing them in the plastic bags. It took just over twenty minutes for him to finish that, and by the time he was done he had filled six bags and part of another.

He whistled while he worked, and after he set the bags of waste outside in the dumpster, he got out the vacuum cleaner and the dust mop. The place had to look like it always had. Which meant it had to be cleaned.

No suspicions needed to be aroused. And so far, he thought none had.

The place had to be cleaned, and so he cleaned.

He didn't want anything to seem out of the ordinary, or out of place, when it was found that his ex-wife had been murdered.

*****

Part Four

On the Realm of Death

Three may keep a secret,
if two of them are dead.

—Benjamin Franklin
Poor Richard's Almanac

1

September 16, 4:35p.m.

In the early hours of the one evening that would stay in Paul Frazier's mind forever—even though it would be years before he would finally be able to convince himself to accept the events had actually happened and were real, and not simply something that his tired mind invented—he decided on the spur of the moment to visit his neighbor and friend.

Something was not right with Richard. Paul had become convinced the television was largely responsible for his friend's condition, but he thought there might be something else wrong, as well. And so his sudden visit this evening was more than just one man's urge to share the companionship of his best friend. It was a visit caused by a curious mind. A curious mind, yet one which was slowly becoming convinced it was breaking, wearing down, traveling somewhere beyond such cultured things as mere curiosity.

It was also a mind with a new nose for certain dangers—such as visiting someone while their television set was on.

So, when he strolled up the short walk to Richard's front door and rang the bell, he already had a solution invented, on the chance the TV set was on. It was a ploy George had told him might work: he would stand out on the walk and politely invite Richard over to his place for a few drinks, all the while thinking as hard as he could about his wife's smiling face—a face he had fallen in love with the first time he'd seen it.

Such thoughts ran through his mind as he waited for

Richard to come to the door, and when he did Paul was surprised to hear music wafting out from inside the apartment.

"Hey, Richie," he said, trying his best to sound nothing more than casual as the door was opened.

"Paul," Richard said, smiling. "Come on in, guy." He opened the door further. "What brings you over here so far from home?"

Paul couldn't help but smile. That was an old joke the two of them had shared ever since they'd become next-door neighbors. Paul held up the six-pack of beer he'd picked up on the way home from work that day. "Thought you might join me for a beer."

Richard eyed the beer speculatively and grinned. "Sure. Come on in," he said, stepping back and allowing Paul access through the door.

Richard had a habit of having both the TV and the stereo on at the same time, so the first thing Paul looked for as he walked into the apartment was the television set. There it was by the bookshelves—and it was off, the green screen dark and mute. The second thing he noticed put his guard up and surprised him at the same time. Yesterday morning the living room looked as though Richard had literally *lived* in it for days—bottles, cans, and trash all over the furniture and floor, and, through the doorway into the kitchen, Paul had seen a gigantic mess in there, as well.

Now, however, the whole place—at least the front room where he stood—looked as neat and orderly as it ever had. The room still had that partially full look, as though someone was only halfway finished moving in (or out), but it was in great shape. It was picked up, vacuumed, dusted, and looked fairly cozy in spite of the missing furnishings.

The change in it was a complete turnaround.

Richard closed the door and Paul gathered his thoughts enough to hand him the beer, after pulling one from the plastic ring. "Here you go, man. Grab one and stick 'em in the fridge. They aren't as cold as they need to be."

"I," Richard said and smiled, "would have to agree on that one. But a luke-warm beer is better than no beer." They both laughed as Richard went into the kitchen—and Paul realized with a faint glimmer of hope how their joint laughter was not forced, or filled with the slightest amount of tension. Instead, it rolled from them effortlessly, as though it were the most natural thing in the world. *Which is the way,* he thought fleetingly, *it should be.*

He sat down on the sofa and Richard returned with a beer, taking a seat across from him in the easy chair.

"So, what's up?" Richard said.

Paul squirmed backward a little on the sofa, into a more comfortable position. "Not a whole lot," he said. In his mind, he wanted to say: *A lot is up. You're in the middle of it, too, whether you know it or not, and for some reason I think you* do *know it. It's on your face.* Because it *did* seem that way. He thought in just a few short seconds about the past two minutes since he'd been here, and it seemed Richard's trite mannerisms (the joke included) and his conversational tone of voice was totally wrong. It wasn't forced—the laughter certainly hadn't been—but instead it seemed contrived; as though he was being his typical self in order to hide something atypical of him. Squirming on the sofa some more, Paul said the only thing he could think of now that he'd caught what he felt to be the true nature of Richard's behavior. "I'm sorry, again, about your job, man."

For a second, Richard only stared at him with vacant eyes, although the smile remained on the lower part of his face. Then he said, "Oh, hell. Don't worry about *that.* It wasn't your fault, you know."

"Have you found anything else yet?" He half-expected the same fury from Richard he had shown yesterday, when Paul had apologized about his job. Instead, Richard surprised him by turning the conversation in yet another direction.

"Nah," Richard said. He took a sip of beer. "I have plenty of time for that, and I *do* have three weeks of severance pay coming. Besides, I've been too busy to even think about it much."

But what have you been busy doing? Paul wanted to ask. "It sure *looks* like you've been busy," he said innocently, glancing around the room.

A light seemed to come on in Richard's eyes, almost an excited look. "Yeah, I guess I got tired of looking at it all damn day. I'm not a very good bachelor. But hell..."

"So *that's* what it is!" Paul said jokingly. "Got a little female company coming over later, huh?" He laughed and took another drink. He knew he was taking a chance by cracking a joke and kidding around, but he thought it might soften Richard up a bit. He could clearly feel the tension lurking behind the excited look that had come into his eyes.

He was just horsing around, but now he saw Richard was grinning, almost shyly.

"Am I right?" Paul said. "Is that what it is?"

Richard's grin broadened into a smile. "Well, I guess you could say it's something like that. I've got a date." He rose from the chair and went into the kitchen.

Paul noticed the lines of thought on Richard's face as he did this, but only passingly. He was too awestruck with what he had just told him. A date. He actually had a *date*. All Paul could think about was the way Richard had avoided talking to him about the divorce. This had worried him at first, and he had come to the conclusion that Richard would talk to him about it only after he'd worked it out himself first. Evidently, he had worked it out pretty well. Paul could hardly believe it.

And another thought struck him. Stout in its brevity, it passed through his mind in less than a second; maybe Richard *was* getting back to his old self. Maybe George Morrison, whom Paul had only known, he reminded himself, a short time, was wrong. Wrong about everything. Perhaps he, George that is, was nothing but some sort of scam artist, and he had yet to figure out what he was being scammed about.

This led to other thoughts, and no matter how Paul looked at it, he inevitably came back to the same conclusion—no matter how good this other idea sounded: He *believed* what George had told him. He believed every bit of it. He knew it was irrational to indulge in such ways of thinking, and even worse to believe in something for which there *was* no rational explanation, but if there was one thing he was certain of—no matter how much Richard's actions made him want to believe otherwise—it was that George Morrison had not lied to him about the television.

It was easier to believe George than it was to believe Richard had made a complete turnaround literally overnight.

Richard returned with another beer, and Paul decided to keep the conversation on the same road it was currently traveling.

"Well?" he said.

"Well, what?"

"Who's the lucky girl?"

Richard turned his head and looked at the floor to the left of him, and although he was still grinning, the grin was not as broad. And to Paul, this one *did* look forced.

"You wouldn't know her," Richard finally said. "Just someone I met the other night."

But where *did you meet her?* Paul thought. *I haven't heard your truck go anywhere at night in nearly a week. So,* where *did you meet this mysterious woman?*

"Oh," he said, sensing Richard's desire to drop the subject.

"How are things at the office?" Richard said. "Patrick still the same 'ol shithead?"

Paul managed a smile even though he didn't feel like smiling just now. "Yeah, I guess so. You know Patrick. He'll probably never change."

"I know you're right, there," Richard said.

Paul visited another thirty minutes, having two more beers. Richard stopped after his second one, saying he didn't want to 'smell like a brewery' all night. The two of them talked about a variety of things, most of them events that had happened at the agency over the years, and Paul thought Richard became more relaxed as it neared, then passed, five o'clock. The only times Richard became fidgety, and less involved in the conversation, was when he glanced at his television set, sitting dark and silent.

The third time this happened, Paul grew uncomfortable and made up an excuse to go home, citing the fact that 'Margie will be worrying about me.'

Now Richard stood framed in the doorway and Paul stood in front of him on the walk outside. A light breeze had kicked up, and in the gathering twilight several dark clouds were rolling in from the northwest.

"No need to hurry off," Richard said for the second time.

Paul noticed a look in Richard's eyes. It was there for only a second and then gone, but to Paul it looked like a plea: Richard really wanted him to stay.

Yet, it had only been there for a second, and maybe not even there at all. He thought he quite possibly could have imagined it—wishful thinking, perhaps—and so he cast it from his mind without another thought. "I'd really better go," he said. "Besides, I'm sure you want to get ready for your date."

"Yeah," Richard said, and now Paul *did* see something in his friend's eyes, and this time it wasn't his imagination—whether the other was or not. Richard's eyes seemed to look *through* him, as though he was looking at something or someplace far away.

When the detached look lingered, Paul took the opportunity to fill the vacuuming silence. "I'll see you later, man."

"Yeah," Richard repeated.

As Paul turned to walk home, he noticed Richard's eyes still held that vacant look.

As he made the short walk, Paul thought about his visit. All in all, he thought Richard had done a decent job of trying to be his old self—the old self Paul had hoped to see—but in the end had not succeeded. Not really.

But what he thought about the most was the fact—because he knew it, *felt* it, to be true—that he was hiding something; some secret Paul didn't care to know—didn't *want* to know. It was bad enough knowing that his best friend had lied to him.

But why?

Although he wasn't yet aware of it, he would find out before the evening was over, and he would realize long before then what he should have seen, and known, on the brief visit to Richard's home.

2

7:15p.m.

Although it hadn't rained all evening, it had threatened to since four-thirty or so, when dark, heavy clouds began to move into the skies over Jonesboro. Now, at a quarter past seven o'clock, the cloud cover blanketed the entire city, although it was too dark to see it from Tina's car as she began the trip across town to Richard's condo. It might not have rained yet, but she had listened to the weather forecast before leaving her small apartment, and she knew it called for rain later in the evening.

This was not the primary thing on her mind, though. Her

mind was on what lay ahead of her tonight. She was only four blocks from her apartment, but for the fifth time patted her purse with her right hand. The purse lay on the seat next to her, and her hand traced the hard shape of the .357 Magnum concealed inside it.

The feel of the gun brought her comfort, but she was nevertheless filled with anxiety. It had hit her almost the instant she got into the car. *Are you really going through with this?* She asked herself. It was funny, but for the last eight hours or so she hadn't thought about *not* going through with her plans. Now, however, with the reality of what she was contemplating hitting home in her mind, she found herself really looking at that question, and looking at it hard.

She tried to remind herself to think about the money, but the portion of her mind she was telling would have no part of it. That part was thinking about why she was planning to hurt—to kill—a person she'd once cared for deeply, had loved as her husband.

She remembered the day, shortly after their honeymoon, when he had taken her across town for her first look at the condominium that she, at the time, knew nothing of. She recalled how coy he was about where they were going that day, how he said he was taking her on a joyride. She had reached over, between his legs. He'd had an erection. "Ooh, this *does* feel like it could take me for a ride," she said. He had laughed and told her, "Not *that* kind of ride. Later, though..." and he leered at her. They had both laughed, and right after that he had pulled into a driveway and stopped. "So, what do you think?" he asked. Tina had looked up and seen they were parked in the driveway of a beautiful condo in a wealthy neighborhood. Confused, she asked, "Who lives here?" To this day, she could not forget what he said next, nor the happiness and excitement it had brought her. "We do," he said. "Welcome to our new home." She hugged him then. Hugged him hard.

They got out of the car and he produced a key from his pocket. "Want to look inside?" She had, and they did. It culminated with the two of them making wild, passionate love on the living room floor. For her, it had been the best sex of the whole marriage.

When did it go bad? she often wondered.

Now, in the confines of her car, she realized she finally had an answer to that question. *You know when. It started with Kerry.* Yes, maybe so, but Richard had become so preoccupied with his work at the time, and paid little attention to her sexual needs and wants. The lovemaking had been cursory for a while, one or two nights a week, with little satisfaction for her. She was a highly sexed individual. She understood he had just started the best job of his career, at JAC, but she'd told herself over and over for the last year or so that he should have been able to sense her needs, and act on them. Not only in the sex department, but by just spending good, quality time with her, building their relationship in a strong way, a block at a time, until it would be unbreakable. Later, in retrospect, she halfway entertained the idea that maybe she should have told him these things, or at least thrown a few brick in there, herself.

At the time, however, she convinced herself it wasn't her fault, and had then proceeded to…what? Take revenge? Everything else aside, that's exactly what it had been. Richard had always been a satisfying lover—was great in bed, in fact—but still…

And was this—what she was contemplating and carrying out now—any different than simple revenge?

"Maybe it isn't," she told herself out loud as she pulled the car onto Crestwood. "but that bastard deserves this. He *hurt* me." And he had. He had left her (kicked her ass out was closer to the truth), and taken away everything she needed to get by in the world. Especially money.

Think of the money, she told herself again.

But it was more than just the money, now.

She had been with more than a few men since the divorce, sure, but she was well on the way to cleaning up her act with Biff Larento. She had been well on her way to falling in love with him. Now he had been taken away from her, along with everything else.

And was Richard responsible for *that?*

Not possible, she told herself. But she for some reason still believed it *was* possible, that he *was* responsible for Biff's death. The feeling had been with her from the time she had found out her lover was dead. It was like a tiny flame inside her; one she could feed and fuel at will into a blazing inferno. She had no physical way to prove it, but she *knew* Richard was to blame.

He was to blame for that, and for everything else she'd been through.

She told herself this with total conviction, and with that conviction—contrived or not, true or not—was able to lay past thoughts about Richard to rest for good. The way he had been, the way he could have been, didn't really matter. It was all his fault.

He was going to pay.

He was going to die for what he'd done.

She swore it.

Thinking these thoughts, she pulled her car into his driveway, a few minutes early for their seven-thirty dinner date.

3

7:35p.m.

Paul Frazier and George Morrison sat around the table in the small kitchen of George's combination repair shop and home. The table this evening was bare except for two cups that held steaming coffee. The untidy stacks of newspaper clippings and notebooks were now tucked into a drawer in George's office. They had no need of them tonight.

After leaving Richard's place earlier in the evening, Paul had sat at home for more than two hours, thinking about what Richard might have been hiding, and coming up with very little that seemed to fit. The first thing he thought—and also the most logical—was that he was trying to hide the television set. Of course, he hadn't done that physically, but he thought Richard might have been nervous because of what the TV could do. Or, put more aptly, what the *man* in the TV could do. But, as far as Paul could see, that made no sense, because he himself had yet to see what the man could do, and Richard certainly hadn't shown him.

The second thought was that Richard was hiding something out of guilt. Guilt about the date? Paul didn't think so. More than likely it was guilt over what he knew about the TV.

But somehow that didn't sound quite right, either.

The more he thought about it, the more he began to believe it *was* something about the date. Richard had not volunteered the name of the lucky lady, for one thing. Paul could see no clear reason for this. He and Richard had been friends for years and Richard had never, with the exception of the divorce and its aftermath, had reservations about telling him *anything,* once he got started talking about it. At least Paul didn't *think* so.

So, with whom did Richard have a date? And did it even matter? He may just be overthinking that part.

Paul had gone through a mental file of every woman who worked at JAC and came up empty. With the exception of two secretaries, all of the women there were married. Besides, the woman was someone Richard said he had just met 'the other night.' Another dead end.

Finally, after two hours, Paul decided on a course of action. He got into his car and drove over to the appliance shop. Maybe George would have some insight into what all of this could be about, even though Paul believed he knew Richard a *hell* of a lot better than George did. But it would be worth a shot.

Now, the two of them sat at George's small table, sipping coffee, and Paul told him about his visit with Richard.

"So, you're worried Richard is hiding something about his *date?*" George asked. Paul didn't notice it at first, but George's tone was nearly incredulous; as though he was asking him something he should already know—like his first name.

Paul meticulously put into words everything he thought about it, and all the different ways he had looked at it; each separate angle and idea, all the theories he had considered and discarded.

"Finally, I decided to come over here and see if you could make anything of it," he finished.

George was looking at him with an almost stunned look, but one which also seemed to hold some morbid sense of excitement and dawning knowledge. Slowly, he said: "I'm glad you did, Paul. I only wish it had been sooner. I'm afraid we might have wasted precious time. I hope we haven't."

Paul was confused. "What? What do you mean?"

George rose from the table in a hurry, and that confused him even more. "What is it?" he was now beginning to think that the old man was having a heart attack or something.

George walked rapidly to the sink and drained his still-full cup of coffee into it. "Don't you see?" he said, running a liver-spotted hand through his hair. "Don't you *see?*"

But Paul didn't. He was honestly puzzled. Later he would think he'd spent too much time worrying about his relationship with Richard and had failed to see the obvious. To a certain extent, he was correct. "See *what?*"

"*Tina* is Richard's date. *Tina!* That's why he wouldn't tell you," George said. He looked up at the ceiling, his eyes moving rapidly, as if following the flight of an angry fly.

"Oh, it all fits so well. We already know Tina is planning to kill him."

Sudden comprehension swept over Paul. "Then this also fits in with what Tina told me on the phone several days ago, when she called the office for Richard."

"And what was that?" George asked.

Paul recounted his and Tina's phone conversation. "And what fits," he said when he finished, "is her saying the two of them were thinking seriously about getting back together."

"Why didn't you tell Richard this?" George asked sternly. "You just left his house. Why didn't you *warn* him?"

"Why didn't you warn any of the people in those notebooks of yours?" Paul returned angrily. It was a low shot and he knew it, and part of his anger—a very large part, in fact—surfaced because he knew he *should* have told Richard. And no one should have had to tell him to do it.

The room was silent for what seemed like hours, although it couldn't have been more than a few seconds. Paul calmed down a bit and said: "I told you what he said to me about her. Richard was furious with Tina."

"Then why? Why didn't you tell him what she said?" George countered calmly.

Paul dropped his head. Here was the moment of truth, then. He had known this was coming as soon as the conversation turned in this direction, and inside he regretted his anger toward George a moment ago, even though he knew it was justified. "I couldn't," he said finally. He raised his head and looked at George. "She blackmailed me."

"She *what?*" Now George's voice was *really* incredulous. He plopped down into his chair.

Paul said: "Over the phone she mentioned an incident to me which happened a few years back, at my boss's New Year's Eve party, only he wasn't my boss then. She told me if I mentioned to Richard what she had told me about the two of them getting back together, she would tell him what happened at that party."

George was quiet, and Paul went on, speaking slowly: "It was a New Year's Eve party and everyone was drunk, to say the least. I know *I* was. It was early in the morning, about one-thirty. The new year was in, lots of people had already left, and even more were passed out in various places in the house. Richard was among those who were out for the night. He'd been out before the old year. Tina and I were among the handful or so who hadn't left and were still awake, although everyone was too drunk to know it, or care.

"I had gone upstairs to the bathroom—someone was passed out in the one downstairs—and as I was zipping up my pants, in walked Tina. I guess I'd forgotten to lock the door. But, instead of turning around and leaving, she turned around and shut the door—and locked it."

Paul took a sip of his coffee. "She had this look in her eyes," he continued. "It wasn't a drunk look. I had seen this one before. She had made what I thought were passes at me several times before this night, and I had turned her down repeatedly, one way or another, even getting almost rude about it. I knew it made her angry when I did, but there was just no way I would ever do that to Richard. But for some reason, that night at the party was different. Call it whatever you like. It wasn't that I *wanted* to do anything, because I had sworn to myself I never would. Maybe it was the excessive amount of liquor I had drunk, maybe it was the atmosphere, who knows? At any rate, I didn't say anything as she advanced toward me, and neither did she. She may have caught me off-guard, but I didn't say anything."

Paul stopped and exhaled a long breath. "Before I knew it, she had undone my pants and was down there...you know...giving me...a blowjob. I don't know. I've always heard that a stiff peter has no conscience, and I guess it's true. Anyway, she took me all the way, and when it was over she left, looking back at me and smiling before she closed the bathroom door. There was some…c—, you know, on her chin. I'll never forget that. After she left, I sat down in the corner formed by the bathtub and the wall, and I cried. I might have been drunk, but I felt terrible at what I had let happen. It was something that could never be taken back. It had happened. And the way she smiled at me as she left…a secretive smile, as though she somehow knew the experience would come in handy some time down the road when she needed it to. And I guess it did, because there was no way I could *ever* tell Richard about that. I would never be able to handle the guilt.

"And I guess I haven't," he finished. "Because when she mentioned the party on the phone, I knew that I *still* couldn't bring myself to tell Richard about what happened. After finding out his wife was sleeping around with more than one man, it would have devastated him to know that *I* had been one of those men."

He fumbled with his coffee cup and then finally looked up at George. "Now do you see why I didn't tell him about what she said when she called? Why I couldn't?"

George nodded. "I understand. And I also see that you really love your friend."

Paul was surprised to feel a strong sense of relief now that someone else knew what had happened at that party, and he was even more surprised to find himself close to tears. He wiped one hand absently down the side of his face. "So, why would Richard make a date with Tina, after the way he talked about her to me, the way he said he *felt* about her?"

"That," George said, "is why we have to hurry. I'm afraid we don't have a lot of time to stop it." He left the kitchen and went into another room. Paul heard a door open, heard him rummaging around, and then the door clicked shut.

When he returned, he was cradling something in his arms. Paul was shocked at the three items George put on the table in front of him—two handguns, and a grenade. He had never seen a grenade before, not in real life, but he had watched enough TV and movies to identify one. The guns were not revolvers. They had magazines that slid upward into the grip. He noticed George sticking two more of these magazines into the pockets of the heavy jacket he had come out of the room wearing.

Paul found it hard to say anything, but he finally found his voice. "What is all of *this* for?"

George sighed. "This," he said, handing one of the guns, grip first, to Paul, "is a .44 Magnum, and it's for you. *"This,"* he said, holding up the other, identical gun, "is *also* a .44 Magnum...and it's for me." He tucked the handgun into one of the oversized pockets of the jacket.

"What about that?" Paul asked, pointing to the Army-green grenade.

"This," George said, holding up the grenade, being very delicate with it, "is a hand grenade, compliments of the United States Army and the Korean War. And *it*...is for the TV. Now, let's go. Let's stop it all, before it's too late." He started for the door.

Paul got up and followed him. "But who or what are the guns *for?*"

"For protection," George said as he opened the door to the back parking lot. "We have to stop Tina, for one thing, and she has a gun. I don't know about Richard."

Paul grabbed him by the shoulder and spun him around. *"What do you mean?"*

George sighed again. "Don't you get it? Do I have to spell it out for you? Tina is planning to kill Richard, but *he* is planning to kill *her!* Now, let's go. You'll have to drive." George got into the passenger side of Paul's vehicle.

Paul, walking numbly to his side of the car, was again

shocked, this time by what George had just said. He wanted to chide himself for not having seen all of this himself, but he didn't have sufficient time; George was impatiently honking the horn.

No matter, there would be plenty of time for such thoughts later. At least, he hoped.

He got in and the two of them headed across town in the direction of Richard's apartment.

And mine, too, Paul thought. *Mine, too. What a mess. What a royal mess!*

It was 7:50.

4

7:29p.m.

Richard got into his ex-wife's car at 7:29p.m. He had met her at the door, jacket in arm, ready. He hadn't invited her inside because he didn't want her to see the television. But not only that—he didn't want her inside his apartment at all. For some reason he felt she knew what he had planned, and he feared if she entered the premises, she might intentionally plant something in there, some shred of evidence, on the off-chance that her plan failed and his was successful. Paranoid thinking, but there it was.

But more than that, he didn't want her trying to execute her plan in the place they had shared for more than three years— and he didn't want to kill her in his own home. That, he knew, would be hanging himself.

The two of them said their cordial 'hello's' at the door (Richard wincing inside at how attractive she looked in a pleasant outfit that accented her long legs), and then he got into her car.

One thought played over and over in his mind as he did this: *Why didn't you tell Paul the truth while you had the chance?*

This thought bothered him because, although he'd earlier felt resentment toward his friend, he had, in the end, wanted Paul to stay. He had felt a sudden and overwhelming urge to tell him everything that had happened since he'd bought the television set. Part of him wanted to put aside all of the weird tendencies he'd been feeling, and just cry on his friend's shoulder; talk to him in the way the two of them always had before the divorce. His rational mind recognized how he had alienated Paul since the moment he'd walked in on Tina and another man and found them entwined in a lover's embrace (and his mind said as it always did, *No, they weren't "entwined in a lover's embrace." They were* fucking). He had subsequently found out about the other men—during a loud argument, when Tina had laid it all out, similar to events in his dream more than a week ago—and from that point on, until he purchased the television, he had pictured her, in his mind, with virtually every man he saw, and that included Paul. He knew he was wrong to think that about his friend, but at the time he'd been in a jealous rage which he had, fortunately, been able to keep suppressed.

While Paul was visiting this afternoon, Richard had been more than a little nervous about him being in the same room as the TV. Wasn't *that* silly, he told himself. Soon after that, he was able to convince the tantalizing part of his mind that the only reason he was nervous was because the TV was off, and Jerry was not with him.

Outside his apartment, however, his nervousness had been abruptly replaced with anxiety, and a lot of the old feelings came back. He'd seen in Paul the friend he had, and he wanted him to stay. Perhaps for the chance that the night's inevitable events could be thwarted somehow. Part of him was frightened at the task that lay ahead of him.

"So, how have you been?" Tina asked as she drove down Crestwood to the intersection of Dregger Boulevard. She looked the way she always had—picture perfect. Her hair was styled back and up in a long, feathered ponytail (which had always been his favorite look), and she had the perfect amount of makeup applied to her high cheekbones and her pouty mouth. Yet in her eyes, Richard saw an awareness; he saw that she wasn't able to effectively hide the story her eyes showed—everything was just a put-on, as he'd been told.

"I've been okay," he answered her. "Just sitting around the house, reading, drinking." He shifted in his seat. "How about you?" He knew this was nothing but false formalities and he found he hated it.

"Work has been keeping me pretty busy," she said and laughed girlishly.

"Where are we headed, anyway?" he asked. The irony of the question never entered his mind. If it had, he might have asked it sooner—like two years ago.

"I thought we'd go to The Faria. If that's okay with you," she added.

"That's fine," he said, and settled back more comfortably in his seat. He forced a smile. "The Faria it is."

They arrived there within ten minutes, and soon were being seated by the Maitre'd.

They were given a table just two over from the one Richard and Paul had shared nine days ago, when they'd celebrated the successful presentation over expensive champagne. This fact did not escape him. Briefly, he looked back on that day with a feeling not unlike a dreary homesickness. It had been his first opportunity to tell Paul about the television, and what he had seen on it. Paul had certainly been willing to listen to anything he said that day. He had just blown the opportunity.

Now he found himself wishing he could take back that chance. Perhaps he wouldn't be in the situation he was now in;

dinner with his ex-wife, and then...what? Death? Certainly. But whose—his, or hers? He would have to stay alert the rest of the night if he wanted to avert his own end.

Their waiter brought two menus to the table, along with glasses of water, and in a few minutes came back and took their orders. Richard ordered a medium-rare steak, baked potato, and a salad. After just the slightest pause for consideration, he ordered a bottle of *Corona* as well. Tina ordered a garden salad and iced tea, and while they waited for their food they talked idly.

"A salad is all you're having?" Richard said casually.

"Yes. But you know me. I'll be lucky if I can finish even that." She laughed that girlish laugh again. Richard thought the laugh was a mask, hiding her nervousness. It was not her usual laugh, and he didn't think something so natural as a laugh could be changed easily. But one thing that hadn't changed was her appetite—she had never been a big eater.

The waiter brought their drinks, and as Richard took the first sip of his beer, Tina excused herself and made her way to the far side of the room, where the restrooms were located.

Nervousness, he thought, noticing with more than a little surprise that she had left her purse on the table.

5

Once inside the ladies' room, Tina immediately peered into each of the five stalls lined along one wall. Empty. She was alone in the small room.

She went over to the wash basins and gripped one of the porcelain sinks with both hands, looking at herself in the large mirror on the wall above it. She was shaking all over and could feel a think sheen of sweat break out beneath her clothes.

She ran water into the basin, letting it run over her hands and wrists. In the past, this always stopped sudden sweats such as this one. It helped some now, but she still shook visibly. "Calm down, girl," she told herself out loud. Her voice seemed to echo and boom in the deserted restroom.

The fact was, she was frightened. Richard certainly couldn't know what she had planned, but what frightened her—what made her so nervous she shook—was the uncanny feeling she had that he just *might*. In fact, she was almost to the point where she was certain he *did*.

That feeling had first crept into her mind when Richard got into her car. He looked nice, dressed in a cashmere sweater and twill slacks, his hair combed back neatly, and she had admired—not for the first time—his youthful looks and his strong sex appeal. Those had always been a turn-on for her.

But his eyes.

His eyes were full of what looked like either knowledge of some sort, or a strange curiosity; she could sense that his guard was up. But shouldn't it be, after what they'd been through in recent months? Her feeling had ultimately formed itself into a coherent thought: *He knows! He knows!*

But that was ridiculous, wasn't it? There was no way he could know. It just wasn't possible.

After they were seated in the restaurant, she remembered that she'd had that same eerie feeling yesterday, when they talked on the phone. Her rational mind entertained the idea—and she thought it a probable one—that these thoughts were more than simply imaginary feelings or paranoia; perhaps they were attributed to instinct. Yet, although she usually trusted her instincts, she feared trusting this particular one; she feared that the feeling would turn out to be true.

However, she realized there was a first time for everything and if, by chance, her instincts were wrong, she didn't want to blow everything by being a nervous wreck all evening. If he *didn't* know or suspect anything, she certainly didn't need to let her actions give her away.

She had to calm down before she could even *think* about returning to the table, and she would have to do it quickly. Their food would arrive shortly, and she had already been in here longer than was normal for her. No need to let him think she was doing anything more than freshening up.

She splashed cold water on her face and that helped bring some of her color back. It also marginally soothed her nervousness and she found, after taking a few deep breaths, that she would be able to leave the restroom and return to the table. She might, even, be able to carry out the rest of her plan. The confident tone of the thought caused her abated shakes to slow, and then stop completely.

Finish dinner, she thought. *It won't be very long before it will all be over.*

She tacked a smile on her face—the sort of smile she often used at work—and left the ladies' room.

6

When Tina returned, the food was being put on the table and Richard was crushing out a cigarette in a crystal ashtray. She took her seat, a slight look of embarrassment on her face.

Richard gave the waiter a ten-dollar bill. "Thank you. Could you bring me another *Corona?*"

"Certainly," the waiter said, and bowed slightly. "And thank you."

They began to eat, and Richard was surprised at how ravenous he was. Earlier he hadn't felt all that hungry, but his appetite had apparently been laying dormant, waiting for the first bite of steak to bring it roaring to life. He ended up ordering a side of baked shrimp.

They finished their meal and Tina sipped her tea while Richard smoked and nursed his third beer (he'd used the second one to wash down his meal).

"I've never been so full," he lied. "That was delicious."

"Yes, it was," Tina said. The waiter came and removed the dinner dishes, and she propped her elbows up and leaned forward slightly. "Remember the last time we were in here together?"

"How could I forget?" Richard said as he remembered.

The two of them had eaten dinner one night in early winter of last year, washing down crab legs and lobster with more than three pitchers of beer. Soon they had both been singing horribly modified renditions of several *Lynyrd Skynyrd* songs. They had subsequently been asked to leave by the Maitre'd, and they laughed and sang all the way to the door, feeling the other customers' frowns and not caring. He had yet to find out about her infidelity, and he thought now that night had been the last time the two of them really had fun together, in total enjoyment of each other's company.

He ordered another *Corona*, and they spent the next thirty minutes recounting other things they'd done together in the past, none of them as glamorous as the night at The Faria last year. There *were* better times in their history, but both seemed to stay away from those by unspoken mutual agreement, and stick to the neutral events that wouldn't hurt or scar. While Tina prattled on, his mind wandered repeatedly away from the conversation and focused instead on what might happen next this evening. After careful consideration, he took the initiative and told her that he was ready to leave.

She agreed, and stood back to let him pay the bill when they got to the cashier. *And she was the one who asked* me *out,* he thought to himself. He paid the bill.

Rain was forecast for the evening, and outside the first drops began to fall, and thundered rolled off to the north. The wind also picked up, and it blew fat drops onto the pavement and their skin with stinging force. Tina held her purse over her head and the two of them dashed to her car as the rain came down harder. They closed the doors just as a thunder-clap shook the sky and the rain became a downpour.

Tina started the car, and although she didn't tell him where they were going—and he didn't ask—Richard was not surprised when she turned left out of the parking lot, onto a route that would take them outside the city limits.

It was nine o'clock.

7

8:00p.m.

As Paul and George pulled into the driveway in front of Richard's apartment, they felt their faint hopes of saving Richard lifted: his truck was in the driveway. Also, it looked as though the lights were on in the front room. The light from the bay window spilled out onto the concrete drive in an orangish glow that seemed to blend in not at all with the gray, dark, cloud-covered night.

"Looks like he's still here," Paul said as he turned the motor off and doused the headlights.

"Maybe," George said. "But maybe not." To Paul, he looked tired and drained, as though he was a five-year-old boy who had just spent the last eight hours or so walking doggedly around a twelve-acre carnival and was now ready to go home.

"We'll see," Paul said.

They got out of the car.

Later, after that evening's event finally ended, Paul would think back to when he and George walked up to the front door of the apartment. He would recognize in this retrospection that the feeling that ran through his body was not one of hopeful relief, as he thought at the time. Instead, it was a precognitive flash of some sort. Or, perhaps it was only intuition. Either way, it amounted to the same thing—he had known Richard would not be home, and that they were too late.

He knocked tentatively at first, to no avail, and now his hand fell away from the pounding it rendered to the face of the oak door. "He doesn't answer. I don't think he's here."

He noticed George's face didn't show as much worry as his own probably did. It held a look of grim determination. "Try the door."

Paul knew Richard never left the house without locking up, and this time would be no different; if he was gone, the door would be locked. And so he was surprised when the handle turned easily and the wood door swung inward with a sigh.

George put one hand in his jacket pocket and nudged him. "Go on in."

He entered the lighted front room and George followed, closing the door behind them. "Richard?" Paul called. "You here, man?"

Silence answered him, in the same unique voice that had defined it for eons.

"I'm going to check his bedroom," Paul said. "You check the bathroom and the spare bedroom. Come on, they're this way."

George nodded and the two men strode down the hallway, Paul turning on lights as they went. Richard was not in any of the rooms, and they made their way back toward the living room, stopping in the spotless kitchen.

Paul looked puzzled. "His truck is here, but he's not." He thought about calling his own apartment to see if Margie had seen Richard leave, and then remembered she had left for her

Bridge night with the girls just before he'd drove over to George's shop. It was a fortuitous break. If she was home, it would only be a matter of time before she glanced out the window and saw his car next door.

"Tina must have picked him up," he said after a moment.

"That would be my guess," George said.

"Where do you think they went?"

"Remember when I told you about Tina buying the gun at Milo's Pawn?"

"I remember."

"When I talked to Milo, he told me she had asked about a good place to practice shooting it. He told her about the old Miller Homestead. Ever been there?"

"Sure," Paul said. "It's a good place for hunters to practice their marksmanship before deer season."

"Do you think there are any hunters out there tonight, on the brink of a thunderstorm?" George asked.

"Doubtful," Paul said. "Do you think that's where they went?"

"I'd bet the house and lot on it," George said. "If you know the way, let's go. If you don't, I'll show you."

"I know where it is."

The two of them had been standing in the kitchen, and now they moved into the living room, planning to leave. But something caught Paul's attention and he stopped abruptly.

It was the television, of course. At least that's what the shape beneath the heavy wool comforter suggested it was. It was over near the corner, between bookshelves.

"That's the TV," he said, and pointed. "But what's he got that blanket over it for?" He walked toward the set.

*****

A dread feeling came over George. How could they be so

stupid? Hadn't he felt a slight, relentless pull at the back of his head the minute he'd come through the front door? A tingling along his scalp that he had mistaken for adrenaline? The television should have been the first thing they looked for, not its owner. "Paul. Wait!" he yelled.

But it was too late. Paul already had both hands wrapped in the comforter, and as George spoke, he pulled it away in one swift movement, yanking up and back.

The light from the television spilled onto the floor and over the men's faces. "Well, well," the man on the TV said with a smiling face. "If it isn't Mr. Morrison and Mr. Frazier. I'm so glad you could stop by."

8

9:09p.m.

The rain pelted the windshield in what seemed like a solid sheet, driven by a wind that was gusting from the northwest at over twenty-five miles an hour. In the car, Tina turned the heater on to ward off the chill cause by her wet clothes, while back at Richard's apartment a brutal battle was almost over.

Richard and Tina talked sparingly; it was too much trouble to try and out-talk the driving rain. It hammered against the roof of the car like thousands of drumming fingers.

As they passed the city limits *(Now Leaving Jonesboro, Arkansas,* the sign said. *COME AGAIN!),* Richard asked the question he hadn't asked at The Faria while they were exiting the parking lot. He felt more comfortable asking it now. Jerry had all but fingered their course in this direction, and the frightened feeling he'd had earlier was now gone entirely. That, he knew, was because of what was in his right front pocket. He could feel the comfortable weight against his thigh. "Where are we going, anyway?" He had to talk loudly to be heard above the constant hammering of the rain.

"I thought at first we would drive around for awhile and talk," Tina said loudly. "But maybe we should pull over out of the rain until it slacks off. The Miller Homestead is just up ahead. We could stop there until it slackens up." She paused for only the slightest of seconds, and then added hurriedly: "If you want to, that is."

She looked back at the road and began to squint through the windshield again, but she had looked at Richard long enough for him to see—with the aid of the light from the instrument panel—the anxious look on her face.

You don't fool me, Tina, he thought, and a smile formed on his lips. It couldn't be seen in the interior darkness of the car, but it was there. *You don't fool me at all. But maybe, just maybe...I have you fooled.*

He put a concerned look on his face with surprisingly little effort and said: "I think that sounds like a good idea. I don't know how you can even see to drive in this mess. I know *I* can't."

He thought she smiled then. Fine. That was okay. He tacked one on his own face. It was a small one but, he thought, more convincing that hers—and more secretive, as well.

Almost immediately they were in front of the Miller Homestead and Tina slowed the car to a crawl. She pointed to her right, past Richard. "That barn over there doesn't have a door on it. Think the car will fit in there?"

He looked to his right. There was the shape of a barn there, all right, and a large entrance in the front. The dark doorway looked to him like a black, gaping mouth in the pelting rain. There were no lights on in there, nor were there any on in the tall house that stood directly opposite it, across the road. Richard hadn't expected any, and he guessed Tina hadn't, either. The place had been empty for over a decade.

In a brief flash, he found himself remembering what Jerry had told him: *"Richard, I can only tell you this much for sure—if she takes you to an unpopulated area, if she drives toward the city limits, then she only plans to take you away from where there might be people and shoot you like a dog...and when you get there, you* kill *her! You do it any way you want, but* don't *let her catch you with your guard down..."*

Then something else came to mind, which Richard decided was more important. This he filed into the foremost part of his mind, and it was what ultimately made his decision for him: *"Remember to show no knowledge that you know what she's up to...the element of surprise is your best weapon...so try to keep that in mind."*

Right, Jerry, he thought now. *I hear you, buddy. No-o-o-o problem.*

He glued another smile to his face and looked at Tina. "I think the car will fit just fine. Pull in."

Tina did.

9

8:15p.m.

The first thing to enter Paul's mind as he stared fixedly at the TV was a feeling of wonder; the picture on this set was in color, and for some reason that thought held its grip on him seconds before a feeling of fear, a feeling of being caught doing something he shouldn't be doing, and a feeling of sheer panic all stole into him at once. *He knows my name! He knows my name!*

What brought him out of it was a noise from behind him. It was a hoarse, choked sound, coupled with short intakes of air.

He turned away from his thoughts, and from the face of the

man on the screen. George was stumbling backwards in slow steps. One hand held the left side of his chest, and for a moment he reminded Paul of Redd Foxx having one of his 'big ones' on *Sanford and Son*. "George!" he said, grabbing hold of him. "Are you okay?"

George slicked his lips and Paul noticed with relief that the wheezing sound from his throat had nearly stopped. "I'm okay…it's just…" He went into a coughing fit then. "It's just my lungs…too much air. I'll be fine."

Good thing it wasn't his heart, Paul thought. *Thank God.*

"I'll say it's a good thing," a voice said, and Paul jerked back around and faced the TV screen. "If it was his heart, you would be up a tall tree, my man."

The man on the screen had a look of rapt interest on his face. He was wearing a solid black suit, and an even darker shirt with a bright white tie draping down the center of it. His hair was close-cropped and combed back neatly. Paul noted with a kind of wonder that it was the sort of hairstyle Richard favored. "A tall tree, indeed," the man said. He lit a cigarette and then leaned his head back and howled loud, braying laughter.

"Where's Richard?" Paul asked the man. *"Where is he?"*

"Tsk, tsk, what a temper," the man said. "And this from the man who calls himself Richard's friend."

George had gotten his breath back, and now he came forward and stood beside Paul. "You bastard," he said to the man on the screen.

The man veered his gaze over to George. Paul saw the red fury in them, and realized he was looking into the eyes of a demon of some sort. Perhaps it was the devil himself.

"If it isn't Mr. Morrison!" the man exclaimed. "What brings *you* here, George? I always took you to be the cowardly type when it came to dealing with me." He grinned then, his teeth growing decidedly pointed and long, and to Paul it was the evilest grin he'd ever seen.

"You know why I'm here," George said. "I'm here to end this thing. I should have put a stop to it long before now. Where's Richard, you son of a bitch!" He put a hand inside a pocket of his jacket and rested it on the Army issue grenade.

"I don't think you'll need that for me to tell you where your friend is, Mr. Morrison. In fact, you already know." The man leaned back in his chair and puffed his cigarette. "The two of you are smart for figuring it out. But *you* are *especially* smart, George. Saving and clipping, clipping and saving—*thinking* all these years. Yet...still too much of a coward to do anything about it."

George looked struck by these words, almost hurt, but he composed himself quickly, and Paul was impressed by it. Apparently, so was the man on the screen, whose eyebrows raised a notch. "Those days are over and behind me," George said in a stern voice. *"Over!"*

"Who...who *are* you?" Paul asked. Going through his mind was yet another thought filled with more than a little wonder: George was right. He was right about *everything.*

"I," said the man, leaning forward over his desk, his eyes a blazing red, "am the embodiment of injustice in this world. I put blame in the proper place, where man has often failed to put it. My people are those who have been killed unjustly, and who seek the revenge they need to depart the phase of the afterlife they find themselves in—a purgatory of sorts, if you will. I am the key to finding their lost revenge, I am the door that leads to the path they crave. I am *justice!*" The man relaxed some and leaned back in his chair. "I am," he said in a smooth, soft voice, "the rarest form of death...the right one."

There was a tinkle of broken glass from the far side of the room, at the window along that wall.

"And those who interfere with my Network must die, for their deaths are justified."

Now there came a loud crash at the window, and Paul and

George looked in that direction. Shards of broken glass covered the carpet, sparkling in every direction in the light from the living room. But what they stared at wordlessly was what was coming *through* the window. It (for that is all you could call it) wore a long, grimy trench coat with two large holes near its center. What was beneath this long coat looked to have once been a man. Now, though, most of its skin hung in fluttering flaps, and where there was no skin, white bone glimmered dully in the lit room. It stepped through the window and into the room, grinning luridly at the two men.

Before either man could react, another window shattered noisily. This time it was the one behind and to the left of them. Another creature was struggling through it. It looked as though the top of its head had been ripped right off; jagged chunks of bone stuck out in a sharp oval shape.

It made a grunting sound—"Hm-mnt. Hm-mnt"—as it heaved its way inside, and Paul noticed that two fingers were missing from its left hand; from where they had been jutted stumpy fragments of chipped, white bone.

George was the first to react. He reached into the over-sized pocket of his jacket and found the .44 Magnum. There came more shattering glass, this time from down the hall in one of the bedrooms. "Paul!" he yelled. "Your gun!"

Before Paul even remembered that he *had* a gun, there was a bucking roar right beside his head as George unloaded two rounds at the zombie in the trench coat. When Paul turned to look in that direction, he saw Trenchcoat holding its head with two rotted hands that were mostly bone. A large hole had appeared in the center of its forehead, and through it—with brief astonishment—Paul could see the far wall.

It fell to its knees, trembled slightly, and then pitched forward, face down, to the floor.

But he didn't see it fall. The second zombie—Spike—had made its way fulling into the room, and Paul found himself with his gun held up in front of his face, pointing at it. He could not remember the last time he'd fired a handgun. He owned several rifles and shotguns, and he used these seasonally for hunting. But the barrel of a shotgun was longer, and he knew if he was going to hit the thing before it got to him, his aim would have to be true. Spike shuffled towards him. Paul noticed with a slight sickening to his stomach that…things, were squirming around inside the creature's ripped head. They resembled worms. In his fear he did not notice the light nausea that came upon him.

He heard George's gun go off again—thunder—as the zombie who had entered through a bedroom window began to make its way down the hall. It fell backwards with the shot and there was a thud as it hit the floor.

But Paul saw none of this—only registered it with a part of his mind which was still in tune with things other than the walking dead man currently coming for him. For all he knew, George had just killed the first zombie…or had perhaps turned the gun on himself.

Spike's hands were outstretched now, reaching for him. Paul closed his eyes, prepared himself for the jolting recoil that would follow, and squeezed the trigger.

But nothing happened. The trigger resisted the pull of his finger. It wouldn't budge.

10

The old Miller Homestead stood on a plot of land five miles from the city limits of Jonesboro. The twenty-two acres which made up the property contained a large cedar house (although it was now old, and crumbling with disuse), a weather-worn hay barn, and several patches of thick woods. In between these small patches of woodland were clear strips of land that started at the rear of the barn and ran roughly four acres in length. Targets had been set up at irregular intervals along these swatches of flatland, and it was here that hunters came to sharpen their shooting skills in the early fall.

The land had once been owned by a man names Troy Miller, a man whom no one in town cared for. His father had owned the land before him, and his father before him, for four generations. Troy Miller had been dead for over a decade now, but the attorneys who were hired by the state to handle his estate (alas, the man had no formal will) shortly after his death had failed to find a buyer for the property. There had been a sign in the front yard of the house for nearly two years, but there had been no takers. Apparently, people thought the dislike toward Troy Miller might be contagious for whomever moved into the old house. The sign had finally fallen over and was soon covered up by a tall growth of Timothy grass that ran wild on the lawn. Five years later, a group of deer hunters had begun to call the place 'The Miller Homestead,' and the name had stuck. Soon after that, it became the popular place it was today—a place where men got together to swap hunting stories and lies, and drink beer while polishing their techniques and skills.

On nights such as this, with rain pouring down, thunder rumbling loudly, and lightning leaving white trails across the blackened sky, the property would be deserted.

Tonight, however, a vehicle was parked inside the hay barn. The door to the barn had been torn off by a group of kids several years back who had outgrown the frightening look of the old building, but only the headlights of this car were visible from the road. Soon, they too became invisible, as they were extinguished.

"Whew!" Tina exclaimed. "That's better." She turned the wipers off and shut off the engine. The rain battering the tin roof of the barn was loud, but it was a sound she associated with good things. That in itself was good, because she thought it might make talking to Richard much easier. The feeling that he knew something was still with her, but it wasn't as strong as it had been at The Faria. A part of her knew there would be paranoia involved, but she felt now that maybe things were going to work out as she'd planned after all.

Initially, she'd had no exact plan for getting the two of them to the Miller Homestead. She'd just driven towards it, hoping to come up with something on the spur of the moment. But the rain had been a real help there. She had thought she would just suggest pulling the car over to the side of the road until the rain quit. She could then pull the gun on Richard and make him go into the barn with her. In spite of the natural cloak of the howling wind and rain, she didn't want to kill him out in the open. No good could come of that; someone might see her.

And then he had asked her where they were going. That couldn't have come at a better time, and things had gone smoothly since then. Tina took it as an omen of how the whole night was going to turn out. So far, things looked to be in her favor.

She touched her purse lightly in the darkness and ran her fingers over the hard, unyielding surface of the .357 Magnum, and that boosted her confidence even further.

*****

Richard rolled his window down and the smell of old hay and manure wafted into the car. The smell was not particularly strong, but he was nevertheless surprised that it lingered after more than a decade. "Must have never cleaned this barn out," he remarked, almost to himself.

"Want to get out?" Tina said. "I'd like a cigarette, and I hate to smoke in a car."

"I know," Richard told her. "I haven't forgotten. Do you have a flashlight in here anywhere?"

"There should be one in the glove box. At least there was last time I looked." She leaned across the seat and bent forward, opening the glove compartment. Richard could smell the fragrance of her hair, the tangy smell of wild apples. She had switched brands of shampoo, to one different than she'd always used when they were married, and he found the aroma exciting. Her head was almost in his lap as she rooted around in the glove compartment, the interior light reflecting off her shiny hair.

He became aroused, and abruptly his mind was filled with the image Jerry had shown him on the TV—Tina's head bobbing at the midsection of her boyfriend. This caused another bout of embarrassment...and also a mad flash of jealous anger. He pushed her aside in slight anger, but also because he feared her head would bump into the swell of his erection. "I'll get it," he said.

He looked into the glove compartment and immediately spotted the flashlight. It was between the car registration papers and an old roadmap. He picked it up and flicked it on. "Here it is." He thought she had seen it all along. *You're pretty smooth, Tina,* he thought. *If I didn't know what you were up to, I probably would have sat there enjoying my hard-on while you looked for this damned thing. I probably would have been content to sit there all night.*

He tilted the beam up to his face and smiled. "Looks like the batteries are good."

"They should be," Tina said. "I just put them in a few weeks ago." She grabbed her purse and got out of the car.

You are *smooth, aren't you?* Richard thought. *I'd bet you got fresh batteries just for this occasion. Maybe as long ago as this afternoon.* He got out on his side and pulled a pack of cigarettes from his shirt pocket. He put the flashlight on the hood of the car, and there was a small flash as Tina lit her own cigarette.

He took a drag and then picked up the flashlight, a small two-cell, shining it around the barn. Tina walked up and stood beside him as he played the beam around the place. There were two rooms off to his right. There were empty wooden bins in one of them that may have held cattle and horse feed at one time. The other room had a door. It was closed, But Richard guessed that it was a tack room. The owners would have kept saddles and bridles and things of that nature in that room.

Tina had backed the car into the barn, and the wall behind the car had several hooks on it. All of them were empty except for one, and a thin piece of leather hung over it, looking forlorn and lonely. He shined the light to the right of the hooks and it landed on an old set of wood stairs. A few of the steps were bent or broken off, but the steps remaining looked sturdy. These most likely led to the hayloft. A few bats fluttered as Richard shined the light along the beams supporting the roof. Directly above the two rooms was a jagged rail that resembled a balcony. This rail went around roughly half the barn, in an L-shape. The area behind this rail would be where hay was once stored.

"Remember the barn at my Uncle Raymond's place?" Tina said, breaking the lingering silence. The rain was slowing, and the drumming on the roof was softer.

Richard smiled. He couldn't help it. "Yeah, I remember." The two of them had spent one hot summer afternoon in the loft of Raymond Pullen's barn while he and his wife, Millie, were on vacation up north to visit Millie's sister. After making love three times in the sun-strewn hay, Richard and Tina had both been slick with sweat and 'hay scratches,' and the itch hadn't gone away entirely for two weeks. Their other itch had lasted even longer. "That was some time, wasn't it?"

Tina grabbed his arm lightly with one hand. In the other she clutched her purse. "Let's look around up there."

"Tina—"

"Just for a few minutes, I promise. I just want to see what's up there. Please? she added in her poutiest voice and tugged softly but more insistently at his arm.

Richard sighed and grinned falsely. "Okay," he said. He aimed the beam at the old stairs and started up. He stopped on the second step, turning to look at her. "Be sure to catch me if one of these breaks and I fall."

Tina giggled girlishly and the two of them began to make their way up the wood steps.

11

8:51p.m.

The safety, Paul thought. *How could you be so stupid?* He released it with a flick of his finger…but it was too late. The zombie had reached him. Before he could squeeze off a shot it wrapped two moldy, flaking hands around his throat. The hands began to squeeze.

Paul's oxygen was cut off immediately. He was astonished that the rotted hands possessed such strength. The zombie stank of dirt and rot, and he tried screaming, but no sound issued from his restricted throat. He sensed vaguely that another creature was making its way into the room through the same window this one had entered through, and somewhere in the room—although it sounded much further away from him—he could hear a mad, panicky voice: "How dare you! *How dare you!"*

Paul punched weakly at the thing at his throat and its grip lightened for a brief moment, allowing him to suck in one good breath of air. Then the vice-like grip was around his throat once more. The room began to spin and darken. *This is it,* he thought crazily. *This is how it ends.* Shit.

Just as he was about to pass out, he heard George's gun roar a third time, dangerously close to his right ear, and the creature's hold was suddenly released. In Paul's fogged state of mind, he didn't realize immediately that the creature had been shot. That realization came only when he saw the gaping hole in the zombie's head, just above its left eye. *George sure knows where to hit them,* he thought fleetingly. He mustered his concentration on pulling in huge lungsful of air, and winced at the pain it caused in his swollen throat.

There was yet another shot, then a second, causing him to jump, as George shot the zombie that had climbed in behind Spike. It fell over with a thud on the carpet, just in front of the door.

Paul had his breath back fully now. He scanned the window in front of him for more zombies but there weren't any. That is when he heard the dry click of George's gun, followed by a hoarse scream: "Paul! Get it off me, Paul! *Get it off!*"

Paul turned and saw that another zombie had come through the window on that side while George had been shooting the zombies on Paul's side of the room. It was short, about four-feet tall, and he realized this creature had once been a child. It's dirty blonde hair was matted against a skull that was covered with moss. It hung from the bony face in clumps, some of them dropping wetly to the floor. It had sunk its teeth deeply into one of George's legs, and it clawed at his stomach with one bony hand, digging deep furrows that immediately began to seep bright red blood.

*****

George beat furiously at the small zombie's head, but to no avail. Its rotten yet firm teeth had a grip like an iron fist on his right thigh.

The pain shooting up his leg and through his abdomen was like a white fire, hot and all consuming. It felt as though someone had poured gasoline over his leg and stomach and thrown a match to it.

He beat the thing unsuccessfully with his free hand, and now he brought the empty .44 around and swung it against its head with all the force he could muster. If anything, its grip seemed to tighten. He realized he couldn't reach the pocket of his jacket, where the spare magazines were located.

"Paul!" he shouted again.

*****

Paul stared at him, unable to move. It seemed as though George's voice was coming from far away—across galaxies, instead of the distance of the room.

And there was another voice there as well, blending in and swirling with George's. *"You cannot do this. The pattern of the network cannot be broken,* won't *be broken. You are only wasting your time!"* It was the same voice Paul had heard seconds ago, while Spike choked him. He dimly realized the voice belonged to the man on the television.

This understanding brought him out of his temporary shock, and he brought the gun up in front of him, putting the creature's head in his line of vision at the end of the sights. But the thing's head dipped as George clubbed it again with the .44, and now Paul's gun was aimed at George's bloodstained leg. His finger had already tightened against the trigger, and it was only with a great amount of will that he managed to relax his finger. In his mind, in a flash of what could have been, he saw the gun exploding in his hands and George's leg being ripped off just above the kneecap by the impact of the bullet. *That ankle was painful anyway, prosthetics would have done wonders for him,* his mind tried to scream. *Why didn't you go ahead and shoot, for Chrissakes? If you wait much longer it won't matter if you hit the zombie or not, because George will be dead. No one can lose that much blood and live for long.*

And that voice was right, Paul saw. An ungodly amount of blood spread in a widening pool around George and the child-zombie. It made a crude red wrestling ring for the two as they struggled on the carpet in front of him. Paul's mind also had time to register that George's struggles were weakening. The creature had bitten into his femoral artery.

This got him moving, and instead of aiming the gun for another shot, he ran to the zombie, screaming, and shoved the barrel of the gun to the creature's decayed head. *"You son-of-a-bitch!"* he yelled, and pulled the trigger three times in quick succession. The zombie's head exploded into fragments with the impact.

Paul dropped down to the floor, and immediately felt a warm wetness as his knees squished in the drenched carpet. He leaned over the old man. "George! George, are you okay?" It was a stupid question, but it was all he could think of to say. There was so much *blood.*

George muttered something, and that is when a hellish scream came from the window directly behind him. Paul looked up and saw another creature dragging its way through the window, this one as decayed as the rest, but female. Perhaps it was the mother of the thing that had attacked George and now lay dead and unmoving on the floor.

Paul brought the gun up without even thinking and fired twice into the head of the female zombie. A large hole appeared in the creature's forehead. The second bullet had followed the same path as the first, and the zombie was thrown backward through the window, shattering a few remaining pieces of glass as it went. No more creatures entered through the window, and he glanced quickly to the other one. None there, either. Curtains blew around the shattered window, billowing in a cool breeze that crossed through the open living room. Paul was suddenly cold.

"Paul," George croaked, and Paul immediately leaned over him.

"It's okay, George. They're gone. They're all gone." He grimaced as he looked down at him. The pool of blood around his body had widened even more, and now blood trickled out of his mouth as well. Paul saw clearly that the man was dying. "I'm so sorry, George. So sorry."

"The TV," George managed. He spat up a glob of thick blood, and Paul lifted his head as gently as he could so he wouldn't choke. "The TV."

Paul looked at the television, some fifteen feet or more away. The man on the screen now had his head down on his desk. He raised it slightly and then brought it down hard. He did this again and again. "Stupid fools. Stupid fools," he said. Paul didn't know if he was talking about the two of them or his zombies, who had managed to get shot and killed before their job was completed.

"It's still there," Paul said. Perhaps George had thought the television would disappear with the lives of the dead creatures.

"Richard," George said. "G—ah!"

"Easy," Paul said.

"Go," George said. "Save Richard." He vomited blood in a red gush, and it helped clear his drowning lungs, which had been punctured by the child-zombie's sharp fingers. "It may not be too late. I don't think it is, but you...hurry." He screamed again as another spasm wracked him.

"What about you?" Paul asked him. His eyes scanned frantically over George's mangled body, and he knew he had asked another stupid question. There was no question at all what was going to happen to George; he was going to die.

"The TV," George said again. "Take me to it."

"Don't you *dare,"* the man on the screen said. Paul looked and saw the man had sat up straight in his chair. The look on his face was one Paul recognized instantly—it had been on his own face long enough tonight, and he guessed it still was. It was a look of unadulterated, naked fear.

"Do it!" George said. "And be quick. I don't have much time."

Numbly, Paul rose to his feet and got behind George, pulling him into a sitting position by hooking his hands beneath his armpit. George let out a painful groan, and Paul clenched his teeth, trying to close his ears to it.

With some effort, he dragged George to the television set. The man on the screen was now backed up against the wall behind his desk. *"No!"* he yelled. "You can't do this! You *mustn't!"*

Paul looked down at George. The dying man had a hand in the shredded, blood-soaked pocket of his jacket, and he seemed to be feeling for something. After a moment he pulled the hand out and it held the grenade.

"Squeeze the handle, Paul, and place it in my hand. I think I can hold it for a while. "You'll have to pull the pin for me, too." He spat another clump of blood onto his jacket.

Paul, seeing what George intended, reached over and removed the grenade from his liver-spotted hand. His first thought had been to suggest they get George to a hospital, but inside he knew that even the best of all hospitals couldn't save his friend now. For Paul *had* begun to think of him as a friend. It was a new friendship, and an unspoken thing, but that feeling was there. And he had failed his new friend miserably. George had saved his life minutes ago, and instead of attempting to return the favor, he had wasted precious time asking stupid, pointless questions. He would waste no more. He owed the old man that much, at least.

He squeezed the handle of the grenade and removed the pin. He looked down at George, who was laying on his back, next to the television. "Are you sure?"

"I've never been more sure about anything in my life,"

George said in a wheezing voice. Although he must be in extreme pain, Paul saw the shadow of a smile touch the corners of his mouth.

"You did good here, Paul. Don't ever think any different. You did what you could—the *best* you could—and that's all you can do." He coughed, and it sounded as though his lungs were full of water. "None of this should have happened in the first place. Now..." He made a gesture with his left hand and Paul handed him the grenade, being careful that his grip on it was firm, and then he let go.

"I'm so sorry, George," he said.

"No need for you to be sorry about anything," George wheezed. His voice was weaker now. "Only me. Now I have a chance to atone for some of it. Probably not enough, though." Amazingly, he laughed lightly. "I guess I still have a front row seat reserved for me in hell." He grimaced but didn't scream as another flash of pain racked his body. "Now go," he said. "I can't hold on to this thing much longer. Go, and save Richard. Save your friend."

"George," Paul said. He went to the front door, opened it, and began to walk out, already thinking about what had happened here, and what might happen when he found Richard —*if* he found him.

"Paul!"

Halfway out the door, Paul looked back. George lay on the floor, the hand with the grenade in it outstretched, laying directly under the TV. There was no sound coming from the set. "Yes, George?"

Now George Morrison's face lit up in a true smile. There was also sadness and fear written there. "Thank you," he said.

Paul nodded, surprised to feel a tear roll down his right cheek. He didn't know it, but he had been crying for the last minute and a half. "Good-bye, George."

He closed the door and ran to his car. He had to find

Richard, but he had to be quick. George was dying, and Paul didn't know how long he would be able to hold the handle on the grenade.

12

After the door closed, George looked up at the TV screen. The man there was mouthing something but George couldn't hear him; he had turned the volume control all the way down. The cool air coming through the broken windows made him shiver all over. At least it *felt* like he was shivering. His body lay still, too weak to move. All of his remaining strength was being used to hold the handle against the body of the grenade.

"One-thousand-one," he said in a whisper. That proved too painful, so he counted to himself. *One-thousand-two.*

He heard the door of Paul's car open, and a moment later it shut. *One-thousand-five.* The sound of a motor cranking, once, twice, and finally catching. *One-thousand-seven.*

His grip on the grenade was weakening.

"Dammit!" he said aloud in an effort to muster more strength. He found he had just enough.

One-thousand-nine.

Tires squealing as the car pulled away from the driveway. Sirens in the distant, growing louder by the second.

"A little redemption," George said, and released the handle.

13

Paul backed out of Richard's driveway. As he did, he glanced at his own apartment, worry for his wife seizing him. He was relieved to see that her car was still gone. It felt like he and George had been in there for hours. He put the gear lever in drive, tore out of there, and ten seconds later the front half of Richard's place exploded in a huge ball of fire and broken debris that shook the street beneath the car.

"George," he said out loud. And on the heels of that: "Richard."

I could have saved him, he thought. *He saved my life, but I couldn't do the same for him.*

What's done is done, an interior voice told him. *You have to find Richard. Save him, and you can save yourself.* To Paul, there was no mistaking whose voice that was—it certainly wasn't his. It was George's. How he knew that, he didn't know, but he *felt* it, and that was enough. He believed it to be true.

He had failed to save George, yes, but a part of him now realized that the TV had to be destroyed, and what George had done was the only way under the circumstances. Perhaps it was fate. Maybe it was something more than even that.

He thought George would have preferred dying that way to dying at the hands of one of the zombies. He would have wanted to die knowing that the television—the one he had sold and catered to more than a handful of people, knowing their outcome though not courageous enough to do anything about it—had been destroyed. It was less than ironic for George to be the one to destroy it, but Paul felt that he would have preferred that, too. He had found the purpose in his life and had died for the opportunity to grasp it.

Paul might not have been able to save George, but he planned to do better by his best friend.

He headed toward the old Miller Homestead.

It was 9:12.

14

Near the top of the wooden stairs, one of them gave way with the exertion of Richard's weight, and his right leg fell through, causing him to lose his balance. He put his hands down in front of him to break the fall, but before they found purchase his nose hit the edge of the top stair. There was a sudden burst of pain between his eyes, and after sitting up to where his knees supported him on the riser below the broken one, he put a hand to his nose and felt the wetness there. The flashlight had not fallen from his right hand, and as he pulled his left one away from his nose, he shined the beam of light on it. He was not too surprised to find blood dripping from it—it felt like his nose was broken.

"Shit!" he said.

*****

"Richard? Are you all right?" Tina asked. She put a hand against his shoulder, trying to pull him around so she could get a better look at his face. Some concern swept her when she'd seen his nose smack against the edge of the stair, but it hadn't lasted long. Inside, she celebrated that it happened. In fact, she almost had to stifle a laugh. Richard had taken the lead up the stairs, carrying the flashlight, and when he'd done that, all thoughts about him possibly knowing what she was up to left her head. If he'd known what she had planned for him once they reached the loft, there was no way in hell he would have let *her* follow *him* up the creaky stairs. He wouldn't have risked getting shot in the back.

And the thought had even crossed her mind; just shoot him in the back as he climbed the stairs. Get it over with.

But the stairs were too close to the door of the barn—which of course was open—and that didn't seem like the safest place in the world to kill somebody. Besides—shoot him in the back? Not a chance. She wanted to see the look on his face when she ended his life. The insurance money aside, that is where the *real* satisfaction would come from…the look on his face.

*****

"I'm fine," Richard said. He stood up and climbed to the top of the stairs, skirting the broken one as he ascended the last two.

Tina was in the loft a few seconds later. "Is it broken?" she asked. There was concern in her voice, but Richard detected notes of anxiety and a dark hopefulness there, as well.

"I don't know. I don't think so, but it sure feels like it."

*****

Tina reached into her purse, letting her fingers bypass the gun—*not just yet,* she told herself—and found the cloth handkerchief that was tucked against the bottom. Only a day and a half ago there had been a set of wedding rings lying atop the hanky. "Here," she said, handing it to Richard.

"Thanks," he said.

*****

Richard held the hanky against his nose, wiping away blood. The flow had slowed remarkably, and he knew he'd been lucky. It wasn't broke.

The flashlight in his hand bobbed around the loft randomly as he attended to his nose, allowing only glimpses of the room, which smelled like sweet Bermuda hay. "Kind of creepy up here," Tina said.

Richard held the handkerchief to his nose and shined the beam slowly around the dusty loft.

The floor was slightly covered with hay and wheat straw, and there were cracks between most of the boards. As they walked across the loft pieces of hay and straw slipped through these cracks, falling down to where the car was parked. To their left was a solid wood wall covered with dust and cobwebs. Ten feet to their right was one of the rails they had seen from below. It didn't look very sturdy, and some sections of it leaned forward or back, depending on which way the wood had warped. Ahead of them, the loft stretched the entire length of the barn. Huge support beams rose through the floor at regular intervals, rising to meet equally massive cross-beams at the roof of the structure.

As he played the light on some of the beams, bats fluttered around angrily, fleeing the invading light. At the end of the loft, he could see what looked like about fifty or so bales of hay silhouetted against the loft's only window. Most of the foggy squares were broken. The bales of hay were stacked unevenly, creating a loose-looking pile of dried grass. A few bales sat on the floor of the loft in various places, and most of these bales were still bound with rope or wire. To the right of the pile of hay the loft ran back to the right, the lower portion of the L-shape. Because the hay smelled fresh, Richard guessed some one kept a supply here for the archery targets located on one of the strips of land.

They walked slowly to the far end of the loft, and Richard sat down on one of the bales that was still held together with baling wire. It made a good seat. The smell of hay rose around him, but he could only smell it faintly. What he *could* smell of if reminded him of times as a child when he had spent summer weekends on his aunt and uncle's farm near Lafe, Arkansas. The loft in their barn had been a place full of wonder and adventure, the perfect place for playing hide-and-seek, king of the mountain (using hay as the mountain) and other games, most of which would ultimately be forgotten as he grew older and found other avenues of adventure and pleasure. He felt a deep, fleeing ache for those times. Kids could see the goodness in things that grown-ups couldn't. Through his adult eyes, this loft looked more along the lines of what Tina had just said; it was creepy.

"I guess it's a little creepy, all right," he said, dubbing his nose with the hanky and checking it for blood. The flow had almost stopped entirely now, and the pain had subsided to a tolerable throb. He silently cursed what had happened. He hadn't worried about leading them up the stairs. He'd reflected that if they had come here first instead of going to The Faria, he would have *insisted* she go up the stairs first. But because of what he had in the front pocket of his slacks, he'd decided that Tina following him up provided no real threat, although the thought was tedious and could be entirely wrong. He hadn't thought it was, however, and got a bloody nose for thinking so.

The rain beating against the tin roof slackened even more, and the drumming noise was much softer. Thunder rolled in from the southwest, in the direction of the city.

"I'm sorry about your poor nose," Tina said, walking to where he was and sitting down beside him on the bale of hay. She put her purse on the floor in front of her and put an arm around Richard's shoulders, massaging the taut muscles of his neck. "Is there anything I can do for it?" she pouted.

"It's okay," he told her.

Before he could say anything else, Tina rose, knelt in front of him, and kissed him hard on the lips. Despite the situation the two of them were in—each wanting, literally, to kill the other one—Richard found himself responding. He sighed through his hurt nose as her tongue darted between his lips, searching for his own. Her hands rubbed his body all over; his face, his chest, his thighs—*high* on his thighs.

"Tina—" Richard began.

There was a sound like a snapping board at the other end of the loft, near the stairs. "What was that?" he said.

Tina quit kissing him long enough to look behind her toward the stairs. "Probably just an animal seeking shelter from the rain," she said. She turned around again and began planting more kisses on his wet lips. One talented hand stole to his crotch and moved against the fabric.

There was another sound then, a shuffling movement. Richard locked his hands around her arms and pushed her away. "I'd better see what that was."

*****

Tina took this opportunity to make her move. Getting him lulled into complacency with sex—she had decided to use the tools she possessed and knew—now seemed to be the wrong approach. Richard was getting edgy, and when he got that way it was usually because he was suspicious of something.

She grabbed the flashlight from his hands in one fluid motion. When she had it, she shined the beam directly into his eyes, kneeling to her purse and slowly backing away from him.

He threw an arm up, shielding his eyes against the piercing light. "Tina, what are you doing?"

She wrapped her hand around the .357 Magnum and pulled it free of the purse. "What I should have done a long time ago, you bastard," she spat. She backed up a little more and let the beam of light drop to his chest.

*****

Richard blinked at the sudden change of light. His pupils

weren't adjusting to the darker light quickly enough for him to see clearly what she was doing, but he thought he knew.

"What are you talking about?" he asked, stepping forward.

"You know what I'm talking about. How come you never mentioned the life insurance policy to me? How come you insisted on making my life miserable? Was that your way to get back at me for what I did? *Is it?"* she yelled.

Richard didn't answer. He only came forward another step. His eyes looked down at what she held, but his face registered no surprise.

"Don't come any closer!" she nearly screamed.

"What are you going to do with that gun?" he asked, taking yet another step toward her. He was less than ten feet from her now.

*****

The big pistol began to shake slightly as Tina held it. Her mind was suddenly reeling in shock and fear. It was not a fear of being afraid of anything (she still felt like she had the situation under control—after all, *she* had the gun), but more a feeling of being found out. The feeling that he knew what she had planned this night was back again, stronger than ever, and she didn't think it would just fade away this time. *How could that be possible? He* can't *know.*

"Tina," Richard said.

He took another step toward her and then...and then he was smiling. *Smiling!* Tina looked into his eyes and saw the gulf of knowledge there.

He *did* know. Somehow, he knew.

Tina didn't have time to stop and wonder how this had come about. If she was going to kill her ex-husband it would have to be now, before he took too many more steps her way.

She threw the safety catch with her thumb, took a step back, and aimed the gun at Richard's head.

15

Rain began to fall before Paul reached the end of Crestwood. Even through this heavy rain—which fell in a downpour at once, with no forewarning of light spatters—he could see, through his rearview mirror, the heightening flames of the fire that now engulfed Richard's apartment. He didn't think the fire department would get there in time to save it, but the rain might help, and that was something. At least it should keep it from spreading to his own apartment.

He was just three blocks away when a police cruiser passed him, speeding up the avenue with its lights flashing and sirens wailing in the night. He supposed that someone had called in the sound of gunfire, and he further supposed there was a chance someone had noticed him leaving Richard's place, and would be able to easily identify him for the police. *"Yes, sir, I recognized the man in the getaway car. He lives right next door to that flaming mess."* Not only, Paul thought, was that a possibility, it was a probability.

But he pushed these thoughts out of his head. What happened later was something that would just have to happen. Right now, he had to save Richard if it wasn't too late. He couldn't waste valuable time—for he felt he didn't have much—worrying about whether or not he was in trouble with the law.

He turned the wipers on full speed as he made the turn off Crestwood, but he still had to lean over the wheel and squint into the rain and darkness to make out the yellow and white lines on Dregger Boulevard.

Two miles later the rain slackened and he was able to see better. As he drove out of the city limits he pushed the car up to the legal fifty-five, although he knew that on a night like this, with rain falling and the roads slicker than usual, he might still be pulled over if he passed a police officer who was gauging traffic.

He decided he would simply have to chance that. The old Miller Homestead was just up ahead another mile or two, and he would have to concentrate on looking for it. He couldn't afford to miss it and have to backtrack. He felt there wouldn't be time for such mistakes.

Two minutes later he spotted the silhouette of a barn in a flash of lightning. He slowed the car to a stop on the shoulder of the road about a hundred-fifty yards away from the barn, and killed the engine. If Richard and Tina were somewhere on the Miller property, he didn't want them to see him. He decided to look in the barn first, because it was the closest building. From there he could move across the road to the house. He hated wasting time walking to it, but he would hate it even more if one, or both of them, saw him coming before he could make out what, if anything, was going on. *You know what's going on. George laid that out for you as neatly as rolling out a new carpet. Don't kid yourself.*

But *did* he know?

On a night like this, Tina would have a hard time getting Richard to come all the way out here with her. The rain would have been a deterrent and would likely have spoiled any chance of that.

But remember. Tina has a gun. He might do anything she says if she has it pointed at him, or has threatened him with it.

And what about Richard? Did *he* have a gun? Paul thought about it briefly, but decided that he had never seen him with one. Richard didn't own one, as far as that went. Whenever the two of them went hunting, he always borrowed one of Paul's.

He had always said that, for a once-a-year thing, it didn't seem worth it to spend money on a gun. So, if Richard didn't have a gun, then perhaps it *was* possible that he and Tina were here somewhere.

He tucked the .44 firmly into the waistband of his jeans, wrapped his light jacket around his upper body, and opened the car door.

He was dripping wet before he got fifty feet from the car, but he hardly felt the change against his clothes and skin. They were still slicked with George's blood. He ran as fast as he dared toward the barn, his shoes slapping wetly against the pavement.

As he came to a halt in front of it, he realized two things at once: the Miller Homestead was creepy, and it looked deserted. There was no vehicle parked in front of the barn, nor was there one in the driveway that climbed its way up a small hill to the house directly across the road from it.

The trees in the front yard of the old house cackled secretly, their nearly-empty branches bumping against each other in the howling wind.

Not here, he thought. *But where can they be?*

He turned around to begin making his way back up the road to his car when a bright, jagged bolt of lightning split the sky overhead. As it did, he caught a quick glimmer of something through the broad, open door of the barn. It was only a flash, but it roused his curiosity.

He gripped the butt of the .44 with one hand—after what he'd already had to deal with tonight, he was taking no chances with *anything*—and walked down the muddy dirt drive that led into the barn. Another bolt of lightning flashed and now he could make out clearly what the glimmer was; the front bumper of a car. Not only could he see that much in this second flare of electrical light, but he could also make out the color and model of the vehicle. His heart picked up a quicker pace when he realized he was looking at Tina's car.

He walked up to it slowly, trying to glance in all directions at once in the darkness, and placed his hand on the hood. It was warm to the touch. As he moved across it, intending to walk to the rear of the vehicle, he felt his hand brush at light pieces of something. He gathered a few of them and knew immediately what it was—hay.

He looked up and saw a light prodding the beams at the roof of the barn. Then the beam of light swung away and he couldn't see it anymore.

He heard voices, muffled by the slowing rain, but voices just the same. He didn't have to guess more than once to know whose voices they were. Richard and Tina were in the loft above him.

He remembered seeing, in the second flash of lightning, an old set of wooden stairs ear the door of the barn, and now he made his way to them, walking as quickly as he dared in the darkness and trying not to make an excessive amount of noise.

He tested the bottom step with his left foot. It felt sturdy enough to hold him and, better yet, it didn't squeak when he put his full weight on it But that didn't mean the others wouldn't. He was almost to the top when a small piece of board snapped and his foot almost fell through the hole (it was the same step Richard had fallen through).

"What was that?" From where he was, near the top of the old stairs, it would have been hard for him to miss the sound of Richard's cultured voice. He felt his stomach turn in a nervous knot. What were the two of them doing up there, anyway?

He made the top of the stairs (checking each one carefully now for unwelcomed holes) and could now see, at the far end of the dusty loft, a light down close to the floor...and Richard and Tina. But it was what the two of them were doing that threw his mind into a stumbling confusion.

Tina was knelt down slightly in front of Richard, her hands roaming all over his chest and legs. Their faces were locked together in a lover's kiss. Paul couldn't believe his eyes. He just couldn't process what he was seeing. His first coherent thought was that George had been wrong about everything. His second thought was that this was not the first time he, Paul, had entertained this particular idea. He'd thought it briefly earlier that day, when he visited Richard.

How could he have been such a fool? How could he have believed what George had told him about Richard? Right now, it looked as though Tina was righter than George. Maybe the two of them *were* getting back together. Maybe Richard was embarrassed about it, and played off an anger he didn't feel. The thought made Paul feel like an intruder and he felt his face redden.

But you saw the man on the TV yourself! his mind screamed at him. *Explain that!*

Explain that, indeed. He *had* seen the man. Had heard him talk. The man had even known his *name*. And there had been the zombies.

So, why didn't that jive with what he was seeing right now? He felt as though there was once more piece of information about the whole thing that he didn't know, something George hadn't told him—or hadn't been able to. He didn't know. It was like knowing you were missing one piece to a jigsaw puzzle, and you couldn't find it anywhere, no matter how hard you looked.

He jumped at a noise ahead of him and slightly to his left. If was a shuffling, dragging movement. He saw Richard rise from the bale of hay he'd been sitting on and push Tina away. "I'd better see what that was," Richard said. Paul was beginning to wonder himself what that sound had been. But before he could think any more about it, what he thought he'd been seeing in front of him, near the end of the loft, took a sudden left turn. In his confused state, Paul still had time to realize that George had been righter than he had moments ago given him credit for.

16

The dry click of the .357 Magnum echoed loudly in the stillness of the barn as soon as Tina pulled the trigger. She had stiffened with the expectation of a powerful recoil, and when it didn't happen her mouth formed an 'o' of surprise.

She looked at Richard, the expression still on her narrow face.

Now he not only smiled; he began to laugh, as well. He delved his right hand into the front pocket of his slacks and pulled out the assemblage of bullets he had removed from the gun when Tina had gone to the ladies' room at The Faria. "Looking for these?" he asked, holding up the fistful of bullets playfully. He would have looked the same if he'd been dangling a set of keys to a car she wanted badly and could only dream of owning.

*****

In a fraction of a second, Tina realized why Richard's behavior tonight had been so cognitive. He *had* known what she had planned for him. But the question gnawing at the back of her mind was: *how* did he know?

She never had time to give the question more thought. In an instant, the gleeful look on Richard's face turned into a savage snarl. He flung the handful of bullets over his shoulder, where they made a muffled landing on the hay strewn floor. And then he was running at her, arms outstretched. The fury on his face was so great that Tina thought for a second he had somehow been transformed into some sort of demon; a creature sent from hell to claim and torture her. But as his hands clamped around her exposed throat and began to squeeze, she saw that it was only Richard ...and that he meant to kill her.

She tried desperately to pull air into her straining lungs, but the pressure on her throat was crushing, and she could only move her mouth up and down, like a fish out of water.

"Isn't this *what you* really *wanted to do to me?"* Richard hissed. *"Isn't* this *what you thought I deserved, you bitch!"*

The words floated aimlessly in Tina's ears. Her head was beginning to feel light with the lack of oxygen, as though it was floating. Richard's angry face was fading in and out of her vision. He was becoming blurry. His vice-like hands exerted even more pressure on her constricted throat, and just when she thought she was finally going to pass out the grip loosened, the hands falling away, as a voice spoke from behind them.

"Let her go."

17

When Tina pulled the gun from her purse, Paul immediately became apprehensive. George had been right, after all. No matter how silly the idea of Richard and Tina plotting to kill each other had sounded (and how illogical), he saw now that at least half of George's theory was true. It appeared as though Tina was carrying out a plan right along those lines.

Paul went for his own gun, pulling it from the waist of his jeans. But before he could pull it all the way out, he heard the dry click of Tina dry-firing the big gun she had pointed at Richard.

"Looking for these?" he heard Richard ask. Paul didn't like the sound of his voice. He didn't like it at all. The voice was teasing, mocking.

Then Richard was at Tina's throat, and even from across the length of the loft, by the low lighting cast from the flashlight the lay on the floor between them, Paul could see he was choking her, and hard.

Before he could react, however, a quick shadowy movement ahead of him and to his left caught his eye. He tracked the shadow as best he could in the darkened loft, and before it even spoke he could make out a dark figure standing midway between him ad where Richard and Tina were struggling. "Let her go," the figure said.

18

Richard's hands fell away from Tina's throat when the voice spoke and she fell limply to the floor, where she began to kick feebly while she gasped for air. The flashlight had fallen from her hands in their struggle and it now lay on the floor of the loft, shining off to Richard's right, but providing a dim illumination. He bent over, retrieved the light, and shined it in the direction from which the voice had come. What he saw caused him to take two steps backward. He tripped over a small pile of loose hay and landed on his rear. He could do nothing but shine the light as Biff Larento strode into view, walking toward him.

Biff's skin was a dull gray color in the small beam of light and all of his skin was visible, for he was naked. There was a dark, wet stain at his crotch, and Richard realized sickly that it was where the man's penis had been.

He shambled toward the place where he sat, but Biff's eyes were on Tina, who sounded as though she was recovering. "Tina," Biff said now, and Richard understood that he was dead, that this was his corpse speaking. With dawning knowledge, he knew that Biff Larento had become a part of Jerry's unseen audience—an audience about whom he had previously only speculated.

*****

Tina looked up when she heard the voice speak her name. Her breath still came in wheezy bursts, but now she struggled to find her voice. Her mouth opened and closed, as if Richard was still choking her. "Biff?" she finally managed to say. She could say nothing else. What she was seeing couldn't be real. Her swimming mind tried to tell her that she was dead—that Richard had succeeded in killer her after all—and that she was seeing her former lover because, of course, he was also dead. But what Biff said next caused her confused mind to come fully awake.

"I've come for you, Tina. You killed me, and now I've come for my revenge," Biff said as he shuffled toward her. "And I'll have it, you fucking *bitch!*"

"Biff?" Tina said, frightened. She looked down at his crotch and saw what had killed him. She glanced quickly behind her, saw Richard, and knew she was not dead. When she turned back around Biff was less than four feet from her, and before she could utter a single sound, even one scream, Biff's arm swung toward her at an angle, and there was instant pain at her battered throat.

She felt cool, brittle air enter her throat, and it wasn't until she put one shaking hand there that she realized it had been ripped wide open. The loft began to swirl in front of her as she collapsed onto the floor, and she found she couldn't even put a hand out to break her fall. There was a warm, sticky wetness down the entire length of her blouse. A dark tunnel opened in front of her, hands beckoning her to enter it. She felt instinctively that she would find relief from the pain inside that tunnel, and she leaned toward it, a smile forming on her face.

The last sounds she heard before the welcoming darkness surrounded her was the heavy thud of running footsteps, a loud yell, and the thundering roar of a gun, echoing loudly in the receding loft.

19

As Richard watched, the Biff-creature gouged out Tina's throat with one swiping hand. There was an immediate jet of blood, and it coated Biff's naked torso in a fine sheen. The creature began to lean over Tina, as if to examine her, and then he heard the sound of running footsteps, and heard another voice. This one sounded oddly familiar to him. *"Get down, Richard!"*

He ducked instinctively, and just as he did there was a tremendous roar. He thought at first that he'd been hit. There followed a solid thud, and as he looked up he saw Biff Larento lying on top of Tina's dead body—saw the gaping hole in the creature's head. And then...and then the dead body began to slowly fade. But not only the body that had belonged to Biff; Tina's body beneath the creature began to faded, as well. They became fuzzy, transparent, and then vanished completely, as if they had never been there at all.

"Richard?" the new voice asked tentatively.

Richard shined the light in the direction of the voice, and was utterly surprised—and relieved—to see Paul Frazier walking toward him. Paul held a big gun low to his side, and the hand holding it was shaking.

He looked up at Paul's face and saw the sad smile there. It was perched between two glistening streams that were tears.

"Richard?" Paul said again. He let the big gun fall to the floor and then dropped to his knees.

Richard glanced at the floor, and when he looked up again there were tears in the narrow corners of his own eyes, threatening to spill over. A lipless smile touched his face.

"Paul," he said.

20

At 9:35 p.m., Richard Raines and Paul Frazier walked through the door of the old barn on the Miller Homestead and into the night outside. The rain slackened to a light drizzle, and big drops fell from the slanted roof of the barn, plunking hollowly into puddles that were formed on the wet ground. The moon broke through a gap in the clouds, and its pale light shimmered on the water.

The two men walked up the drive and onto the shoulder of the road, in the direction of the vehicle that belonged to Paul.

"How did you find out?" Richard asked. It was the third time he'd asked that question since Paul had shot Biff Larento. Paul hadn't answered him the first two times.

"It's a long story," Paul said. "and it starts with a man I met. A *good* man," he said, after a slight pause. He thought of George, and what he had gone through to help save his friend. He recalled briefly the notebooks and stacks of clippings. George had known what was going on and had told the story to Paul, even though he hadn't been sure what to do about it. Yet what he had done worked out fine.

Paul smiled to himself then, and thought that at least the story he would tell Richard had an ending to it. At least it was over.

"I'll tell you about it sometime," he said. He threw an arm

over his friend's shoulder and the two men walked down the road together, toward whatever future awaited them.

*****

EPILOGUE

The fire at Richard's apartment burned for only a short period of time before the driving rain and a prompt city fire department quelled the flames. No other homes in the area were harmed, including the one belonging to Paul and Margie Frazier.

When Richard and Paul returned home that evening, both of them were able to feign ignorance to the amazingly few questions asked by police and fire officials who, the next day, would attribute the cause of fire to lightning.

No foul place was suspected, and no bodies were found in the charred remains of the condo. People had been inside their homes due to the weather, and if anyone had heard gunfire, none was reported.

The fire was pretty much an open and shut case.

*****

A week later, on the twenty-third of September, Paul Frazier inserted a key into the lock on the front door of George Morrison's small shop. He'd gotten the key from one of

George's friends, Larry Vincent, on the premise that he had left some personal items with George—mainly paperwork for a future advertisement that hadn't panned out. The sun shone brightly outside the shop, but inside the place was gloomy, dusty.

Paul walked slowly around the place, looking at the old toasters, VCRs, and other small appliances that were beginning to collect dust, wondering what would become of them. George had left everything to Larry in his will, and Paul guessed the man would sell everything off, including the building.

He kicked at a few pieces of paper that were strewn across the floor, and then he went into George's small apartment. The notebooks and ledgers were still inside a drawer in the kitchen. After a short, inner debate with himself, Paul gathered them up and tucked them under one arm. He wasn't sure why he wanted to keep these things, but he felt it would be best if he did.

He wished he could have gotten to know George better. He turned and left the small living area and went back through the shop.

He was almost to the door when he caught an image of something from the edge of his vision. He turned slowly and almost dropped the load of papers.

It was the television; the one that had been in the living room of Richard's apartment.

Not possible, he thought.

It sat in the far corner of the shop, seeming to stare at him with one pale green eye.

The screen blinked into life, only for a second; white, snowy static filled the screen and then flickered off, and the screen was blank once again.

Paul stared hard at the television, believing he was only seeing things, and that this was *not* the same television.

Yet for a brief second or two, when the screen had flickered into life—if it really had at all—Paul felt his scalp tingle as though being massaged by invisible fingers.

He looked at the television a moment longer, but nothing happened. It stared back at him with idiotic indifference.

Only a television set.

And it *was.* He could see now that it was a newer model *RCA,* nothing at all like the one Richard had purchased here.

He opened the front door and walked out onto the sidewalk, into the welcoming sunshine. He looked up at the cloudless blue sky and breathed deeply. It was a beautiful day.

He walked toward his vehicle. He had to take the key back to Larry Vincent, and after that he had a date with a friend.

He and Richard were going to a basketball game this afternoon, and he knew Richard would want to get there early. So would he.

Paul got into his car and drove away.

Acknowledgments

I would like to gratefully acknowledge the help I received from the following people:

Kerry Pugh, who, other than the actual writing, put almost as much work into the preceding story as the author. He helped make this novel much better than it was in its original form. Any mistakes you see are mine alone.

Thanks most of all to my wife, Melissa, for faith and support that is exceeded only by her love.

About the Author

Ivan Tritch lives in northern Arkansas, with his wife, Melissa. He is the author of several novels, a story collection, and one work of non-fiction.